RANSLEIGH ROGUES

Where these notorious rakes go, scandal **always** *follows…*

Max, Will, Alastair and Dominic Ransleigh—cousins, friends… and the most wickedly attractive men in Regency London. Between war, betrayal and scandal, love has never featured in the Ransleighs' destinies—until now!

Don't miss this enthralling quartet from Julia Justiss.

We met Max and Will in
THE RAKE TO RUIN HER
and
THE RAKE TO REDEEM HER

Now follow Alastair's journey in
THE RAKE TO RESCUE HER

And look out for Dominic's adventures in
THE RAKE TO REVEAL HER
coming soon

AUTHOR NOTE

Is there anything more satisfying than love the second time around?

When I first envisaged my *Ransleigh Rogues* I knew that Alastair had suffered a broken heart and, as a poet and dreamer, felt the tragedy more deeply than an ordinary man. When I later envisaged the lady who'd wounded him I realised a love like theirs was once in a lifetime; somehow they *had* to get back together.

Diana returned Alastair's love with the same passion. But to safeguard the two men she loved—her father and Alastair—she was forced into marriage, and forbidden to tell Alastair why she'd repudiated him.

Eight years later they meet by chance, after the death of her husband, and Diana takes the opportunity to explain what she did. When she admits to Alastair that there is nothing she can do to make it up to him, he angrily suggests she become his mistress.

Expecting to be rejected, he is amazed when Diana agrees. An affair begun to purge her from his heart soon gives him glimpses into the horrors of her marriage—and makes him determined to free the woman he's never stopped loving from the demons of the past and protect her from present danger.

For the embattled Diana, stripped of everything and everyone she loved, recovering from her bleak existence is difficult. Under Alastair's fierce protection she gradually comes to trust and love again.

I hope you will enjoy their journey.

THE RAKE TO
RESCUE HER

Julia Justiss

First published in Great Britain 2015
by Mills & Boon, an imprint of Harlequin (UK) Limited,
Large Print edition 2015
Harlequin (UK) Limited, Eton House, 18-24 Paradise Road,
Richmond, Surrey TW9 1SR

© 2015 Janet Justiss

ISBN: 978-0-263-25554-6

Harlequin (UK) Limited's policy is to use papers that are natural, renewable and recyclable products and made from wood grown in sustainable forests. The logging and manufacturing processes conform to the legal environmental regulations of the country of origin.

Printed and bound in Great Britain
by CPI Antony Rowe, Chippenham, Wiltshire

Julia Justiss wrote her first ideas for Nancy Drew stories in her third-grade notebook, and has been writing ever since. After publishing poetry in college, she turned to novels. Her Regency historicals have won or been placed in contests by the Romance Writers of America, *RT Book Reviews*, National Readers' Choice and Daphne du Maurier. She lives with her husband in Texas. For news and contests visit juliajustiss.com

Books by Julia Justiss

Mills & Boon® Historical Romance

Ransleigh Rogues

The Rake to Ruin Her
The Rake to Redeem Her
The Rake to Rescue Her

Silk & Scandal

The Smuggler and the Society Bride

Linked by Character

The Wedding Gamble
A Most Unconventional Match

Stand-Alone Novels

From Waif to Gentleman's Wife
Society's Most Disreputable Gentleman

**Visit the author profile page
at millsandboon.co.uk for more titles**

To the Evelettes:
You've hugged me, cried with me,
and been there for me every step of the way
on the long twilight journey of the last two years.
I love you guys!

Chapter One

It was *her.*

Shock rocked him like the blast of air from a passing cannonball. Struck numb in its wake, Alastair Ransleigh, late of His Majesty's First Dragoons, stared at the tall, dark-haired woman approaching from the other side of Bath's expansive Sidney Gardens.

Even as his disbelieving mind told him it couldn't be her, he knew on some level deeper than reason that it *was* Diana. No other woman had that graceful, lilting step, as if dancing as she walked.

Heart thundering, he exhaled a great gasping breath, still unable to move or tear his gaze from her.

So had she glided into the room the day he'd first met her, bringing a draught of spring air and enchantment into the Oxford study where the callow collegian he'd once been had gone to consult her father, a noted scholar.

Memory swooped down and sank in vicious claws. *Just so he'd watched her, delirious with delight, as she walked into the Coddingfords' ballroom eight and a half years ago. Awaited her signal to approach, so her father might announce their engagement to the assembled guests.*

Instead, she'd given her arm to the older man who had followed her in. The Duke of Graveston, he'd belatedly recognised. The man who then announced that Diana was to marry him.

A sudden impact at knee level nearly knocked him over. 'Uncle Alastair!' his six-year-old nephew Robbie shrieked, hugging him around the legs while simultaneously jumping up and down. 'When did you get here? Are you staying long? Please say you are! Can you take me to get Sally Lunn cakes? And my friend, too?'

Jolted back to the present, Alastair returned the hug before setting the child at arm's length with hands that weren't quite steady. Fighting off the compulsion to look back across the gardens, he made himself focus on Robbie.

'I've only just arrived, and I'm not sure how long I'll stay. Your mama told me you'd gone to the Gardens with Nurse, so I decided to fetch you. Yes, we'll get cakes. Where's your friend?'

Still distracted, he followed his nephew's pointing finger towards a boy about Robbie's age, dressed neatly in nankeens and jacket. The child looked up at him shyly, the dark hair curling over his forehead shadowing his blue, blue eyes.

Diana's eyes.

With another paralysing shock, he realised that Robbie's friend must be her son.

The son that should have been his.

Pain as sharp as acid scalded his gut, followed by a wave of revulsion. Buy the boy cake? He'd as soon give sustenance to a viper!

Shocked by the ferocity of his reaction, he hauled himself under control. Whatever had occurred between himself and Diana was no fault of this innocent child.

It was the suddenness of it, seeing her again after so long with no warning, no time to armour himself against a revival of the anguish of their bitter parting. The humiliation of it, he thought, feeling his face redden.

Certain there must be some mistake, he'd run to her. Desperate to have her deny it, or at the very least, affirm the truth to his face, he'd shouted after her as the Duke warned him off and swept her away. Never once as he followed them did she glance at him before his cousins dragged him, still shouting, out of the ballroom...

Hurt pierced him, nearly as sharp as on that night he remembered with such grisly clarity. An instant later, revitalising anger finally scoured away the pain.

Ridiculous to expend so much thought or emotion on the woman, he told himself, sucking in a deep, calming breath. She'd certainly proved herself unworthy of it. He'd got over her years ago.

Though, he thought sardonically, this unexpected explosion of emotion suggested he hadn't banished the incident quite as effectively as he'd thought. He *had*, however, mastered a salutary lesson on the perfidy of females. They could be lovely, sometimes entertaining, and quite useful for the purpose for which their luscious bodies had been designed, but they were cold-hearted, devious, and focused on their own self-interest.

So, after that night, he had treated them as temporary companions to be enjoyed, but never trusted. And never again allowed close enough to touch his heart.

So he would treat Diana now, with cordial detachment.

His equilibrium restored, he allowed himself to

glance across the park. Yes, she was still approaching. Any moment now, she would notice him, draw close enough to recognise him.

Would a blush of shame or embarrassment tint those cheeks, as well it should? Or would she brazen it out, cool and calm as if she hadn't deceived, betrayed and humiliated him before half of London's most elite Society?

Despite himself, Alastair tensed as she halted on the far side of the pathway, holding his breath as he awaited her reaction.

When at last she turned her eyes towards them, her gaze focused only on the boy. 'Mannington,' she called in a soft, lilting voice.

The familiar tones sent shivers over his skin before penetrating to the marrow, where they resonated in a hundred stabbing echoes of memory.

'Please, Mama, may I go for cakes?' the boy asked her as Alastair battled the effect. 'My new friend, Robbie, invited me.'

'Another time, perhaps. Come along, now.' She crooked a finger, beckoning to the lad, her glance passing from the boy to Robbie to Alastair. After meeting his eyes for an instant, without a flicker of recognition, she gave him a slight nod, then turned away and began walking off.

Sighing, the boy looked back at Robbie. 'Will you come again tomorrow? Maybe I can go then.'

'Yes, I'll come,' Robbie replied as the child trotted after his mother. Grabbing the arm of the boy's maid, who was tucking a ball away in her apron, his nephew asked, 'You'll bring him, won't you?'

The girl smiled at Robbie. 'If I can, young master. Though little notice as Her Grace takes of the poor boy, don't see that it would make a ha'penny's difference to her whether he was in the house or not. I'd better get on.' Gently extricating her hand from Robbie's grip, she hurried off after her charge.

Alastair checked the immediate impulse to follow her, announce himself to Diana, and force a reaction. Surely he hadn't changed that much from the eager young dreamer who'd thrown heart and soul at her feet, vowing to love her for ever! As she had vowed back to him, barely a week before she gave her hand to an older, wealthier man of high rank.

Had he been merely a convenient dupe, his open devotion a goad to prod a more prestigious suitor into coming up to snuff? He'd never known.

Sudden fury coursed through him again that the sight of her, the mere sound of her voice, could churn up an anguish he'd thought finally buried. Ah, how he *hated* her! Or more precisely, hated what she could still do to him.

Since the night she'd betrayed him, he'd had scores of women and years of soldiering. He'd thrown himself into the most desperate part of the battle, determined to burn the memory of loving her out of his brain.

While she seemed, now as then, entirely indifferent.

Mechanically he gave his nephew a hand, walking beside him while the lad chattered on about his friend and his pony and the fine set of lead soldiers waiting for them in the nursery, where they could replay all the battles in which Uncle Alastair had fought. It required nearly the whole of the steep uphill walk from Sidney Gardens across the river back to his sister's townhouse in the Royal Crescent for him to finally banish Diana's image.

Damn, but she'd been even lovelier than he remembered.

Sending Robbie up to the nursery with a promise to join him later for an engagement with lead soldiers, Alastair turned over his hat and cane to his sister's butler. He'd placed boot on step to follow his nephew up the stairs when Simms halted him.

'Lady Guildford requested that you join her in the morning room immediately upon your return, Mr Ransleigh, if that is possible.'

Alastair paused, debating. He'd hoped, before meeting his all-too-perceptive sister, to return to the solitude of the pretty guest chamber to which he'd been shown upon his arrival early this morning, where he might finish piecing back together the shards of composure shattered by his unexpected encounter with Diana. But failing to respond to Jane's summons might elicit just the sort of heightened interest that he wished to avoid.

With a sigh, he nodded. 'Very well. You needn't announce me; I'll find my way in.'

Moments later he stepped into a back parlour flooded with mid-morning sunlight. 'Alastair!' his sister exclaimed with delight, jumping up from the sofa to meet him for a hug. 'I'm sorry I was so occupied when you arrived this morning! Though if I'd had any inkling you were coming, I would have had all in readiness,' she added, a tinge of reproof in her tone.

'Do you mean to scold me for showing up unannounced, as Mama always does?' he teased.

'Of course not! I assume you're not here for some assignation, else you'd not come to stay with me.'

'Assignation?' he said with a laugh. 'You'll make me blush, sister mine! And what would a proper matron like you know about assignations?'

'Nothing whatever, of course, other that you're

rumoured to have many of them,' Jane retorted, her face flushing.

'You shouldn't listen to gossip,' Alastair said loftily. 'But let me assure you, if I did have an "assignation" in mind, I'd choose a more convenient and discreet location than Bath to set up a mistress.'

'It pains me that you've become so cynical. If only you'd become acquainted with any of the lovely, accomplished and well-bred girls I've suggested, you'd find that not all women are interested only in title and position.'

'Of course not. You married Viscount Guildford out of overwhelming passion, the kind you'd have me write about,' he said sardonically.

Her flush deepened. 'Just because a match is suitable, doesn't mean there can't be love involved.'

'Oh, I'm a great believer in love! Indulge in it as often as I can. But I could hardly make one of your exemplary virgins my mistress,' he said, then held up a hand as Jane's eyes widened and she began to sputter a reply. 'Pax, Jane! Let's not brangle. I came to see you and Robbie, of course, and I do hope I'm welcome.'

'Always!' she said with a sigh, to his relief letting the uncomfortable topic go. He loved his sister and his mother dearly, but the succession of women with whom he'd been involved since his break with

Diana—with their attempted claims on his time, his purse or his name—had only strengthened his decision never again to offer his heart or hand.

Jane looped her arm with his, leading him to a seat beside her on the sofa. 'Of course you may come and go as you wish! But if the ladies in your life would prefer to prepare a proper welcome and perhaps cosset you a bit, you must forgive us. We waited too many long anxious years while you were in the army, not sure you would ever make it back.'

'But I did, and I wager you find me as annoying as ever,' Alastair pronounced, dropping a kiss on the top of her head. 'So, was it my unannounced visit that I've been summoned to answer for? I thought, with Guildford off in London toiling away for some Parliamentary committee, you'd be delighted to have me break the tedium of marking time in Bath while your papa-in-law takes the waters. How is the Earl, by the way?'

'Better. I do think the waters are helping his dyspepsia. And I can't complain about being in Bath. It may not be the premier resort it once was, before Prinny made Brighton more fashionable, but it still offers a quite tolerable number of diversions.'

'So which of my misdeeds required this urgent meeting?'

To his surprise, despite his teasing tone, his sister's face instantly sobered. 'Nothing you've done, as well you know, but I do need to make you aware of a…complication, one of some import. I'm not sure exactly how to begin…'

Brow creased, Jane gazed warily at his face, and instinctively he stiffened. 'Yes?'

'It's…'

Though Alastair would have sworn he neither moved a millimetre nor altered his expression in the slightest, Jane's eyes widened and she gasped. 'You've already seen her! You have, haven't you?'

Damn and blast! He was likely now in for the very sort of inquisition he'd heartily wished to avoid. 'If you mean Diana—the Duchess of Graveston, that is—yes, I have. At any rate, I believe it was her, though we didn't speak, so I'm not completely sure. It has been years, after all,' he added, trying for his calmest, most uninterested tone. 'A lady who looked like I remember her came to Sidney Gardens when I went after Robbie, to fetch her s-son.' Inwardly cursing that he'd stumbled over the word, Alastair cleared his throat.

Distress creased his sister's forehead. 'I'm so sorry you encountered her! I just this morning discovered her presence myself, and intended to warn you straight away so you might…prepare yourself. *That woman*, too, has only just arrived, or so

Hetty Greenlaw reported when she called on me this morning.' Her tone turning to annoyance, Jane continued. 'Knowing of my "close connection to a distressing incident involving my maternal family", she felt it her duty to warn me that the Duchess was in Bath—the old tattle-tale. Doubtless agog to report to all her cronies exactly how I took the news!'

'With disinterested disdain, I'll wager,' Alastair said, eager to encourage this diversion from the subject at hand.

'Naturally. As if I would give someone as odious as that scandalmonger any inkling of my true feelings on the matter. But,' she said, her gaze focusing back on his face, 'I'm more concerned with *your* reaction.'

Alastair shrugged. 'How should I react? Goodness, Jane, that attachment was dead and buried years ago.'

Her perceptive eyes searched his face. 'Was it, Alastair?'

Damn it, he had to look away first, his face colouring. 'Of course.'

'You needn't see her, or even acknowledge her existence. Her whole appearance here is most irregular—we only received word of the Duke's passing two days ago! No one has any idea why she would leave Graveston Court so quickly after his death, or come to Bath, of all places. With, I understand, almost no servants or baggage. I highly doubt a woman as young and beautiful as Diana means to set up court as a dowager! If she's angling to remarry, she won't do her chances any good, flouting convention by appearing in public so scandalously soon after her husband's death! Although if she did, I'd at least have the satisfaction of being able to cut her.'

'That might not be feasible. Robbie has struck up a friendship with her son,' he informed her, making himself say the word again without flinching. 'He invited the boy to meet him again in the gardens tomorrow.' Alastair smiled, hoping it didn't appear as a grimace. 'So I can take them both for cakes.'

If he hadn't been still so unsettled himself, Alastair would have laughed at the look of horror that passed over his sister's face as the difficulty of the situation registered.

'I shall come up with some way to fob off Robbie,' Jane said. 'It's unthinkable for you to be manoeuvred into associating with her.'

Recalling the strength of his nephew's single-mindedness when fixed on an objective—so like his mama's iron will—Alastair raised a sceptical eyebrow. 'If you can succeed in distracting the boy who chattered all the way home from the Gardens about his new friend, I'll be surprised. Besides, if Diana goes about in Society, I'm bound to encounter her from time to time.'

'You don't mean you'll chance seeing her again?' his sister returned incredulously. 'Oh, Alastair, don't risk it!'

'Risk? Come now, Jane, this all happened years ago. No need to enact a Cheltenham tragedy.'

Pressing her lips together, Jane shook her head, tears sheening her eyes. 'I know you say you're over her, and I only pray God it's true. But I'll never forget—no one who cares about you ever could—how absolutely and completely *bouleversé* you were. The wonderful poetry you wrote in homage to her wit, her beauty, her grace, her liveliness! The fact that you haven't written a line since she jilted you.'

'The army was hardly a place for producing boyish truck about eternal love,' Alastair said, dismissing his former passion with practised scorn. Besides, poetry and his love for Diana had been so intimately intertwined, he'd not been able to continue one without the other. 'One matures, Jane, and moves on.'

'Does one? Have you? I'd be more inclined to believe it if you had ever shown any interest in another *eligible* woman. Do you truly believe all women to be perfidious? Or is it what I fear—that your poet's soul, struck more deeply by emotion than an ordinary man's, cannot imagine loving anyone but her?'

'Don't be ridiculous,' he said stiffly, compelled to deny her suspicion. 'I told you, that childish infatuation was crushed by events years ago.'

'I hope so! But even if, praise God, you *are* over her, I shall never forgive her for the agony and embarrassment she caused you. Nor can I forgive the fact that her betrayal turned a carefree, optimistic, joyous young man almost overnight into a bitter, angry recluse who shunned Society and did his utmost to get himself killed in battle.'

To his considerable alarm, Jane, normally the most stoic of sisters, burst into tears. Unsure what to do to stem the tide, he pulled her into a hug. 'There, there, now, that's a bit excessive, don't you think? Are you increasing again? It's not like you to be so missish.'

His bracing words had the desired effect, and she pushed him away. 'Missish! How dare you accuse me of that! And, no, I'm not increasing. It's beastly of you to take me to task when I'm simply concerned about you.'

'You know I appreciate that concern,' he said quietly.

She took an agitated turn about the room before coming back to face him. 'Have you any idea what

it was like for your friends, your family—witnessing the depths of your pain, fearing for your sanity,
your very life? Hearing the stories that came back
to us from the Peninsula? You volunteering to lead
every "forlorn hope", always throwing yourself into
the worst of the battle, defying death, uncaring of
whether or not you survived.'

'But I did survive,' he replied. *Far too many
worthy men had not, though, while he came through
every battle untouched. 'Angry Alastair's luck' the
troops had called it. He'd discouraged the talk and
turned away the eager volunteers for his command
who listened to it since that famous luck never
seemed to extend to the men around him.*

'Please tell me you will not see her,' Jane said,
pulling him back to the present.

'I certainly won't seek her out. But with Robbie
having befriended her son, I imagine I won't be
able to avoid her entirely.'

'I must think of some way to discourage the
friendship. I really don't want my son to take up
with any offspring of hers. He's probably as poi-
sonous as she is!'

'Come now, Jane, listen to yourself! You can't
seriously hold the poor child accountable for the
failings of his mother,' Alastair protested, uncom-
fortably aware that, initially, he'd done just that.

'He's the spawn of the devil, whatever you say,' Jane flung back. 'You don't know all the things that have been said about her! I never mentioned her when I wrote you, feeling you'd been hurt enough, but there were always rumours swirling. How she defied the Duke in public, showing no deference to his friends or family. Turned her back on her own friends, too, once she became his Duchess—the few who remained after she jilted you. They say she became so unmanageable the Duke had to remove her to his country estate. I know she's not been in London in all the years since my marriage. I've even heard that, as soon as the Duke fell seriously ill, she took herself off to Bath, refusing to nurse him or even to remain to see him properly buried!'

'Enough, Jane. I've no interest in gossip, nor have I any intention of being more than politely civil to the woman, if and when the need arises. So you see, there's nothing to upset yourself about.'

At that moment, a discreet knock sounded and the housekeeper appeared, bearing news of some minor disaster in the kitchen that required her mistress's immediate attention. After giving his sister another quick hug, Alastair gently pushed her towards the door. 'I'll be fine. Go re-establish order in your domain.'

After Jane had followed the housekeeper out,

Alastair walked back to his room, trapped by his still-unsettled thoughts. It was sad, really, that the girl he remembered being so vivacious, a magnet who drew people to her, had, if what Jane reported was true, ended up a recluse hidden away in the country, the subject of speculation and rumour.

Did she deserve it? Had she duped him, cleverly encouraging his infatuation so he might trumpet her beauty to the world in fulsome poetry, drawing to her the attention of wealthier, more prestigious suitors? Whether or not she'd deliberately led him on, she *had* obsessed him completely, inducing him to lay his foolish, naive, adoring heart at her feet.

He ought to thank her for having burned out of him early so unrealistic an expectation as eternal love. Still, something of that long-ago heartbreak vibrated up from deep within, the pain sharp enough to make him clench his teeth.

As before, anger followed. He would offer her nothing except perhaps a well-deserved snub.

Though even as he thought it, his heart whispered that he lied.

Chapter Two

Entering the modest lodgings in Laura Place she'd hired two days previous, her son and his nursery maid trailing obediently behind her, Diana, Dowager Duchess of Graveston, mounted the stairs to the sitting room. 'You may take Mannington to the nursery to rest now,' she told the girl as she handed her bonnet and cloak to the maid-of-all-work.

'Will you come up for tea later, Mama?' the child asked, looking up at her, hope shining in his eyes.

'Perhaps. Run along now.' Inured to the disappointment on the boy's face, she turned away and walked to the sideboard by the window, removing her gloves and placing them precisely on the centre of the chest. Only after the softly closing door confirmed she was alone, did she release a long, slow breath.

She should have hugged Mannington. He would have clung to her, probably. Like any little boy, he needed a mama he could cling to. And she *could* hug him now, without having to worry over the consequences—for him or for her.

Could she find her way back to how it had once been? A memory bubbled up: the awe and tenderness she'd felt as she held her newborn son, a miracle regardless of her feelings about his father.

The father who, little by little, had forced her to bury all affection for her child.

She remembered what had happened later that first day, Graveston standing over the bed as she held the infant to her breast. Plucking him away, telling her he'd summon a wet nurse, as a duchess did not suckle her own child. He'd cut off her arguments against it, informing her that if she meant to be difficult, he'd have a wet nurse found from among one of his tenant farmers and send the child away.

So she'd turned his feedings over to a wet nurse, consoling herself that she could still watch him in his cradle.

A week later, she'd returned to her rooms to find the cradle gone. The child belonged in the nursery wing, Graveston told her when she'd protested. It wasn't fitting for a woman as lowly born as the wet nurse to spend time in the Duchess's suite. If she insisted on having the child with her, he'd end up hungry, waiting for his supper while he was dispatched to the servant's quarters.

Of course, she hadn't wanted her son to go hungry. Or to have his balls taken away, as Graveston had done months later when she'd tarried in the nursery, rolling them to him, and been late for dinner.

Though for the first and only time in their marriage, she had tried to please her husband, nothing she did was enough. The day she'd learned her toddler son had been beaten because their laughter, as she played with him in the garden under the library window, had disturbed the Duke, she'd realised the only way she could protect him was to avoid him.

And the only way she could do that was to harden her heart against him as thoroughly as she'd hardened herself to every other instinct save endurance.

She remembered the final incident, when having noticed, as he noticed everything, that she'd had little to do with the boy of late, Graveston threatened to have the child whipped again when she'd not worn the new dress he'd ordered for her to dinner. He'd watched her with the intensity of an owl honing in on a mouse as she shrugged and told him to do as he liked with his son.

She'd lost her meal and been unable to eat for three days until she'd known for certain that, no longer believing the boy a tool to control her, he'd left the child alone.

Only then had she known he was *safe*.

She sighed again. Having worked so hard to banish all affection, she'd not yet figured out how to re-animate the long-repressed instincts to mother her child. Now that he was older, it didn't help that she couldn't look at the dark hair curling over his brow or the square-jawed face without seeing Graveston reflected in them.

With a shudder, she repressed her husband's image.

Her *late* husband, she reminded herself. That liberation was so recent, she still had trouble believing she was finally free.

Living under his rule *had* perfected her mask of imperturbability, though. Lifting her eyes to the mirror over the sideboard, she studied the pale, calm, expressionless countenance staring back at her. Despite unexpectedly encountering Alastair Ransleigh after all these years, she'd not gasped, or trembled, or felt heat flame her face. No, she was quite sure the shock that had rocked her from head to toe had been undetectable in her outward appearance and manner.

The shock had almost been enough to pry free, from the vault deep within where she'd locked them away, some images from that halcyon spring they'd met and fallen in love. Had she truly once been unreserved, adoring him with wholehearted abandon, thrilling to his presence, ravenous for his touch? She winced, the memories still too painful to bear examining.

She took a deep breath and held it until the ache subsided. Sealing her mind against the possibility of allowing any more memories to escape, she turned her mind to the more practical implications of their unexpected meeting.

She supposed she should have expected to run into him eventually, but not this soon—or here. What was Alastair doing in Bath? His family home, Barton Abbey, was in Devon, and though he'd also inherited properties elsewhere, what she'd gleaned from news accounts and the little gossip that reached Graveston Court indicated that he'd spent most of his time since returning from the army either at his principal seat or in London.

Would she have fled to Bath, had she known he was here? She'd had to go somewhere, quickly, as soon as Graveston's remains had been laid to rest, somewhere she could live more cheaply and attract less notice than in London, but fashionable enough to attract excellent solicitors. Go while the servants were in turmoil, uncertain what to do now that their powerful master was no longer issuing orders, and before Blankford, her husband's eldest son and heir, had time to travel back to Graveston from hunting in Scotland.

What would she do if the new Duke, not content with claiming his old home, was bent on retribution against the woman he blamed for his mother's death and his father's estrangement? What if he pursued her here?

Putting aside a question for which she had no answer, Diana turned her mind back to Alastair. What was she to do about *him*?

She wouldn't remember how many years it had taken to lock his image, their love, and the dreams she'd cherished for the future into a place so deep within her that no trace of them ever escaped. All she had left of him was the pledge, if and when it was ever possible, to tell him why she'd spurned him without a word to marry Graveston.

She might well have that opportunity tomorrow if she accompanied Mannington to the park, where he hoped to encounter his new friend again. Should she take it?

Of course, the other boy might not come back, and if he did, Alastair might not accompany him. So rattled had she been by Alastair's unexpected appearance, she'd not even caught the boy's surname, though he must be some connection of Alastair's. Even his own son, perhaps.

That Alastair Ransleigh had managed to disturb her so deeply argued for avoiding him. The process of locking away all emotion and reaction, of practising before her mirror until she'd perfected the art of letting nothing show in her face, had been arduous and difficult. She wasn't sure how to reverse it, or even if she wanted to. Should that barrier of detachment ever be breached, whatever was left of her might crack like an eggshell.

As if in warning, despite her control, one memory from her marriage surfaced. The hope that she might some day speak to Alastair again had been the only thing that had kept her from succumbing to despair, or heeding the insidious whisper in the night that urged her to creep through the sleeping house to the parapets of Graveston Court and free herself in one great leap of defiance. Besides, though Alastair had almost certainly expunged her from his heart and mind years ago, in fairness, she owed him an explanation for that nightmare night of humiliation.

Very well, she thought, nodding to herself in the mirror. She would accompany her son to the park, and if Alastair did appear, she would approach him. He might well give her the cut direct, or slap her face, but if he allowed her to speak, she would fulfil her vow and tell him the story.

At the thought of seeing him again, a tiny flicker of anticipation bubbled up from deep within. Holding her breath and squeezing her eyes tightly shut, she stifled it.

Having awakened before dawn to pace his room until daylight, Alastair chose to avoid breakfast, knowing he wouldn't be able to hide his agitation from his eagle-eyed sister. When mid-morning finally came, Alastair set out from the Crescent, his exuberant nephew in tow.

Much as he'd tried to tell himself this was just another day, a trip to the park with Robbie like any other, he failed miserably at keeping his mind from drifting always back, like a lodestone to the north, to the possibility of seeing Diana again—a possibility that flooded him with contradictory emotions.

The defiant need to confront her and force a reaction, and curiosity over what that reaction might be, warred with the desire to cut her completely. Overlaying all was a smouldering anger that she had the power to so effectively penetrate his defences that he'd been required to employ every bit of his self-control to keep the memories at bay—a task he'd not fared so well at while half-conscious.

He'd slept poorly, waking time and again to scattered bits of images he'd hastily blotted out before trying to sleep again.

Fatigued and irritable, he tried to focus on Robbie's eager chatter, which alternated between enthusiastic praise of the horse his uncle had ridden to Bath, a wheedling plea to be allowed to sit on said horse, and anticipation at meeting his new friend again.

'The boy may not be able to come today,' Alastair said, the warning as much for his own benefit as for Robbie's. 'You may have to settle for just the company of your dull old uncle.'

'Uncle Alastair, you're never dull! And you will let me ride Fury when we get back home, won't you? We can still stop for cakes, can't we? And I'm sure James will come again. His nurse promised!'

'Did she, now?' Alastair raised a sceptical eyebrow, amused out of his agitation by the ease with which his nephew turned a possibility into a certainty, simply because he wished it. How wonderful to possess such innocence!

But then, maybe it wasn't. He'd had his innocence torched out of him by one splendid fireball of humiliation.

Whatever reply Robbie made faded in his ears as they entered Sidney Gardens—and Alastair saw her. Shock pulsated from his toes to his ears, and once again, for a moment, he couldn't breathe.

Dressed modestly all in black—at least her critics couldn't fault her there—Diana sat on a bench, as her son tossed his ball to the nursemaid on a nearby verge of grass. While Alastair worked to slow his pulse and settle his breathing, Robbie, with a delighted shout, ran ahead to meet his friend.

Now was the moment, and with a sense of panic, Alastair realised he still wasn't sure what he wanted. If Diana turned to him, should he speak with her? Ignore her? If she did not acknowledge him, should he go right up to her and force his presence on her?

Before he could settle on a course of action, with a grace that sent a shudder of memory and longing through him, Diana rose from the bench—and approached *him*.

'Mr Ransleigh,' she said as she dipped a curtsy to his stiff bow. 'Might I claim a moment of your time?'

A reply sprang without thought to his lips. 'Do you think you deserve that?'

'I am sure I do not,' she replied, the serenity of her countenance untroubled by his hostile words. 'However, I vowed if I were ever given a chance, I would explain to you what happened eight years ago.'

The violet scent she'd always worn invaded his

senses. Unconsciously, he looked down, into eyes as arrestingly blue as he remembered from the day they first captivated him. No lines marred the softness of her skin, and the few dark curls escaping from under her bonnet made him recall how he'd loved combing his fingers through those thick, sable locks. Desire—powerful, potent, unstoppable—rose up to choke him.

He had to get away. 'Do you really think, after all this time, that I care what happened?' he spat out. 'Good day, Duchess.' Pivoting on one boot, he paced away from her down the gravelled path.

He heard the crunch of her footsteps following behind him. Torn between a surge of triumph that this time, *she* was pursuing *him*, and a need to escape before he lost what little control he had left, he could barely make sense of her words.

'Although I may not deserve to be heard, since you are a gentleman, Mr Ransleigh, I know you will allow me to speak. Infamous as I am, it's best that I do so here, now, out of sight and earshot of any gossips.'

'I have never paid any attention to gossips,' Alastair flung back, turning to face her. She halted a step away, and he couldn't help noticing the flush in her cheeks, the rapid breathing that caused her bosom to rise and fall beneath the modest pelisse— as if she were recovering from a round of passion.

Desire flared again, thick in his blood, pounding in his ears. Curse it, why must the Almighty be so cruel as to leave him still so strongly attracted to this woman?

But what she said was true—if she was determined to speak with him, it was far better here than at some ball or musicale or—worse yet—a social function at which Jane was also present. 'Very well, say what you must.'

'Walk with me, then.'

In truth, some tiny honest particle of his brain admitted, he wasn't sure he could have turned away. Curiosity and lust pulled him to her, stronger than reason, common sense, or his normal highly developed sense of self-preservation.

Despite the volatile mix of anger, confusion, pain and desire coursing through him, he also noted that, though she asked him to walk with her, she did not offer him her arm.

Not that it mattered. So intensely conscious was he of her body a foot from his, he could almost hear her breaths and feel the pulse in her veins.

'I met the Duke of Graveston at one of the first balls of my debut Season,' she began. 'He asked me to dance and accorded me polite interest, but I thought nothing of it. He was older, married, and I had eyes for only one man.'

Her words struck him to the core, despite the fact that she said them simply, unemotionally, as if stating a fact of mild interest. Swallowing hard, he forced his attention back to her narrative, the next few words of which he'd already missed.

'…began seeing him at home, visiting Papa. They had similar scientific interests, Papa said when I asked him. It wasn't until some months later that I learned just what those "interests" truly were. By that time, the Duke's wife had died. To my astonishment, he proposed to me. I politely refused, telling him that my heart and hand had already been pledged to another. He…laughed. And told me that he was certain I would change my mind after I carefully measured the advantages of becoming his Duchess against marrying a young man of no title who was still dependent upon his father.'

Though they walked side by side, Alastair noticed Diana seemed increasingly detached, as if, transported to some other place and time, she was no longer even conscious of his presence. 'He returned a week later, asked me again, and received the same answer. In fact, I urged him to look elsewhere for a bride, as, though I was fully aware of the honour of his offer, it did not and would never interest me. He said that was regrettable, but he had chosen me for his wife, and marry him I would.'

Alastair had to laugh at that fantastic statement. 'Are you truly trying to persuade me that he "gave you no choice"? That horse won't run! This isn't the Middle Ages—a girl can't be forced into marriage.'

She nodded, still not looking at him. 'So I thought. But I was wrong. You see, those "visits" to Papa hadn't just been spent in scientific discourse. They'd also been gaming together—a pleasant match among friends, Papa later called it when I taxed him about it. But the Duke was a very skilful player, and Papa was not. When I refused again to marry him, he produced vouchers Papa had signed—vouchers worth thousands of pounds. Unless I married him, he said, he would call them in. Of course, there was no possible way Papa could have repaid such a sum. He would be sent to debtors' prison, the Duke said. How long did I think, with his delicate health, he would last in Newgate? At first, I was certain the Duke was joking. He soon convinced me he was not. He warned that if I said a word about this to my father, he would have him clapped in prison, regardless of what I did. I didn't dare call his bluff.'

Scarcely about to credit anyone capable of perpetrating such a Byzantine scheme, Alastair retorted, 'Why did you not come to me, then? True, I'd not yet inherited, but I could have persuaded my father to advance me a sum, and borrowed more on my expectations.'

'He threatened to ruin you, too, if I gave you even a hint of what he intended.'

'Ruin me? How?' Alastair replied derisively. '*I* was never a gamester, and though I was certainly no saint at university, I'd done nothing serious enough to dishonour my name, no matter how the facts might be distorted.'

She paused a moment, as if to say more, then shook her head. 'This would have.'

'No, it's all preposterous!' Alastair burst out. 'Graveston did have a sinister presence about him, but I can't believe he convinced you he would do what he threatened.'

She turned to give him a sad smile. 'Do you remember my little spaniel, Ribbons?'

'The black-and-white one with the ears that trailed in the wind?'

'Like ribbons, yes. After the Duke revealed his intentions, he gave me a day to think it over. When he returned the next day, he asked me how my dog was. I'd not seen Ribbons that morning, and when I looked, I found him—dead. The Duke merely smiled, and told me as his Duchess, I could have as many dogs as I liked.'

Despite himself, Alastair felt the implication of those words like a blow to the stomach.

She continued, 'As you know, we were a small household—just Cook and two maids and a man-of-all-work, all of whom had been with us for years. I questioned each one, and they all swore they'd seen—or done—nothing unusual. I realised then, if the Duke could bribe one of my own household to harm an innocent dog, or infiltrate someone who would, he was perfectly capable of forcing Papa into prison and ruining you. That the only thing to prevent him extracting retribution upon the people I loved would be for me to marry him. His final requirement in leaving you both unharmed was to never tell either of you the truth. You must both believe I married him of my own free will.'

Struggling to decide whether to accept the story she'd just told, Alastair shook his head. 'It's...it's unthinkable that someone would act in such a fashion.'

'Very true. Another reason why the Duke didn't worry about my confiding in anyone but you or Papa. Who *would* believe such a story?'

'Well, I don't,' Alastair retorted, making up his mind. Feeling both betrayed and disgusted that she would try to fob off on him such a Banbury tale, he said, 'Besides, do you really think your apology now makes any difference to me? Frankly, I would respect you more if you just admitted the truth—that the lure of a duchess's coronet outweighed whatever I could offer you.'

She turned to him, for a long moment silently studying his face. 'I have told you the truth. I cannot make you believe it, of course. But I did want you to know that it was not for any lack in you that I wed another man.'

'I never thought it was.'

'I don't expect your respect. I'm rather certain you despise me, and I can't blame you. Nor is there anything I could ever do to make up to you for the embarrassment and humiliation of the Coddingford ball.'

The words exited his lips before he was even aware he meant to speak. 'Well, since I'm currently between mistresses, you could fulfil that role until I tire of you.'

Aghast, he waited for her to gasp with outrage or slap his face. To his astonishment, after staring at him for another moment, she said, 'Very well. Make the arrangements and send me word. Fifteen Laura Place.'

Before Alastair could respond, two small boys

pelted up from behind them, one grabbing his hand. 'Can we go for cakes now, Uncle Alastair?' Robbie asked. 'James and I are powerful hungry.'

'Yes, Mama, may I go today?' Diana's son asked her.

'Today you may go,' his mother responded. While the two boys whooped and slapped each other's backs, without another glance at Alastair, Diana turned and walked away.

Stunned, incredulous—and incredibly tempted— Alastair gazed after her until the turn in the pathway took her from view.

Chapter Three

After admonishing the boys that the hoydenish behaviour allowed in the park would not be tolerated in an establishment that served cakes, Alastair shepherded his young charges and Lord James Mannington's nursemaid across Pulteney Bridge, down High Street, around the Abbey and into the bakery off North Parade that served the famous buns. In a mechanical daze, he ordered cakes for the boys and the blushing maid, dismissing with a distracted wave her protest that he need not include her in the treat.

It was good that both boys had learned their manners well—or that the presence of the nursemaid restrained them. For with his mind whirling like a child's top, he could not afterwards recall a single thing they'd said or done at the shop.

Melted butter congealing on the bun set before him, Alastair went over again and again in his mind the exchange between himself and Diana—particularly the last bit, when he, incredibly, had offered her carte blanche and she, even more incredibly, had accepted.

If he'd had more time after that fraught final exchange, he probably would have retracted the hasty words, perhaps covering the naked need they'd revealed by delivering the stinging response that he'd only been joking, for Diana did not meet the minimum standards for beauty, wit and charm that he required of a mistress.

Instead, he'd done nothing, standing mute as a statue while she walked away.

Regardless of how he felt over her former treatment, he should be ashamed of himself for tendering such an insulting offer. To a dowager duchess, no less, who now outranked him on the social scale by several large leaps! As soon as he arrived back at his room at the Crescent, he should write her a note of apology, recanting the offer.

And yet... For the first time, he admitted to himself what meeting Diana again had made only too painfully clear. Despite the bold assertion to the contrary he'd given his sister, he had never really got over losing her. Every woman he'd met since had been measured against her and found lacking; every mistress he'd bedded had been physically reminiscent of her, unconsciously chosen to blot her out of his mind and senses.

None ever had.

Since Diana *had* accepted his offer, maybe he should go through with it. After all, there was no way the real woman could measure up to the romantic vision his youthful, poetic soul had once idolised...especially after how she'd treated him. Marrying a duke to 'save' him? What kind of dupe did she take him to be?

Maybe possessing her now would finally burn out of him the pain and yearning that had haunted him so long.

Like a thief lured into a dwelling through an unlocked window, now that his mind had tumbled on to the possibility of an affair, he couldn't keep himself from exploring it further. The desire she so readily evoked, banked rather than extinguished, raged back into flame.

Anticipation, excitement and eagerness boiled in his blood, and only by reminding himself that two young innocents and their virginal nursemaid sat mere feet away, was he able to restrain his mind from picturing himself possessing her.

He'd do it, then. Unless Diana sent a note rescinding her acceptance, he *would* go through with it.

After sending her son and the maid home in a

sedan chair, Alastair hurried the now-sleepy Robbie up to the heights of the Crescent. As soon as
he'd dispatched the boy back to the nursery, he descended the stairs at a run, bent on finding the most
exclusive leasing office he could.

It was imperative to find just the right property
for their rendezvous—in a location elegant enough
for the purpose, but well-enough hidden that the
ever-vigilant Jane was unlikely to discover it.

An hour later, the bargain concluded, he was escorted out by the beaming proprietor, whom he'd
paid double his usual fee for his silence and to obtain possession of the property immediately. Holding the key to a fine townhouse in Green Park
Buildings, a respectable address but one well to
the west of the most fashionable streets, Alastair
set off back to the Crescent.

He'd wait one night, to see if a note arrived from
Diana, reneging on her initial acceptance. If he did
not hear from her by tomorrow, he'd send *her* a
note, arranging to meet after supper that night.

Excitement shivered and danced in his blood,
sparkled in his mind. He couldn't remember ever
being this consumed by anticipation.

An exalted state that was sure to end in disillusion, once he became better acquainted with the real Diana. Which was exactly what he wanted.

The sooner the affair began, the sooner it would be over—and he would be free of her at last.

In the evening of the following day, Diana sat at her dressing table, a note in hand. As she glanced at her name inscribed in Alastair's bold script, another memory pierced her chest like an arrow.

How many times during their courtship had she opened just such a note, finding within a beautiful verse in honour of her? Praising her wit, her virtue, her loveliness.

How unworthy of them she'd felt.

How unworthy of them she'd proved.

This current missive could hardly be more different. Instead of elegantly penned lines of clever metaphors, similes, and alliteration, there wasn't even a complete sentence. Merely an address and a time—this evening, nine o'clock.

Despite her hard-won self-control, uneasiness and something more, something dangerously like anticipation, stirred within her. Stifling it, she debated again, as she had off and on since receiving the summons this morning, whether or not to dispatch a last-minute refusal of his shocking offer.

It was risky, allowing him to be near her.

Graveston had possessed the power to restrict her activities and movements, to hurt her physically, but had never been able to touch her soul—a failure that had maddened him and represented her only victory in their battlefield sham of a marriage. Alastair Ransleigh would never touch her in anger…but it was the touch of tenderness, the touch of a man she'd once desired above all else, that threatened her in a way the Duke had never managed, despite his relentless cruelty.

She'd certainly have to be on guard, lest he get close enough to threaten her emotional reserve. Still… Once, she'd been so happy with Alastair. Might giving herself to him bring her a glimpse of that long-vanished happiness?

But then, she was reading much too much into this. The insulting nature of Alastair's offer was proof he despised her.

Would it have made any difference, had she explained just how the Duke intended to destroy him? Probably not, she concluded. He hadn't even believed the Duke's threat of debtors' prison for Papa, and what the Duke had promised for Alastair had been far more outrageous.

No, there wasn't any question of warmth or affection between them. She'd humiliated him before all of Society, abused his trust, and like any man, he wanted retribution. She was fair enough to think he deserved it.

Not that yielding her body would prove much of a humiliation for her, not after years of submission to a man who believed he had the right to use her whenever and however he pleased. Whatever his reasons for proposing the liaison, giving herself up to Alastair would be an improvement over the subjugation of her marriage. Alastair, at least, she'd always admired and respected.

In any event, the arrangement probably wouldn't last long. Once Ransleigh had his fill of her, he'd cast her aside, leaving her free to…do what with the rest of her life?

Frowning, she dropped the note on the dressing table and rose to take a restless turn about the room. Alastair Ransleigh's sudden reappearance had distracted her from focusing on how to deal with Lord Blankford, a matter of far more importance.

There was a chance Blankford might simply ignore her and Mannington. With a sigh, she quickly dismissed that foolish hope. Her husband's eldest son had been raised to believe that a duke's desires were paramount, and that he could manipulate, reward or smite all lesser beings with impunity. It was highly unlikely, given how closely the character of the heir mirrored that of the sire, that the injury he believed she'd committed against him and his mother would go unpunished.

At the very least, he would try to take Mannington away from her. Even if he didn't have evil designs upon the child, she wouldn't allow a dog, much less a little boy, to grow up under the influence of such a man. She might not, up until now, have proved herself much of a mother, but she would do everything in her power to prevent her innocent son's character from being distorted by the same despicable standards held by his father and elder brother.

Even as she thought it, she shook her head. How could she, whom her husband had methodically isolated from any friends and family, prevail against one of the highest-ranked men in England?

Putting aside, for the moment, that unanswerable question, then what? Even if she managed to protect her son from Blankford, Mannington needed more than rescue from evil influences to grow into the confident, compassionate, honourable man she'd like him to be.

She first needed to re-establish some sort of normal, motherly link with the boy—something she'd been forced to avoid while Graveston lived. Now that she need no longer fear showing him affection, how was she to retrieve, from the abyss into which she'd buried it, the natural bond between a mother and her child? That she'd hated the man who sired him was not Mannington's fault. Like every child, to grow and thrive he needed love—of which, until now, he'd received precious little.

For the first time in many years, she allowed herself to think about her own childhood—a time so idyllic and distant that it seemed to belong to another person, or another life. Despite losing his wife in childbirth at an early age, Papa had managed to submerge his own grief and create a home filled with love, security, joy and laughter. How had he done so?

Settling back on the dressing-table bench, she stared at her image in the mirror, digging through the bits of memory.

They'd certainly not had the material advantages available to a duke. As a younger son from a minor branch of a prominent family, no objection had been posed to Papa pursuing a career as an Oxford tutor, nor of his marrying for love a gentleman's daughter of great beauty and small dowry. After Mama's death, they'd taken rooms close to the university, where he might more easily mentor his students and pursue his own botanical studies. As both Mama and Papa had no other close kin, it had always been just the two of them.

She'd learned her letters at his knee, studied her lessons in his office, painted and played piano for him in the adjacent studio. Picnics beside the river turned into treasure hunts, often enlivened by games of hide-and-seek, as she helped Papa search for rare plants. Every day ended with him reading to her, or telling her a bedtime story. Later, as his eyesight began to fail and his health grew more frail, she had read to him.

First thing, then, she ticked off on one finger, she'd need to spend more time with Mannington… *James*, she corrected herself. No longer a tool of the Duke to control her, but simply a child. *Her son.*

A frisson of long-suppressed tenderness vibrated deep within her, as barely discernible as the scent of a newly opening rose.

Having deliberately avoided him since he'd been a toddler, she wasn't sure where to start. Other than accompanying him to the park, what did one do with a young boy?

Perhaps she could start by reading to him at bedtime. All children liked being read to, didn't they? If he enjoyed the interaction, his happiness should warm her, too, and begin the difficult process of dismantling the barriers she'd put in place to stifle any feeling towards him.

But the creation of a true home meant more than

just spending time with him. Her father had not been nearly as prominent or powerful as her husband, but he'd been an enthusiastic, optimistic man who inspired love and admiration in everyone with whom he came into contact. Even students not especially interested in botany grew to appreciate the natural universe whose wonders he unfolded to them.

He'd exuded an infectious joy in life, in every little detail of living, from lauding the warmth of the fire on a cold evening, to savouring tea and cakes with her in the afternoon, to the enthusiasm with which he read to her, altering his voice to play all the parts from Shakespeare, or emoting the sonnets with an understanding that brought the beauty of the words and the depth of their meaning to life. He'd loved being a scholar, never losing his excitement at finding and recording in meticulous drawings all the plants he collected.

She could almost hear his voice, telling her how everything fit together in the natural world, with all having its place. She, too, had been designed with particular talents and abilities, her contributions unique, irreplaceable, and a necessary part to the whole.

She swallowed hard and her eyes stung. She hadn't remembered that bit of encouragement for years. Did she have a place and a purpose? Having lost first Alastair and then her father, was there something more for her than mere survival?

She could start by saving her son from Blankford. She could try her best to unlock her feelings and love him again. She could attempt to create the kind of home he deserved, that every child deserved, where he was wanted, appreciated, nourished.

The last would be a stretch. She wasn't her father, or even a pale echo of him. Once, another lifetime ago, she'd been a fearless girl who loved with all her heart and met life with reckless passion...

But how could she, who had forgotten what joy was, offer that to a child she might not find her way back to loving?

Sighing, she raised an eyebrow at the image in the mirror. The reflection staring back at her, the only friend and ally she'd had during the hellish years of her marriage, merely looked back, returning no answers.

She'd just have to try harder, she told the image. Once Alastair Ransleigh finished with her, she could close the book of her past and begin a new volume, with James.

Pray God she'd have enough time to figure it out before Blankford made his move.

But first, tonight, she must begin repaying the debt she owed Alastair. Her hands trembling ever so slightly, she rang for the maid and began to dress.

Chapter Four

Alastair paused in his pacing of the parlour of the small townhouse he'd rented, listening to the mantel clock strike three-quarters past eight. Unless she'd changed her previous habit of promptness, in another fifteen minutes, Diana would be here.

His pulses leapt as a surge of anticipation and desire rushed through him. Too impatient to sit, he took another turn about the room, then set off on yet another tour of the premises.

He'd arrived at eight, wanting to ensure everything was as he'd ordered. The new staff dispatched by the agency, all with impeccable references, had done their jobs perfectly. The immaculate house gleamed, every wooden surface and silver object polished to a soft glow in the candlelight. Taking the stairs, he inspected the sitting room adjoining the bedroom, nodding dismissal to the maid who'd just finished setting out a cold buffet. In the bedroom itself, a decanter of wine stood on the bedside table, and two glasses reflected the flames of the lit candles on the mantel above.

Wine to lend courage to him—or to her? he wondered with a wry grin. Maybe for consolation, if the joke was on him and Diana simply did not show up.

Which would, he admitted, be a justifiable rebuke for his ungentlemanly behaviour.

Even as he thought it, he heard the click of the front door opening, and a murmur of voices as the new manservant admitted a visitor.

So she had come after all.

Alastair descended the stairs nearly at a run.

'I've shown the, ah, lady into the parlour,' the servant told him. 'Will you be needing anything else, sir?'

'Nothing more tonight, Marston. Thank you.'

Expression impassive, the servant bowed and headed off towards the service stairs. Alastair wondered, not for the first time, what the handful of employees thought of their new situation—and how much they'd been told when the agency he'd consulted had hired them. Certainly upon arrival, if not before, they would have realised they were being called upon to staff the love nest of some wealthy man's *chère-amie*. He'd not been able to glean from the behaviour of Marston, the cook or the maid whether they disapproved or were indifferent to the situation.

To tell the truth, he felt a bit uncomfortable. In his previous liaisons, after hiring a house, he'd simply given the lady of the moment the funds to bring or hire her own staff—and had never given the servants' opinions a thought. But this was *Diana*—and how she was regarded by the staff, he realised suddenly, did matter to him.

Rather ridiculous that he was concerned she be treated like a lady, when he'd set up this whole endeavour to humiliate her.

No, not to humiliate—simply to slake his desire for her, so that he might achieve the indifference that seemed to come so easily to her. So he could get over her and get on with his life, as she so obviously had.

Heartbeat accelerating, Alastair walked into the parlour.

A lady stood at the hearth with her back to him, enveloped in a black cape with the hood drawn up over her hair. Very discreet, Alastair thought, glad that she was evidently as concerned as he that this liaison be kept secret.

She turned towards him, and the visceral reaction she'd always evoked flooded him immediately, speeding his pulses, drying his mouth, filling him with desire and gladness.

'Good evening, Alastair,' she said. 'Where would you like me?'

Something almost like…disappointment tempered his enthusiasm. So there'd be no illusion of polite conversation first—just a proceeding straight to the matter at hand. She'd always been honest and direct, Alastair remembered.

Which was just as well. She wasn't here to revive an old relationship, but to bury the long-dead corpse of one.

'Come,' he said, motioning to the hallway.

Obediently she exited the parlour, brushing past him in a cloud of violet scent that instantly revived his lust and determination. She mounted the stairs, pausing at the top until he indicated the correct bedchamber.

He let her precede him into the room, already so taut with arousal that his hands were sweating and his breath uneven. In one fluid movement, she swept off her cloak and cast it in a shimmer of satin on to the chair beside the bed, then turned to him, waiting.

He scanned her hungrily. The full swell of bosom, the graceful curve of neck and cheek, the dusky curls gleaming brightly in the firelight, the lush pout of a mouth…the eyes staring sightlessly ahead of her, the face as devoid of expression as a statue. As if she were bored, waiting for the episode to be over.

While he stood, barely able to breathe, gut churning with eagerness and longing.

Sudden fury consumed him. But before he could sort through his wildly varying impulses—send her away or seduce her into feeling something—she sank to her knees before him and calmly unbuttoned his trouser flap. Wrapping her hands around his swollen length, she guided him into her mouth.

Shocked that she would play the courtesan so unresistingly, he opened his lips to tell her to stop…but at the touch of the exquisite softness of her tongue, moving over and around his throbbing member, thought dissolved into pure sensation. Gasping, he fisted his hands in her hair, every fibre of his being focused on the delicious friction of her mouth and tongue as she pushed him deep within, withdrew to suckle the sensitive tip, laved it with her tongue and took him deep again. Passion built with unprecedented swiftness until mere moments later, he climaxed in a rush so dizzying and intense he nearly lost consciousness.

Staggering backward, he collapsed on the bed, his heart trying to beat its way out of his chest.

Dazed, he dimly noted Diana rising and walking noiselessly over to the washbasin on the bureau.

Sometime later, his heart finally settled back into its normal rhythm and enough rational thought returned that he recognised what had just transpired. He'd meant to slake his lust, not use her like a doxy—or bolt straight to conclusion, like a callow youth with his first woman.

Shame and embarrassment filled him. Looking around, he found Diana sitting silently in the chair, gazing into the fire, her cloak wrapped around her.

'I'm sorry. I hadn't meant for that to be an exclusive experience,' he said. 'I assure you, I can do much better.'

And he meant to. Of the many things that had attracted him to Diana during their courtship, one that had drawn him most strongly was her passion. She'd gloried in his kisses, giving herself to him with wild abandon, guiding his hands to her breasts, moulding her hands over his erection. He might not be able to love her again or truly forgive her, but they could at least have the honesty of pleasure between them.

'It doesn't matter,' she said.

'It does to me,' he replied, and held out his hand.

This time, he vowed as she took it, he would undress her slowly, as he'd dreamed of doing so many times. Kiss and caress each bit of skin revealed. Use all the considerable skill he'd amassed over nearly a decade of pleasuring women to give her the same intense release she'd just given him.

'I didn't hire you a lady's maid,' he said, turning her so he could begin unlacing the ties at the back of her bodice. 'I shall perform that function myself.'

She didn't reply, which was just as well, for as the ties loosened, the bare nape of her neck so distracted him he'd not have comprehended her words anyway. Unable to resist, he bent to kiss her.

That intoxicating violet scent wrapped around him again as he tasted her skin. Desire returning in a rush, he slid his hands into her hair, winnowing out the pins with his fingers until the heavy mass fell to her shoulders and cascaded down her back. Wrapping his hands in the thick lengths, he pulled her closer, moving his lips from her neck to the shell of her ear.

Already fully erect again, he parted the hair and pulled it forward over her breasts, unveiling the pins and lacing that secured bodice and skirt. Making quick work of those, he peeled off the top and nudged her to step out of the skirt, then guided her to the bed.

Seating her on the edge, he tilted up her head and took her mouth, moving his lips slowly, gently over their silken surface as he dispensed with her stays. At the pressure of his tongue, she parted her lips, allowing him entry to the softness within.

While he licked and suckled, he moved his hands to cup her breasts, full and ripe under the thin linen of her chemise. His breathing unsteady now, he thrust a pillow behind her and urged her back against it, then slid the chemise up, baring her from ankle to waist.

Going to his knees, he slowly rolled down her stockings, kissing and licking the soft skin of her knees, calves, ankles, toes, then moving in a slow ascent back up to her thighs. Urging those apart, he kissed his way slowly higher, while his hands moulded and caressed her hips and derrière.

By now, he was more than ready to enter her and find consummation again. But wanting this time to give maximum pleasure to her, holding himself under tight control, he moved his mouth closer and closer to her centre as he slid a finger over and around the nether lips. Another bolt of lust struck him as he found her moist and ready.

Unable to wait any longer, he moved his mouth to her core, parting the curls to run his tongue along the plump little nub nested within. But though his own breathing was by now erratic, Diana did not, as he'd expected, grip his back or wrap her legs around his shoulders. She didn't arch into him, her body picking up the ancient rhythm leading to fulfilment. Eyes tightly closed, she simply lay against the pillow, her face tense, her hands fisted.

Perhaps she'd been schooled that an uninhibited response was unladylike—he'd have to re-educate her about that. Or perhaps complete possession was necessary to trigger her reaction—he was certainly ready!

Murmuring, his hands gentle and caressing, he moved on to the bed and straddled her parted thighs, positioning himself over her. Kissing her, he lowered himself, slowly penetrating her.

He thought she flinched, and halted. But as he pressed carefully downward, her body greeted him in hot, slick warmth. Thrilled, he pushed deeper into the soft, yielding depths, until he'd sheathed himself completely.

Sweat broke out on his brow and his rigid arms trembled as he stilled deep within her, battling the urge to thrust and withdraw, thrust and withdraw in wild rhythm to reach the pinnacle that shimmered just out of reach.

But though her body was obviously primed to receive him, Diana did not moan, or tilt her hips to pull him deeper…or move at all; she lay, eyes still closed, passively beneath him.

Knowing that even remaining motionless, he'd not be able to stave off his own climax much longer, and wanting desperately to bring Diana with him on that journey to ecstasy and back, Alastair wondered what to try next.

Granted, his previous amours had all been experienced, or at least enthusiastic participants. Almost, he was ready to withdraw completely—except that despite her self-control, her body didn't lie. The peaked nipples and liquid heat within told him that she wasn't unreceptive. The tightly closed eyes, clenched fists and rigid posture told him she was exerting all her will to resist responding.

Well, he'd see about that. Slowly he began moving in her, rocking deep, caressing the little nub with every stroke, then bending to suckle the taut nipples.

But though he was soon riding the razor's edge, trying to stave off climax, Diana remained stiffly unmoving. Desperate, he redoubled his efforts.

Only to have her place a hand on his sweaty chest. 'Go ahead, finish now,' she said, her eyes still closed. And rocked her hips to force him deeper.

He wasn't sure he could have resisted much longer anyway. But as she finally moved beneath him, the dyke of his control broke and wave after wave of pleasure crested, washing over him with a force that robbed him of breath and consciousness.

Suddenly aware that his weight must be crushing her, he rolled to the side and up on the pillow.

'May I wash now?' she asked, not meeting his gaze.

Too passion-drugged for coherent thought, he simply nodded. And watched as she slid off the bed, walked to the bureau, and calmly plied the sponge and linen towelling, then turned to face him, still naked.

Despite the perplexing episode that had just transpired between them, she was still so lovely, still called so strongly to some uncontrollable something deep within him, that all he wanted was to pull her back into bed and love her again.

'May I dress now? Or do you require…more tonight?'

That prosaic question dashed whatever remained of his sensual haze, unleashing a boiling cauldron of emotions. Disappointment. Puzzlement. Curiosity. Embarrassment.

Anger.

No previous experience had prepared him to deal with an outcome like this. But he'd not take her again tonight, much as he wanted to, not until he'd had time to figure out what had happened and what to do about it.

'That will be all for now,' he said curtly, the dismissal eroding what little remained of the euphoria. She nodded, seeming entirely untroubled by the cold, transactional nature of the interlude.

In silence he dressed her. 'Have Marston summon you a chair,' he said at last, when the final tape had been tied, the pins replaced and her hair, much too thick for his fumbling attempts to recreate a coiffure, had been thrust under her bonnet.

'Will you require me tomorrow?' she asked, still not meeting his eyes.

'I'll send you a note. You'll make yourself available?'

'As you wish. Goodnight, then, Alastair.'

With a nod, she exited the chamber.

Alastair listened until her footsteps faded down the stairs. Then, with an oath, he poured himself a glass of wine and downed it in one swallow.

What the hell had just happened?

Chapter Five

Frustration boiled up, and Alastair had to exert all his self-control to keep from hurling the unoffending wine glass into the hearth, just for the satisfaction of hearing it smash.

Had Diana been secretly laughing at him, mocking his all-too-evident desire with her ability to resist him?

Oh, how things had changed! After their engagement, she'd tantalised him, trying to drive him wild enough to overcome his refusal to take her before they were wed. He'd insisted she deserved better than some furtive, hurried coupling in the library or garden, where her father or a servant might at any moment interrupt. When they finally tasted consummation, he wanted them to be able to love each other freely, at length and at leisure.

This time, he had been eager and she'd been... indifferent.

If he'd not had numerous ladies testify to his expertise as a lover, he'd have been unmanned by her total lack of response.

But that wasn't quite right, he corrected himself. Her *body* had responded; of that, he was certain. But for some reason, she'd refused to allow herself to experience pleasure.

To punish him for coercing her into this, so he might not revel in her satisfaction at his hands?

He didn't think so. She'd exhibited no triumph at having resisted his skill; there'd been nothing of gloating superiority in her being able to render him helpless with pleasure, while refusing to allow him to do the same for her.

Besides, though he might have had the bad taste to propose the liaison, he'd done nothing to force her into accepting. As she certainly knew, were she to have refused the offer, he would have left it at that.

Instead, it was almost as if she had withdrawn entirely, not permitting herself to experience pleasure.

How had the passionate girl he remembered come to this?

Was this startling transformation her late husband's fault? For the first time he began to doubt his certainty that the account she'd given him of her marriage was a complete, or at least exaggerated, fabrication.

A sympathy he did not want to feel welled up in the wake of that doubt.

Stifling it, he jumped up and began to pace. There had to be some way to penetrate that wall of resistance. Break through to reach the body trembling for completion, and bring it to satisfaction.

If she'd been repulsed by him, or truly unresponsive, he would have, regretfully, dismissed her tonight. Instead, there'd been an intriguing disconnect between her will and her body's arousal.

He'd hoped a few episodes would be enough to set him free of her. But he knew now with certainty that he could never let her go until he'd *reached* her, coaxed forth the response simmering beneath the surface, until she cried and shuddered in his arms with all the passion he'd not allowed himself to taste all those years ago.

How best to tempt her?

Pouring another glass of wine, he set himself to consider it.

Dismissing the sedan chair, Diana let herself into the townhouse and crept up to her chamber on legs that were still not steady. Summoning the maid to help her out of the gown—mercifully, the girl made no comment on hair that looked like an escapee from Bedlam had arranged it—she then dismissed her.

Sleep was out of the question. With her body still humming with awareness and her hard-won calm in tatters, she settled into the chair before the hearth, heart racing as she tried to determine what to do next.

Oh, she had been so right to fear letting Alastair Ransleigh get close to her! She'd thought, after eight years of fulfilling a man's desires in whatever way demanded of her while mentally distancing herself from the activity, she would be able to service Alastair with detachment.

And so she had…but just barely.

The process had been much easier with the Duke, who had no interest in her physical satisfaction. In fact, he'd mentioned on several occasions that he thought it demeaning for a man to have a wife who disported herself in the bedchamber like a harlot; such behaviour was for strumpets, not for the highborn woman chosen for the honour of breeding the offspring of a lord.

Given his opinion, she might have been tempted to 'disport' herself on occasion, had it not meant lengthening the time she had to suffer his touch. As it was, she slowly perfected the ability to wall herself off from what was happening to her. Viewing actions, even as she performed them, as if she were a spectator observing them from afar had allowed her to tolerate the bedchamber requirements of her role.

But Alastair was not the Duke she hated. And hard as she tried to block out what he was doing, ignoring it had proved impossible. Alastair's touch had been more veneration than violation, and it had taken every iota of self-control she'd developed over eight miserable years to keep herself from responding.

He'd always had the power to move her. She'd not allowed herself to remember that. Once she was irrevocably married, it would have been a cruelty beyond endurance to recall the joy of being caressed by a man whose touch thrilled her, while being forced to submit to intimacies with a man she loathed.

She'd given herself up to Alastair completely that halcyon summer, eager for him to possess her, arguing against waiting until after the wedding for them to become lovers.

She smiled wistfully. Would it have made any difference, had she not been a virgin when the Duke sought her out?

Probably not. He'd regarded her as a treasure like

the Maidens of the Parthenon, and like them, she'd have been collected even if 'damaged'. He'd merely have constructed an inescapable cage to prevent any lapses after marriage, and waited to bed her until he was sure she was not carrying another man's child.

And simply disposed of the evidence, if she had been.

But that was neither here nor there, she told herself, pulling her focus back to the present. The problem was how to deal with Alastair Ransleigh *now*.

Perhaps if she *had* remembered how quickly and deeply Alastair affected her, she'd have armoured herself better to resist him. After this evening, she no longer suffered from that dangerous ignorance. So what was she to do to avoid another near-disaster?

Forbidding herself to react had simply not been effective. Especially since, unlike the Duke, he'd clearly *wanted* her to respond. Wanted to give her pleasure…as a gift?

Or was that to be the form of his revenge: making her respond to him, making her burn for his touch, then abandoning her, as she had abandoned him? Would he not be satisfied until he'd succeeded in doing so?

Could he succeed?

She didn't *want* to feel anything. Not passion, not

desire, not longing, not affection. Overcoming the forces ranged against her, doing what she could to safeguard the boy unlucky enough to be her son, would require all the strength she could muster. A wounded bird marshalling all her efforts to lead the predator away from her nest, she couldn't afford to bleed away any of her limited energy in resisting Alastair Ransleigh.

His reappearance was a complication she didn't need.

She could simply not see him again. Send him a note saying she'd changed her mind. Follow the instincts for self-preservation that were screaming at her to run. Unlike the Duke, who had ignored her refusals, she knew with utmost certainty that if she sent such a message, Alastair would let her go.

But that would be taking the coward's way out. All these years, she'd promised herself that if she ever had the chance, she would do what she could to make amends to him. Reneging on their agreement and bolting at the first sign of peril would snuff out what little honour she had left, like a downpour swamping a candle.

Deep within, beneath the roiling mix of shock, dismay, and frustrated desire, a small voice from the past she'd shut away whispered that she *couldn't* let him go. Not yet.

She shut her ears to it. She'd made him a promise, that was all, and honour demanded she keep it. However difficult it proved, however long it took, she would endure, as she always had.

Decision made, she walked over to the dressing table, seated herself on the bench, and regarded her image in the mirror. The forehead was puckered with concern; with fingers she refused to let tremble, she gently smoothed the skin there, beside her eyes, around her mouth, until the woman in the glass looked once again calm and expressionless.

She took a deep breath and held it, held it, held it until she couldn't any longer. Blowing it out, she took another lungful of air, wiping her mind free of anything but the passage of air in and out, the rhythmic ticking of the mantel clock throbbing in her ears.

Over and over she repeated the familiar ritual. Anxiety, foreboding, and worry gradually diminished until all emotion vanished into the nothingness of complete detachment.

She *was* the lady in the glass—a shadow of a real woman, a trick of light and mirrors, untouchable.

Only then did she rise and walk to her bed... squelching the tiny, stubborn bit of warmth that stirred within her at the thought that tomorrow, she would see Alastair again.

* * *

The following evening after dinner, Diana paced the parlour restlessly. Without the Duke's overbearing presence to impose a structure on her days, she was finding herself at a loss for what to do.

Long ago, in another life, she'd enjoyed reading, but she'd had no books to bring with her. It might be...pleasant to resume that activity, or do some needlework.

She should visit the shops and look for a book or embroidery silks. Though she needed to carefully hoard her limited coin against her uncertain future, she could spare enough for a book, couldn't she?

She had gone out today, visiting the park with Mannington—*James*. It was still a surprise, discovering how...*liberating* it was to leave the house and walk about freely, with no possibility of being recalled, lectured, or punished.

And she'd followed through on her resolution to try reaching out to her son. Haltingly, she'd talked to him, even thrown him his ball, to the astonishment of his nursemaid.

She should go up to the nursery and offer to read to him now.

Her cautious mind immediately retreated from the suggestion. Soon she must leave to meet Alastair, and she'd need all the mental and emotional defences she could summon. Having bottled up any tentative reactions after the walk to the park, she didn't dare breach the calm she'd re-established by approaching her son again.

But putting her son's needs on hold, now that it was no longer necessary to do so to protect him from his father, was just another form of the same cowardice that made her desperate to avoid Alastair Ransleigh, she admonished herself.

Mannington had suffered through six years without a mother worthy of the name. She wasn't sure she could ever become one, but she should at least try.

To do so, she'd need to loosen the stranglehold she'd imposed over her emotions. She'd grown so adept at stifling any feelings, she wasn't sure how to allow some to emerge, without the risk that all the rage, desolation and misery she'd bottled up for years might rush out in an ungovernable flood that could sweep her into madness.

Still, finding her way back to loving a boy whose face so forcefully reminded her of his father was likely to be a long process. He needed her to begin now.

Resolutely, she made her way to the nursery.

She opened the door to find her son in his nightgown, rearranging a few lead soldiers near the hearth. The nursemaid looked up, startled, from where she was turning down the boy's bed.

'Did you need something, my lady?' Minnie asked.

'I...I thought I would read Mannington a story.'

Something derisive flashed in the girl's eyes. 'I'm sure that's not necessary, my lady. The lad's nearly ready for bed, and I can tuck him—'

'Would you really read me a story, Mama?' James interrupted, hope in his tone and astonishment on his face, as if she'd just offered to reach out and capture the moon that hung in the sky outside his window.

'If you'd like...James,' she replied, his given name still coming awkwardly to her tongue.

His eyes brightening, he abandoned the soldiers and ran over to her. 'Would you, please? I'd like it ever so much!'

'Could you fetch me a book?' she asked the maid, who was still regarding her with suspicion—as if she had evil designs on the boy, Diana thought with mild amusement.

She couldn't blame the girl for her scepticism. Minnie had been James's nurse for four years, and never before had his mother appeared at his nursery door with such a request.

How many stories had Papa read her by the time she'd reached the age of six? she wondered. Hundreds.

'A book, my lady?' Minnie said at last. 'Don't have any, your ladyship. I—I don't know how to read.'

Diana had abandoned books years ago, and never thought to see that her son had access to them. 'I see. Well, perhaps we can purchase one tomorrow. Shall we say tomorrow night, then, James?'

His face falling, he reached out as she turned to leave and clutched her hand. 'Can't you stay, Mama? You could pretend to read.'

A tiny flicker of humour bubbled up. 'Very well, I'll stay. But I can do better than pretend. I'll tell you a story. That will be all, Minnie. I can tuck him in.'

Still looking dubious and more than a little alarmed, the maid sketched her a curtsy. 'As you please, ma'am. But I'll be right near, if he—if either of you need anything. Goodnight, young master.'

'G'night, Minnie,' the boy called, then ran to hop in his bed. 'See, I'm ready, Mama. Can you begin?'

At first, she'd had no idea what to say, but in a

flash, it came to her. Now that it *was* safe, he should learn about his family—*her* family.

'Shall I tell you about your grandfather? My father, whom you never met. He was a great scholar, and collected plants. One day, when I was about your age, he took me to the river to look for a very special plant...'

And so she related one of the escapades she'd shared with her father, hunting for marsh irises outside Oxford. She'd slipped and fallen into the stream, and while scolding her for carelessness, Papa had slipped and fallen in, too. He'd emerged laughing and dripping. Then he'd wrapped her up in his coat and carried her home for tea by a hot fire.

James was asleep by the time she finished the tale. Looking at his small, softly breathing form, she felt a stirring of...something. Tucking the covers more securely around his shoulders, she slipped from the room.

That had not been so very hard, as long as she avoided looking at the forehead and jaw so reminiscent of...*him*. She did not want to spoil the mild warmth she'd felt by even thinking the name. It had been almost like recapturing some of the sweetness of her own long-ago childhood, when she'd felt safe and cherished.

Regardless of whether or not she could revive her

own emotions, she would do her best to give her son that security.

As she returned to the parlour, the clock struck half-past eight. Apprehension flared in her gut.

Walking to the mirror, she began breathing methodically, until she'd achieved a state of detachment.

She'd do better tonight, she reassured her image. Alastair Ransleigh had shown himself even more susceptible to her touch than she was to his. She had only to begin at once, to use his sighs and gasps to gauge what ministrations affected him the most, and continue them with all the vigour and imagination she could devise until he was so sated by pleasure, he had neither thought nor strength to attempt touching her. Then take her leave, before he recovered.

She would do that tonight, and for however many nights she must until, inevitably, he became bored with her and ready to move to the next conquest.

Her vow to him fulfilled, she could then concentrate fully on reaching out to James—and decide how best to protect him.

But now, there was Alastair. Giving her impassive image one last look, Diana rose to summon a sedan chair.

Chapter Six

Without her mirror friend to reassure her, Diana had lost a bit of her self-assurance by the time she reached the rendezvous. She arrived before the hour specified, hoping to go up to the bedchamber and ready herself, but the impassive servant who admitted her indicated that Mr Ransleigh was already in residence, and would join her in the parlour.

She damped down an initial flicker of alarm as she followed the man into that reception area. The bedchamber would have been easier, allowing her to implement her plan immediately.

Perhaps their sojourn in the parlour was meant to maintain some veneer of propriety for the servants' sakes, though since there could be no doubt of the purpose for which she, and this house, had been procured, it seemed rather a superfluous effort. No lady worthy the name would ever meet a single gentleman at his abode, day or night.

Before she could consider the matter further, the door opened and Alastair walked in.

She sucked in a breath, struck by a wave of attraction and longing. He'd always had a commanding presence, his tall, broad-shouldered figure standing out from the others, even as a young collegian. Time had magnified the sense of assurance with which he carried himself, the air of command reinforcing it doubtless a result of his years with the army and his current role as manager of the large estate he'd inherited.

The dark hair was still swept back carelessly off his brow—she couldn't imagine the impatient Alastair she'd known ever becoming a dandy, taking time over his appearance—and the skin of his face was a deep bronze, a result of much time in the saddle under the hot Peninsular sun, she assumed.

The most notable change between the young collegian she'd loved and the man standing before her was the network of tiny lines beside his eyes—and the coldness in their dark-blue depths that once had blazed with warmth, energy and optimism.

For that chill, she was undoubtedly much responsible.

Suddenly realising she'd been staring, she dropped her gaze. 'Good evening, Alastair. Shall we proceed upstairs?'

'No need to rush off,' he returned. 'Let me pour you some wine.'

She almost blurted that she'd just as soon get straight to it. Clamping her teeth on the words, she nodded before calmly saying, 'As you wish.'

So they were to have civility tonight. She could manage that, and bide her time. Especially since, if he meant this to give the appearance of a cordial call, he was unlikely to try to seduce her in the downstairs parlour.

Slow, easy breaths, she told herself, accepting the glass of wine he offered, taking a tiny sip—and waiting. She might not force the issue, but she certainly didn't mean to draw out this nerve-fraying delay by initiating a conversation.

'I brought you something,' he said, startling her as he broke the silence. He walked to the sideboard to collect a package and offered it to her. 'I hope you'll like it.'

'Brought me something?' she echoed, surprised and vaguely uncomfortable. 'You don't need to get me anything.'

'Nevertheless, I did,' he replied. 'Go ahead, open it.'

She accepted the parcel, willing her heartbeat to slow.

'I've brought you something...' How many times

during their courtship had he said that, his blue eyes fixed on her as he offered a bunch of flowers, a book he thought she'd enjoy, a new poem rolled up and secured by a pretty ribbon?

Breathe in, breathe out. Aware her hands were trembling, she fumbled to unwrap the parcel. And found within an elegant wooden box containing a sketchbook, a set of brushes and an assortment of watercolours.

'I understand you came to Bath in a hurry, and might not have had time to pack any supplies,' he offered by way of explanation. 'I know how much you hate to be without your sketchbook and paints.'

So unaccustomed was she to having anyone give a thought to her desires, she found herself at a complete loss for words. While she tried to think of something appropriate to reply, Alastair said, 'Perhaps you could paint me something.'

'You are...very kind. But I'm sure I couldn't produce anything worth looking at. I...I haven't touched a brush in years.'

His eyes widened in surprise. 'You don't paint any more? Why did you stop? Not lack of time, surely! I should think, in a duke's establishment, there would have been plenty of servants to see to the housekeeping and care for the child.'

Unprepared and not good at dissembling, she

fumbled for a reply. 'Paints were…not always available.'

'What, was the Duke too miserly to provide them?' he asked, a sarcastic edge to his voice.

Not wanting to explain, she said, 'Something like that.'

Caught off balance, her guard down, the memory swooped out before she could prevent it.

One of the first afternoons at Graveston Court, despondent after having been summoned to the Duke's bed the night before, she'd taken refuge in one of the north-facing rooms and set up her easel. Trying to shut out her misery, she focused her mind on capturing the delicate hues of the sunlit daisies in the garden outside.

She had no idea how long she worked, lighting candles when the natural light faded, but when a housemaid found her, the girl had been frantic, insisting she come at once and dress, as she was already late for dinner.

The Duke said nothing when she arrived, merely looking pointedly at the mantel clock. But when she returned to the room the next day to resume her work, easel, paints and all had disappeared.

She'd asked the housekeeper about them, and was referred to the Duke. Who told her that when she could appear at dinner on time and properly attired, he might consider restoring them to her.

She'd never painted again.

She looked up to see Alastair regarding her quizzically. Frustration and alarm tightened her chest.

She couldn't allow him to start speculating about her! He could be as tenacious as a terrier with a rat, and she didn't think she could fend off persistent enquiries without further arousing his curiosity.

She must regain control of this situation immediately.

'I'll just put them back in the box. I'm sure you can return them,' she said, giving him a determined smile. 'Shall we go upstairs now?'

To her further frustration, he shook his head. 'There's no need to hurry. We have all evening. I thought we'd chat first.'

She had to work hard to keep her expression impassive. 'Chat' was the last thing she wanted.

She should give him a flirtatious look, try to entice him, but she couldn't remember how. 'I thought you would be…impatient,' she said, a little desperately, trying to bring his mind back to the physical.

'Oh, I am. But delay just heightens anticipation, making the fulfilment all the more satisfying. Now, my sister said you've spent most of the last few years in the country. What did you do there, if you didn't paint? Although in such a grand manor house, I expect there was an excellent library. Did you re-read the classics, or more modern works?'

Once again, she struggled to find an innocuous reply. 'I…wasn't much given to reading.'

And once again, his eyebrows winged upward. 'But you always loved to read. Was the library inferior?'

Her chest was getting so tight, it was difficult to breathe. 'N-no, the library was, ah, was quite good.'

'Then why did you not avail yourself of it?'

Oh, why would he not just leave it be? 'I didn't always have access to it,' she ground out.

'Not have access? But you were mistress of the household. I can't imagine you letting some old fright of a housekeeper deny you books!'

'It wasn't the housekeeper,' she blurted.

He was silent so long, she thought perhaps he'd finally taken note of her obvious reluctance and dropped the matter. Until he said quietly, 'Your husband denied you books?'

Oh, why had she never learned to tell a convincing lie? 'Yes,' she snapped, irritated with him for his persistence, with herself for not being able to come up with a plausible story to deflect him. 'Whenever I displeased him. And I displeased him constantly.'

Setting down her wine glass with a clatter, she

reached over to seize his hand. 'Please, can we have no more of this? I'd like to go upstairs now.'

Though he continued to regard her with an expression entirely too penetrating for her comfort, he nodded and set down his own glass. 'Far be it for me to deny an eager lady.'

He had no idea how eager, she thought, light-headed with relief as he followed her up the stairs. Eager not for caresses, but to pleasure him and be gone before he could tug out of her any more ugly secrets from her marriage.

At the chamber door, she took his hand and led him to the bed. 'Let me make you more comfortable,' she said, urging him to sit, then attacking his cravat. The sooner she got to bare skin, the closer she'd be to seducing—and escaping—him.

But though he let her unwind the cloth and toss it aside, when she started on the buttons of his coat, he stayed her hands and pulled her to sit beside him on the bed. Tilting her head up to face him, he asked, 'Did he take away your paints, too, when you did not please him?'

Caught off guard again, she couldn't seem to come up with anything but the truth. 'Yes.'

'How long have you been without books and paints?'

She pulled her chin from his fingers, not wanting to meet his gaze. 'A long time.'

'And piano?'

Ah, how she'd missed her music! *She'd hung on the longest to that, sneaking out in the depths of the night, like a burglar who's discovered where the valuable jewels are hidden. In the smaller music room, a location far removed from the servants' quarters and the main rooms, she'd played softly, in darkness or in moonlight...until that last, terrible night.*

She jerked her mind free of the memories. 'I'm not the woman you once knew, Alastair.'

Gently he recaptured her chin and made her look up at him. 'Aren't you?'

He lowered his mouth to hers, barely brushing her lips, his touch butterfly-light. This time, it was she who levered his lips apart with her tongue, then stroked at the wet warmth within.

With a growl deep in his throat, he responded immediately, seizing her shoulders and deepening the kiss. She wriggled her trapped hands down his chest and stomach until she could reach the buttons of his trouser flap, then struggled to open them against the erection that stretched the cloth taut. Finally working two buttons free, she slipped a hand inside, caressing down his length to the silky tip and back.

When he gasped, she broke the kiss, pushed herself off the bed and knelt before him. Before he could countermand her, she quickly popped the other buttons, grasped his member in both hands and took him into her mouth.

With him now beyond words, she ran her lips and tongue over every surface, listening carefully for his responses, deepening her touch or increasing friction when he gasped or thrust against her. Having catalogued his most sensitive areas, she focused on them, sucking, nipping and laving gently, then harder, then gently again, trying to stave off and intensify his climax.

It seemed she had done well, for some moments later he cried out, his nails biting into her shoulders through the fabric of her gown as he reached his peak, shuddering.

Not until he sagged back on to the bed did she gently disengage. Noting that he seemed for the moment insensate, she walked over to the washbasin to refresh herself, planning how she would next attempt to satisfy him.

Undress him, stimulate him, straddle him, she thought, ticking off in her mind the techniques that might leave him most sated. She damped down the shivers of feeling sparking at her breasts and between her thighs as she envisaged pleasuring him.

Pleasuring *him*, she rebuked her stirring senses. This had nothing to do with her.

Hands at her shoulders startled her. 'Come back to bed,' he whispered, nuzzling her neck.

Obediently she turned and allowed him to guide her over. 'Let me undress you first,' she urged.

'Only if I can then return the favour.'

Get him naked and she might avoid that. Murmuring a non-committal response, she turned to seat him at the bedside.

Swiftly, she removed his jacket and waistcoat, then pulled the shirt over his head. And caught her breath, as any woman would, for he was so beautifully made.

Strong arms and shoulders gleamed in the candlelight. The muscles of his chest tensed as she ran a finger over them, down the taut belly to the edge of his trousers, then back up and over the scar that circled one shoulder.

'Sabre slash,' he answered her unspoken question. 'Doesn't hurt any more.'

'Where?' she asked, curious in spite of herself.

'Badajoz.'

She'd read accounts in the newspapers about the battle. Not yet retired from Society, she'd also heard he'd entered the fortress city first, leading the van of the 'forlorn hope' through the breach the engineers had blasted into the walls. Her heart, not yet armoured against him, had swelled with fear at his recklessness, with joy that he'd been spared.

Denying the heat building within her, she ran her tongue along the scarred ridge of flesh, feeling him gasp and flinch under her touch. Encouraged by his response, she kissed lower while her hands caressed the lines of muscle and sinew.

Concentrate on him, she urged herself as her fingers tingled and the tension within her coiled tighter.

She suspended her kisses to strip off his boots, socks and trousers, then urged him down on the bed, pressing him back against the pillows. But when she lifted her skirts to follow him, intending to straddle the erection that sprang up boldly before her, he stopped her.

'My turn.'

She made a murmur of inarticulate protest, but, ignoring it, he stood and turned her so he might access the fastenings of her gown. Not wanting to provoke a dispute by refusing, she allowed him to proceed.

She'd just have to resist as best she could—and resist she would, she promised herself.

Stiffening, she suffered him to unfasten her bodice and skirt, tightening her jaw as he began to caress her breasts through the linen of her chemise. He cupped them in his big hands, dragged his thumbs over the nipples until they peaked, each swipe sparking a flash of sensation that shot right to her core.

Her control already unravelling, she jumped when he hooked a finger at the hem of the chemise and dragged it up, letting cool air flow over the hot, damp place between her legs. Gently he pushed her to the bed, kissing her with insistent, drugging kisses that stole her breath.

Her pulse grew unsteadier still as she struggled to resist the tide of sensation hammering at her. She bit down on her lip to keep herself from rubbing against him when his finger insinuated itself between her thighs, bit down even harder when he slid that finger up to caress the nub at her centre. Her arms ached from holding herself rigid.

Then he slipped that finger inside her, evoking a sensation so intense, she had to hold her breath until she almost lost consciousness to battle down a response.

He bent to kiss her again, suckling her tongue in rhythm to the stroking finger. Everything within her seemed to be melting, building towards some precipice she was desperate to reach.

If she couldn't stop him before she got there, she'd come apart.

Frantic, she broke the kiss, rolled on to the bed and pulled at his hips, urging him over her. 'Now!' she gasped.

Mercifully, he must have thought she was ready to finish. At once, he plunged within, filling her, which was better—or maybe worse. Rocking urgently against him—this time, she simply couldn't remain motionless—she sought to bring him to fulfilment, before the sensations he was unleashing drove her mad.

In deep, penetrating thrusts he drove to the core of her, possessing her through every inch of her body. *So the two become one flesh*, flashed through her disjointed mind.

Never. Never one. Not now. Chance. Once. Lost.

Thoughts disintegrating to chaotic bits, she despaired of holding out any longer, when, buried deep within her, Alastair went rigid and cried out. A few moments later, he collapsed on her, then rolled with her to his side.

Heart hammering a crazy rhythm in her chest, she tried to steady her breathing. *Please, let him fall asleep now, as he had the night before.* Any illusions of courage abandoned, she would steal out as soon as his relaxed body and steady breathing told her he was beyond consciousness.

She couldn't withstand a repetition of that assault on her senses.

With him limp beside her, she wriggled free of his entrapping arm. Silently, she threw on her skirt and fixed the pins of her bodice as best she could—thank heavens for the all-concealing cloak! She was groping for her shoes, ready to tiptoe out, when a hand reached out and grabbed her wrist.

She jumped, startled by his touch. Desperate to escape, she attempted a smile. 'I'm sorry. I didn't mean to wake you. I'm afraid I must…must get home. Right now. My son. I'll…I'll meet you again. T-tomorrow?'

Sweet heavens, she was stuttering, her control a shambles. She had to get away.

'He denied you passion, too, didn't he?'

Unable, unwilling to answer, she stared at him, her eyes begging him for the mercy of release.

'Why won't you let me give you pleasure?'

'Why would you want to?' she shot back, anguish loosening the hold over her tongue.

His lazy eyes widened. 'You can't believe I'd try to hurt you?'

'You have no reason to be kind. Please, Alastair, I'll come tomorrow, I promise, but no more tonight.'

She was trembling now, light-headed with sensations denied, torn between her body's eagerness for what he offered and her need to resist. If she didn't get out soon, the battle might rip her in two, right here in bedchamber.

She nearly let out a sob when he let go of her wrist. 'Very well. I would never keep you against your will. But...tomorrow?'

She nodded, her head bobbing back and forth like a child's toy. This had been bad, much worse than she'd anticipated. But with twenty-four hours of calm reflection, away from his disturbing presence, she could figure out anything. 'Yes, tomorrow.'

'Goodnight, then, Diana.'

Whirling around, she headed towards the door. She could feel the heat of his gaze on her back as she scurried, like a mouse racing from the cat, out of the room and down the stairs.

After Diana's abrupt departure, Alastair stared at the open doorway. Her effect on him had not been lessened after the first possession yesterday. In fact, with the enthusiasm of her ministrations, his climax tonight had been even more intense. So intense, his mind was still not functioning properly, or else he'd not have let her go so easily.

Instead, disturbed and disbelieving, he would have coaxed her to stay and questioned her further.

It was hard to credit that she'd truly been deprived of books and supplies. But years of gauging the veracity of men's accounts from their tone and manner as they related them, a skill essential to an officer in an army at war, argued that what she'd revealed was the truth.

What kind of man would take away what most delighted his wife, only because she'd displeased him?

The same kind who would force her into marriage by threatening her father with debtors' prison and her fiancé with ruin?

When she'd first related to him the reasons behind her marriage, he'd rejected the story with contemptuous disbelief. But from the bits he'd just pried from her, it was just possible that her tall tale might be true.

Another memory surfaced: once during their courtship, he'd read her a piece of effulgent, adjective-laden verse, then waited expectantly for her reaction. After a few moments, her lips opening and closing as she sought a response, she'd blurted, 'Oh, Alastair, that was awful!' After a moment of outrage, he'd laughed and admitted that it was over-written.

He'd teased her that she'd have to marry him rather than some dandy of the *ton*, for as impossible as she found it to prevaricate, she'd never be fashionable. She'd readily agreed, confessing that her mind went completely blank when faced with constructing a polite evasion to mask her real thoughts, especially if pressed by her questioner.

As he had pressed her tonight.

What was he to make of what she'd revealed… and what she'd left out?

Puzzlement and something more than curiosity stirred in him. Something like compassion, and a concern he didn't want to feel.

All he'd hoped for tonight was to have the gift he'd offered relax Diana enough to finally break the hold she was maintaining over her response to him. Still, he had to admit, he'd enjoyed looking for something to tempt her.

He'd always loved giving her gifts. She'd accepted even the simplest with joy, appreciative of the care he had taken in choosing them. He'd been delighted when he hit upon the idea of the paints, sure she would find them impossible to resist. He'd spent a good deal of time looking for the finest pigments and brushes available.

Instead of accepting the supplies with the pleasure he'd envisaged, she'd put them back in the box and recommended he return them.

He tried once again to take in the incomprehensible notion that a girl of her ability no longer painted.

Well, he'd not be returning them. It was a travesty for an artist of her skill to give up the brush, almost an insult to the father from whom she'd inherited her talent.

He'd have to try tempting her with them again.

Which reminded him of her shocking response to his offer to give her pleasure. Though he'd been stung when she'd seemed suspicious of his reasons, he had to concede her instincts hadn't been all that far off the mark.

He hadn't entered this affair for her benefit. Not that he'd precisely *wanted* to hurt her. Indeed, given how indifferent she'd appeared to him the last few times they met, he'd not considered it possible to injure her. He had, however, wanted to reach her and force a response.

He still wanted that. Every instinct he possessed told him that tonight, he'd come a hair's breadth close to sweeping her beyond control. Next time, he was convinced, he would bring her all the way to completion.

But now, he wanted more than physical surrender.

Not just her body had responded to him. He'd caught her staring at him when he entered the parlour tonight; unaware he was inspecting her closely as well, she'd not been wearing the impassive mask behind which she normally retreated. In her unguarded expression, he'd read wonder, attraction, and a vulnerability completely at odds with the controlled, emotionless woman she tried to appear.

Had she truly been coerced into marriage? What had the Duke done to turn the vibrant girl he'd known into a woman who turned an indifferent face to the world, who seemed desperate to maintain a rigid self-control?

Now, he knew he couldn't walk away from her until he uncovered the whole truth about Diana.

Chapter Seven

Having fled Green Park Buildings without waiting for a footman to call her a sedan chair, Diana quickly traversed the dark streets, keeping herself into the shadows. Arrived safely at Laura Place, grateful for the enveloping cloak that had allowed her to travel with her gown not fully fastened and to be able to remove it without having to wake up a maid, she crept up to her bedchamber. Knowing she was too distraught to think rationally or worry over what Annie would think of this sudden ability to get herself out of her gown without assistance, she'd shed her garments, thrown on her night rail and wrapped herself, trembling, in the bedclothes.

With her dissatisfied body humming and her mind racing in panicked indecision, she slept poorly.

Diana woke early, hardly more rested than when she'd laid her head on the pillow. But the last hour before dawn was the only time she'd have alone to think before the household was stirring.

Escaping Alastair and his too-persistent questions last night had been the most temporary of solutions. She was still bound to return to him tonight, where she was likely to face even more pointed enquiries.

She could just tell him everything, rather than waiting for him to trick and dig it from her. But, with Graveston having methodically isolated her from everyone she'd known, she'd lost the knack of making confidences. Besides, how could she revisit those scenes of misery and despair, without the risk that some of the ugly emotions she'd worked so hard to bury might escape the pit into which she'd thrust them?

She was free of that place now, of *him*. She didn't *want* to remember any of it.

She could still send Alastair a note, breaking off all contact.

The possibility tantalised. With no Alastair Ransleigh to challenge her control and distract her thoughts, she could bend all her energies into preparing herself to counter the move from Blankford she knew would soon be coming.

At the cost, of course, of whatever honour she had left.

She tried to talk herself out of that conviction;

after all, 'honour' was a concept invented by the same gentlemen who wrote the laws allowing husbands to beat wives with impunity, assume control of all their assets and property to use or waste as they chose—and take away their children.

She tried to convince herself, but it wouldn't wash; she was too much her father's daughter. The idea that a pledge once given must be followed through, that a wrong done must if at all possible be righted, were precepts ingrained in her from earliest childhood.

But hard upon the swell of despair brought by that thought, a new, much more promising possibility occurred to her. One that set her needy senses racing.

Why not give Alastair what he wanted? What he truly wanted, which wasn't the sordid details of her marriage, or some sloppy flood of emotion, but her physical surrender. If she allowed herself to respond to him, the nights at Green Park Buildings could be pleasant for them both, rather than exercises in frustration, as she tried to resist his touch. After inciting her to passion, he would be too satisfied and replete for conversation.

Excitement feathered through her, dissipating the lingering fatigue. She'd burned and hungered for his touch during their courtship days, eager for the feel of complete possession. What a dolt she was being, to have been offered that and refused it!

Even better, passion would possess her completely, too, eliminating any thought or emotion beyond the physical. No frustration and anxiety, nor any need either to armour herself against a revival of the love for him she'd buried deep, where its loss could no longer hurt her. There'd be only a firestorm of sensation and then the peace of fulfilment.

Best of all, she knew she could do this. Resisting his touch had been an exhausting, nerve-fraying battle of will. Letting go of that control, her secrets and emotions securely hidden, would be sweet as slipping between silken sheets.

Perhaps some day, when she'd learned to love her son again and figured out how to keep him safe, she might risk remembering the joy of that long-ago spring with Alastair. Their attachment had lacked only physical fulfilment to make it complete. If she claimed that now, in that far-away future she might merge the two memories into one shining, jewelled brilliance of a recollection—the image of a perfect love to sustain her the rest of her days.

She *would* do it.

Energised, she leapt from the bed and went to

ring for the maid. Instead of dreading the dusk tonight, now she was almost eager to see the sun set.

On the other side of Bath, having also slept badly and thus not wanting to face his perspicacious sister, Alastair elected to breakfast in his room. Sipping his second cup of coffee, he was feeling more like a rational human being when a footman brought in his correspondence.

Idly he flipped through it, then halted at a gilt-edged note. Disquiet stirred when he read the card: Lady Randolph, who before her marriage had been one of Diana's bosom-bows, had for some inexplicable reason invited him to tea.

Lady Randolph being the same Miss Mary Ellington whom, in the near insanity of his rage and grief after Diana's stunning rejection, he'd subjected to a most improper, most insulting offer of carte blanche.

He felt his face redden at the memory. Luckily for him, the offended lady had merely slapped his face and sent him on his way with the tongue-lashing he deserved. Had she revealed his dishonourable proposal to her brother, he probably would have been shot before ever making it to his regiment.

Mary Ellington had gone on to make a good

match to a viscount's son with political aspirations, and, by Jane's account, was now a happily married wife with a quiverful of children.

He'd neither spoken to nor seen her since that disgraceful afternoon. Why would she invite him to tea?

He debated sending a polite refusal, but given the colossal insult to which he'd subjected her on their last meeting, decided that he owed it to the lady to appear in her drawing room long enough to apologise.

Hopefully, Jane's assessment was accurate, and she wasn't now a bored wife, looking to take him up on that long-ago offer. Though if she were, he could sidestep it, a manoeuvre with which he'd had a fair amount of practice.

One didn't earn a reputation as a man who disdained marriage and preferred pleasant, short-term liaisons without attracting the interest of Society matrons long on available time and short on commitment to their marriage vows. Particularly, he thought cynically, when the potential lover possessed a deep purse she might try slipping a hand into.

With Diana waiting for him, he certainly wasn't interested in another mistress.

But Mary Ellington had also been Diana's closest female friend. Might she have some insight into what had happened to the girl he'd once loved?

With a sigh, he tossed the card back on the tray and rang for another cup of coffee. It appeared he was going to have tea with the chaste virgin he'd once propositioned.

More anxious than he'd like to be, Alastair presented himself at the appointed hour at another elegant townhouse on the Circus. Shown by the butler into a salon, he had only a few moments to wait until his hostess arrived.

'Mr Ransleigh, thank you for coming to see me on such little notice,' she said, nodding to his bow. 'Let me pour you some tea.'

Seating himself where she indicated, Alastair held on to his patience over the next few minutes as they exchanged the conventional cordialities.

Finally, he said, 'If you intend to take me to task over my inexcusable behaviour the last time we met, let me relieve you of the obligation. I behaved despicably, for which I am truly sorry. I do hope you've forgiven me.'

She looked startled for a moment, then laughed. 'Oh, that! No, your, ah, regrettable behaviour then has nothing to do with my reasons for asking you to come today. Or at least, not directly. Besides, we all knew that you weren't yourself, that soon after the…break with Diana.'

That being unanswerable, he merely nodded. 'What did you want with me, then?'

She sighed. 'I'm not quite sure how to begin. Let's just say that I'm…aware you have recently seen Diana.'

Inwardly cursing, Alastair struggled to keep a smile on his lips. Blast! Did everyone in Bath know he'd encountered Diana?

When he said nothing, she continued. 'Please hear me out, for what I'm about to say, you could with justification point out, is none of my business. But knowing Diana so well years ago, I felt it important that you know it.'

Hoping what she revealed might shed light on Diana's situation, but wanting to say nothing that might hint of the renewed relationship between them, he'd not decided what to reply when his hostess forged on.

'I know how deeply Diana wounded you. It would be entirely understandable if you wished to seek some sort of…retribution, especially as she is now in the city without benefit of husband or anyone else to protect her.'

Nettled, he rose. 'Are you suggesting, madam, that I would seek to harm her?'

'No! Not at all!' she protested, waving him back to his seat. 'Only asking, if you should be required to have any dealings with her, that you…treat her gently.'

At his raised eyebrow, she rushed on. 'The manner in which she jilted you was inexcusable, but though she may have captured a duke, save for the son finally granted her, it appears she had little joy of her prize. You may have heard that after her marriage, Diana ignored all those who knew her before she became a duchess.'

'Jane told me as much.'

'So it appeared, but it wasn't true. I was as aghast as anyone after she broke your engagement—and in so shocking a fashion! Though normally, one could believe that a duke's offer of marriage would be preferred over one from a mere mister, Diana had never been interested in social advancement. I truly believed she was as besotted by you as you appeared to be by her. After the hasty marriage, I was curious, of course, but also worried about her happiness. The Duke of Graveston was known to be a cold, forbidding, unapproachable man. So I called on her…and was told the Duchess did not wish to receive me. Then, or at any time in future. I was shocked, and hurt, of course.'

'I can imagine.' *Having received just the same treatment.*

'As I was walking back to my carriage—I'd told the coachman to circle the square, as I didn't intend to remain long—Diana ran up to me. Speaking all in a rush, she told me she'd seen my arrival from a window, slipped out the kitchen door and come through the mews to catch me. The Duke had decreed that since her former friends were not of suitable rank—I'd not yet married Randolph—she was no longer permitted to associate with them. Saying she must return before her absence was discovered, she gave me her love and said goodbye. I—I didn't know what to make of it at the time, but I do know she never received any of her other friends, either.'

'"No longer permitted"?' Alastair echoed. 'Could a husband enforce such a stipulation? Or was that a convenient excuse?'

Lady Randolph shook her head. 'I don't know. I didn't see her again until years later, after Randolph won a seat in Parliament, and we were invited to a political dinner hosted by the Duke. There had already been rumours that the match was a most—unusual—one, and I was quite anxious to have a chance to speak with Diana again.'

She paused, looking troubled. 'Did you speak with her?' he prompted, impatient for her to continue.

She started a little, as if she'd been lost in memory. 'No, for reasons I will soon make apparent. The Duke came down after the guests had assembled, but as the hour grew later, Diana still had not appeared. Finally, just after the butler announced dinner was to be served, she suddenly arrived at the doorway through which the guests must pass to reach the dining room. She wore a striking white-silk gown with a very low décolletage, but neither gloves nor jewels. Instead, circling her neck and wrists were…bruises, the ones beneath each ear clearly fingerprints. In the shocked silence, she walked up to the Duke, and as if nothing out of the ordinary had occurred, said she was ready to go in to dinner.'

'What did the Duke do?'

Lady Randolph laughed shortly. 'What could he do? I'm told he seldom exhibits any emotion, but those near him said his face reddened. Without a word, he offered his arm—and ignoring it, she walked beside him into the dining room. It was the most magnificent bit of defiance I've ever witnessed.'

It was all Alastair could do to guard his expression. To hear of any woman abused would have aroused his anger and pity—but Diana! Sickened, furious, he struggled to find a comment that expressed a degree of outrage appropriate for a former fiancé—rather than a man once again involved with the woman in question.

Giving him a sympathetic look, his hostess continued. 'I know what a shock that news must be, even for one who no longer has any warm feelings for Diana. It's simply wicked, what a wife can suffer without any legal remedy, and makes me daily grateful for my Randolph! Sadly, I've known several poor souls whose husbands treated them…ungently, and without exception they tried to hide the abuse, were embarrassed by it. And afraid. Whereas Diana flaunted the Duke's lack of control for all his world to see, embarrassing *him*. With utter disregard for how he might make her pay for it later.'

The thought chilled him. He'd seen no evidence of current bruises—but her husband might have been ill for months, for all he knew. Had she suffered his hand raised against her through all her marriage?

'As soon as dinner concluded,' Lady Randolph continued, 'the Duke took her arm and escorted her upstairs, saying she was feeling "indisposed", then returned to his guests.' She shuddered. 'I hesitate even to imagine what must have happened later. In any event, it was the last time I saw her. Soon afterward, the Duke took her to Graveston Court, and though he returned to London for Parliament and occasionally entertained there, she never again accompanied him. I heard from guests who dined with them before her banishment that she always conversed freely at table, giving no deference to the Duke or his opinions, pointing out discrepancies as she saw them in his arguments or those of his Parliamentary supporters.'

'Not an ideal political wife,' Alastair observed, before his own words came out of memory like a stiletto to the chest: *You shall have to marry me, rather than some dandy of the* ton, *for as impossible as you find it to prevaricate, you'll never be fashionable.*

Anguish twisted in his gut. Never fashionable. Never appreciated.

Never safe.

'Quite frankly, after what I'd seen and heard, I'm rather surprised she outlived him—but ever so glad! Despite what the malicious are saying about her in Bath, I intend to seek her out and offer her friendship.'

To his surprise, Lady Randolph seized his hands and looked up at him earnestly. 'Diana made a terrible decision that summer so many years ago. But whatever advantage she thought to gain, she's paid a dear price for it. Paid enough, I think. I just ask that you have pity, and if you can't forgive her, at least don't add to her sufferings.'

'I can assure you, I have no intention of doing that.'

Releasing him, she sat back. 'Thank you! Since you are a man of honour—most of the time,' she added with a smile and a pointed look, 'I am satisfied.'

Taking his leave a few minutes later, Alastair scarcely recalled what had been said during the rest of his visit, so preoccupied had he been by what Lady Randolph had revealed—and with not betraying by some comment or expression his full reaction to the information she'd conveyed.

Once free of her restraining presence, though, electing to walk back to his sister's townhouse so he might think uninterrupted, he methodically reviewed her recitation, looking for bits and pieces that fit with what he'd learned himself.

Lady Randolph's account seemed to confirm Diana's assertion that she had never confided to anyone else the account she'd given him of being coerced into marriage. Of course, as he'd told her and she'd readily admitted, the story beggared belief. Even her dearest friend thought it was the temptation of marrying into the highest rank of

Society that had, in the end, induced her to abandon him.

Had it been?

His certainty about that, already shaken, wavered further as he allowed himself to recall more about the Diana he'd known. The Diana who, without question, would never lie. The Diana who, even now, could not come up with a plausible evasion.

Equally without question, the girl she'd been would have been capable of sacrificing her own happiness to save those she loved.

A girl who, heedless of her own safety, had had the courage to publicly defy a duke.

Suddenly he recalled her confusion when he'd offered her the paints. The confusion of someone who had received so little for so many years, she no longer knew how to respond to a gift.

The confusion of one who only knew what it was like to have what she loved taken away.

Feeling sick inside, Alastair halted at the street corner, mopping his face with a trembling hand. Had he been wrong all this time, wallowing in self-righteous indignation over her supposed betrayal?

Common sense rejected that conclusion, and yet... Like snow silently accumulating on a windowsill, the doubts that had begun creeping in to trouble his assumptions over what she'd done, and why, redoubled.

He had to know the truth.

Little by little, he promised himself as he resumed his walk, with a tenderness and concern she apparently had not been shown for years, he would coax her to tell it to him.

But before that, he'd need to get a pianoforte delivered to Green Park Buildings.

Chapter Eight

After a session before the mirror to restore her calm—only in the bedchamber could she permit herself any emotion—Diana arrived at the townhouse in Green Park Buildings. So great was her nervous anticipation she'd had to exercise great self-control not to arrive very early, so she might have time to position herself before Alastair arrived.

She'd filled some of the waiting time reading to James. During a walk down Milsom Street this morning, they found a picture book of soldiers. She'd enjoyed reading to him, and he seemed to like it, too. The interlude had been...pleasant. Perhaps she would be able to revive the tenderness she'd once felt for him.

Precisely at the agreed hour, she knocked at the door of Alastair's townhouse. The same expressionless manservant—having been spied on by her husband's retainers for so long, she was inured to expressionless servants—showed her into the parlour where, this time, Alastair waited to greet her.

Swallowing hard over a renewed attack of nerves, she made herself walk calmly over to him. He rose, and when he angled her chin up for a kiss, she let him.

Feathering her eyes closed, she opened herself to sensation. The soft pressure of his lips brushing against hers was gentle, sweet, and sensual, setting all the nerves of her mouth tingling. When he broke the kiss, she was disappointed—and eager for more.

'I brought you a little something,' he said with a smile, motioning across the room.

So preoccupied was she by this bold new venture of responsiveness, she'd noticed nothing in the chamber but Alastair. Following the direction of his hand, she uttered a gasp. 'Alastair! That's hardly "little"—it's a pianoforte!'

He grinned at her, and a sharp stab of…something struck the barrier she'd erected to restrain her emotions, already shaken by his kindness in remembering how much she loved music. As he stood smiling, the harsh, cynical edge to his expression gone, he looked like the boyish young man she'd once given her heart to.

Good she was about to sweep all thought away with passion, else he might tempt her too much.

'Play for me.'

'I haven't played in years!' she protested. 'I'd likely sour milk and set all the cats on the street to squalling.'

He chuckled. 'I'll risk it. If it's been that long, all the more reason to begin again immediately. It's like riding a horse—you never truly forget.'

'Who told you that?' she asked, swallowing a laugh. 'Certainly no one who played well! Daily practice is essential to remain truly proficient.'

'And you were wonderfully proficient. There might be a few cobwebs to brush off, but I wager that won't take long. So, play for me…please.'

She wanted to refuse, get right to bedroom matters; straying on to the topic of music could bring the dangerous possibility of more prying. But even from across the room, she could tell the pianoforte was a beautiful instrument—trust Alastair to choose only the best. She'd missed music almost as much as she'd missed Alastair, the love for it, like her love for him, suppressed but never extinguished.

'Very well,' she capitulated. 'But you might want to leave the room. I expect I shall be dreadful.'

He merely smiled and gestured towards the instrument. Eagerness bubbled out before she could restrain it as she ran her fingers experimentally along the keys. As the bright tones issued forth, her much-denied, atrophied heart gave a feeble pang.

And so she played, slowly at first, then faster, with more assurance. During her clandestine midnight forays at Graveston, before the instrument had been taken away, she'd memorised many of her favourite works, not wishing to risk leaving sheet music about. She found her fingers returning to one piece after another.

Soon she lost herself in the music. Time ceased to matter, and when the final movement ended and she lifted her hands from the keyboard, she wasn't sure how long she'd been playing.

She looked around to see Alastair in a wing chair by the fire, wine glass in hand, watching her.

Contrition seized her. 'I'm sorry. I…I lost track of the time. So sorry to keep you waiting.'

'Not at all. That was lovely. I've missed hearing you play.'

He looked as surprised as she was by that remark. Not sure what to respond, she rose and came over to him. Now to put her plan into effect before he could initiate any more conversational delays.

'You should have a reward for your patience.' She leaned down to kiss him, her tongue outlining the edge of his lips.

With a murmur, he set down his glass, pulled

her into his lap, and deepened the kiss. This time, she let herself respond to the warmth and heat of him, opening to him, fencing back as they tangled tongues, the soft moist heat stoking the passion rising within her.

She brought his hand to her breast, and he caressed her through the material of her gown and stays. Luscious sensation sparkled and shot through her body, setting off a throbbing at her centre as she envisaged how much more acutely she would feel his touch, once his clothes and hers were removed. Revelling in his caress, she rubbed herself against him.

He broke the kiss, his eyes blazing and his breathing unsteady. 'Upstairs, now,' he urged, setting her on her feet.

Before he led her off, she turned to him and tilted her mouth up for another kiss. When he obliged, sweeping his tongue in to possess hers, she wrapped an arm around him and inserted her other hand between their two bodies, massaging the hardness pressed against her.

'More of that later,' she promised, before taking his hand to tug him towards the door.

Wrapping an arm around her, he caressed her bottom as they walked up the stairs. Once in the bedchamber, she whirled around, offering him access to pins and tapes, which he dispensed of quickly, unpeeling her bodice and helping her step out of her gown. She lifted her hands to let him strip the chemise over her head and stood before him, clad only in garters and stockings.

He ran his gaze slowly over her, from chin to toes. 'Lovely,' he murmured.

Kissing him, she unfastened his trouser buttons and urged the garment down, then pushed him to sit back on the bed. As soon as he'd balanced there, she climbed on his lap, straddling him, then wrapped her legs around his back and guided herself down to enclose his swollen member.

Ah, how good he felt, slick hot steel caressing her inner chamber for all his length. Sighing, she leaned back, offering up her naked breasts. Cupping her bottom to secure her, he bent to them, rolling the hard nipples between his teeth, nipping and suckling.

The sensation was exquisite, every sweep of his tongue and nip of his teeth intensifying the throbbing pressure building deep within her, where his member stretched and pulled and teased. Feeling the urgent need for more movement, she began rocking into him, savouring the friction as she pulled almost free, then sank down on him again.

Pressure built and built, lifting her again towards

the precipice she'd sensed the night before, driving her to intensify her efforts. If she could just force him deeper, rub against him harder...

Suddenly, in a rush of sensation unlike anything she'd ever experienced, the pressure released in a flow of tingling, throbbing delight. She felt she was soaring, flying above all pain and misery and memory, for long, brilliant minutes before settling softly back to earth.

Boneless, she sagged against Alastair, who simply held her, kissing the dampness of her forehead and her ears. His silence was just as well, for her scattered thoughts were too incoherent for speech.

'Thank you,' he whispered at last.

Surprised, her eyes started open. 'Shouldn't I be thanking you? Especially since...' She rocked her hips around the still-hard member still inside her.

'All in good time. Thank you for letting go, giving me the gift of your pleasure.'

'Isn't it time for you to give me the gift of yours?'

'Gladly.' He smiled against her lips before kissing her.

She wanted to finish undressing him, but he wouldn't hear of it. Rising, still almost fully clad, he slid back to the pillows and lay back, holding her in place astride him.

'What would please you most?' she asked disjointedly, hardly able to formulate the sentence for the pressure of him moving inside her, creating little eddies of pleasure.

'Watching you again, as you ride me. But first, this.'

He pulled her close, kissing her—throat, shoulders, silky skin of inner arms, down to her breasts. Though he'd pleasured them before, he began again, even more slowly, a meticulous caress of every surface, licking the pebbly nipples as he massaged the full softness.

By now, her core was throbbing again, too. Murmuring encouragement, he lay back, urging her to move on him. Balanced better on the bed, she could spread her knees wider and take him deeper still. The thrust of his hardness along the whole of her passage, from the depths to the tight nub at the peak, elicited a whole new range of sensations.

Faster and faster she moved, each stroke tightening the coil of pressure until at last, in a splendid blaze of pleasure, they flew over the crest together.

For a while afterwards, they both drifted in somnolent contentment. When at last she rose back to full consciousness, she found herself beside him, his arm wrapped around her, her head pillowed on his shoulder.

A wave of wonder and delight washed through her. How many times had she dreamed of waking like this?

And this time, she had no need to thrust away or bottle up the thought.

Instead, she nestled closer. 'Must I go now?'

'Go?' he echoed. 'Heavens, no, my sweet. We've just begun.'

Her eyes widened at that. 'Just begun?' she repeated cautiously.

Laughing, Alastair rolled out of the bed, swiftly stripped off his clothes, walked over to pour them a glass of wine and brought it back, while she admired his magnificent nakedness.

'Here, drink up. We've hours yet.'

After taking a long sip, she let herself smile. 'That's excellent.'

He chuckled and took back the glass. 'Let me show you how excellent,' he murmured. Smoothing his hands down over her belly, he nudged her legs apart and moved his clever, wicked mouth to that needy place between her thighs.

Slowly Diana emerged from the heavy mantle of sleep, like a sea creature rising from the deep. Her body felt languid, replete with a humming satisfaction. When she finally forced her eyelids open, she saw a dearly beloved visage, smiling at her.

What marvellous dream was this? A sense of wonder escaping before she could cage it, she raised a hand to trace the face from forehead to lips. 'Alastair?' she whispered.

As if his name had evoked it, consciousness returned in a rush, accompanied by a paralysing stab of fear. 'Alastair! You must—I must get away. At once! He mustn't find us!'

As she frantically pulled at the bedclothes, desperate to flee, he stilled her hands. 'Stop, Diana! It's all right. Your husband is dead. He'll never hurt you again.'

The room seemed to swirl around her dizzily. 'He's…gone?' she repeated, trying to focus her muzzy senses.

'Yes. He's gone, and I'm here.'

She struggled to pull herself free from the iron grip of another world. After a moment of frantic concentration, reality began to fall into place. Graveston's death. Coming to Bath. Meeting Alastair again. The bargain.

The luxuriant somnolence of her body clashed with the agitation of emotions still out of control. Responding to the imperative to reel them in, she pushed at the arm he'd wrapped around her.

'Please, I need…I need to sit.' Detaching herself, she slid away and off the bed, looking around wildly for the dressing table. Spying it in the corner, she hurried over, and heedless of her nakedness and his keen observing eyes, seated herself before the glass. The forehead of the face reflected back to her was creased with anxiety, the eyes feral.

With a trembling hand, she smoothed away the lines and began the ritual breathing. *Long slow inhale, hold, hold, exhale.* Applying every bit of mind and will, she forced back the anxiety and buried the panic, until finally the countenance staring back at her was expressionless and calm.

Only then did she turn to Alastair. He was still looking at her with concern—no wonder, after witnessing that performance! Better distract him quickly, before he could begin questioning.

'I'm so sorry!' She managed a smile. 'I can't recall when I last slept so deeply, I awoke with no idea where I was.'

Though his eyes still looked troubled, mercifully, he did not press her. 'Passion satisfied can do that.'

She smiled in earnest. 'What a wondrous gift! I had no idea such feelings existed. Thank you.'

'I should point out, the gift was mutual. Thank you, too.'

Suddenly she noticed that, though the candles had guttered out, a dim light illuminated the chamber. Her relief at recalling that Graveston was gone and she was in Bath abruptly dissipated.

'Goodness, what hour is it?'

'Just past dawn.'

Shocked that she'd slept so long, Diana hopped off the bench and began gathering up her garments. 'I must get back at once, before the servants begin to stir.'

'I'll summon you a chair.'

'No, I'll walk—it's light enough now, someone might notice the chair.'

'I appreciate your efforts at discretion, but it's not yet full daylight and you shouldn't be out on the streets alone,' he countered. 'I'll escort you.'

'What kind of discretion would that be? No, you mustn't be seen by anyone in the house. The servants can't be trusted not to gossip.'

With a sigh, he came over to help her. 'I'm much better at removing these than putting them back on,' he said as he fitted the gown over her chemise and began pinning. 'Why so worried about gossip? I thought you'd brought with you only a few trusted retainers.'

She leaned back against him as he secured the

garment. 'All were hired here but Minnie, James's nursemaid, and she's loyal only to him. The servants at Graveston Court obeyed their master and no one else. Not that I blame them. Had any of them shown sympathy or allegiance to me, they would have been turned out at once without a character.'

'So you truly had no one.'

Deciding, after a moment's hesitation, to ignore the question, she sat to roll on her stockings and slip her feet into her slippers, then stood and twirled before him. 'All put to rights, am I?'

'Sadly, yes. I prefer you in the natural state.'

'Wouldn't give one much chance of slipping through the streets unnoticed, you must allow.' Feeling somehow shyer now in her garments than she had while naked before him in the languid aftermath of loving, she glanced up as she tied on her cloak. 'Will you…want me again tonight?'

The smouldering look he returned sent a little thrill through her. 'You know I will.'

'Then I shall be here.' Stepping towards the door, she paused to look back over her shoulder. 'Alastair, I—I really do thank you. Last night was…magnificent.'

A twinkle in his eyes, he walked over to capture her chin and give her a kiss, long and slow and full of promise. 'Just wait until tonight.'

Warmth bubbled up, and this time, she didn't try to stop it. 'Tonight,' she whispered, parting his lips to delve into his mouth and deliver her promise in return.

Maintaining her vigilance as she slipped through the empty streets, her only fellow travellers a few returning revellers and the last of the night-soil men rattling off with their carts, Diana arrived home to find the kitchen still dark but for the banked embers in the fireplace.

Grateful not to have to manufacture an excuse for appearing downstairs at so odd an hour, she padded softly up to the privacy of her chamber.

As long as she came and went alone, she didn't worry too much about any gossip the staff might exchange about her movements. The servants had already been instructed that she planned to go out most evenings and would let herself back in, so except for the maid who assisted her with dressing, they need not wait up for her. Though she supposed that directive might be unusual, the permission to end their long day when they chose, without having their rest depend upon the vagaries of their employer's social schedule, was attractive enough, none had questioned it.

Once safely within her chamber, Diana seated

herself in the chair before her own banked chamber fire. In a moment, she'd strip off the cloak and lie down on her bed, telling the maid when she came later in that she'd been so weary after returning, she hadn't bothered to ring for her. Now, for the next few moments, she could let down her guard and recall the events of the night.

How wonderful it had been to no longer fight against Alastair's insidious attraction! How exciting to respond freely to his touch, to let passion sweep her away to a satisfaction more powerful and complete than she'd imagined possible. She'd suspected loving Alastair would be magical, but words couldn't begin to describe the all-encompassing power and grandeur of it.

The warmth she'd felt earlier bubbled up again, expanding until it filled her with a sense of peace she hadn't experienced since long ago, in that other life.

Home, safe, content, she slept, to awake later feeling energised. The well-being stayed with her through the morning and well into the afternoon. Until, returning from a walk to the park with James and Minnie, the maid informed her as she entered the house that a solicitor was waiting in the parlour to see her.

Chapter Nine

Dread struck her like a fist to the gut. Surely Blankford couldn't be moving against her this quickly! She'd expected it to take at least a fortnight for him to pack up and decamp to Graveston Court after the news of his father's demise reached him, and some time after that for him to trace where she'd fled.

But she couldn't imagine any other reason a solicitor would be asking for her, here in Bath, barely a week after her arrival.

Whoever it was, she must meet him now. With no more time to prepare, she didn't have the luxury of panic. Pummelling down the fear, she told the maid to announce her.

The man who rose to greet her as she entered the parlour was the image of what one would expect of a peer's solicitor: old, sober of demeanour, garbed in expensive, well-tailored but not ostentatious garments.

'Good afternoon, Your Grace. I'm Feral, solicitor to Lord Blankford—the new Duke of Graveston, that is,' he said, confirming her fears. 'I've brought a letter from his Grace, vouching for my identity and authorising me to collect the boy.'

Though she knew exactly what he meant, she repeated blankly, 'Collect the boy?'

'Lord James Mannington, the late Duke's son by his second marriage to you. The new Duke wishes the boy brought back to Graveston Court—where he can be reared as befits his station,' he added, with a disparaging glance around the modest room.

Anger overlay the fear, sharpening every sense. *Delay, expostulate, distract.* She widened her eyes, gave him an incredulous look. 'You've come to take away my son?'

The solicitor had the grace to look discomfited. 'He'll be well cared for, I assure—'

'My husband dead barely a fortnight, and you want to strip me of my son?!' she interrupted, letting her voice rise to a distraught crescendo. 'No, I cannot bear it!'

Closing her eyes, Diana fell in a dramatic faint to the floor.

'Your Grace!' Feral exclaimed, looking down at her.

From her position on the carpet, Diana remained unresponsive. At length the solicitor grew more concerned and rang the bell to summon assistance.

The maid looked in, gasped and ran back off, then returned with the entire household staff. Several minutes passed as they bustled about, Annie chafing her hands while Cook waved a vinaigrette under her nose and Smithers, the manservant, helped the two females lift Diana off the floor.

During those minutes, she schemed furiously, examining and discarding several courses of action until she hit upon one with the greatest likelihood of success.

'Some tea to restore you, my lady?' Cook asked after she had been propped on the sofa.

'Yes. And I suppose I must offer some to Mr Feral, even though he has come to take away my child.'

Diana doubted she'd earned much sympathy from the staff during her brief stay, but all of them were charmed by James, and the idea of stripping a boy from his mama did not sit well. Though none of the servants were ill trained enough to display overt hostility, the gazes they turned towards the solicitor were distinctly chilly.

'As you wish, my lady,' Cook said, returning to her domain.

'Shall I remain until you have fully recovered?' Annie asked, stationing herself protectively between Diana and her guest.

Her point made, and her visitor now looking distinctly uncomfortable—and as rattled as Diana had hoped—she said, 'No, Annie, you may go. Nothing else Mr Feral says or does could wound me more than he already has.'

As soon as the servants exited, Feral turned to her with an exasperated look. 'Indeed, Your Grace, that was hardly necessary! You'd think I was attempting to send the boy to a workhouse, rather than return him to a life of ease in the home of his birth!'

Pushing away from the pillows, she dropped the guise of distraught mother and switched to imperious aristocrat, a role which, after watching her husband, she could play to perfection.

'How dare you, a solicitor, son of a tradesman no doubt, presume to tell me what to do?' she cried. 'My son remains with me.'

As she'd hoped, the change in demeanour took the solicitor by surprise. Years of serving an employer who would have tolerated nothing less than complete deference and absolute obedience had him stuttering an apology.

'I meant no disrespect, Your Grace. But—'

'But you thought you could simply march into this house, my retreat from grief, and order me about?'

That might have been a bit much, for the solicitor, his expression wary, said, 'Though I have every appreciation for a widow's grief, Your Grace, I must point out it was common knowledge that you and the late Duke...did not live harmoniously together.'

'We did live together, however, which is more than can be said for my late husband and his heir, who, long before his father's death, had broken off all relations between them. Yet now you have the effrontery to assure me that this man, who hasn't set foot inside Graveston Court for years, who refused ever to speak to me, will take good care of my son?'

'Surely you don't mean to suggest the Duke would not treat the boy kindly!' the solicitor objected.

She merely raised her eyebrows. 'I believe he will treat Mannington—and everyone else—in whatever way he chooses. I have no intention of abandoning my son to the vagaries of his half-brother's humours. Besides, there is no need for Mannington to be reared at Graveston; he's not the new heir, or even the heir presumptive. Blankford married two years ago, I'm told, and already has a son and heir.'

'The existence of an heir has no bearing on the Duke's wish that his half-brother be raised in a ducal establishment.'

'Even if Mannington were the heir,' she continued, ignoring him, 'until he's old enough to be sent to school, a child should remain with his mother.'

'If a case for custody were brought forward, the Court of Chancery would likely decide in favour of the Duke,' the solicitor shot back, obviously already prepared for that argument.

Before she could put forth any more objections, he said in a softer tone, 'Your Grace, though I sympathise with a mother's eagerness to hold on to her child, you might as well resign yourself. As you should know from association with your late husband, when a Duke of Graveston desires something, he gets it.'

Nothing he could have said would have enraged her more. Welcoming a fury that helped her submerge a desperation too close to the surface, she snapped, 'He will not get my son. I fear you've made a long journey to no purpose. Good day to you, Mr Feral.'

Before he could respond, Diana rose and swept from the room.

* * *

Her heart thudding in her chest, Diana instructed Smithers—who'd been loitering outside the door—to escort the visitor out, then paused in the doorway to the kitchens, concealed by the overhanging stairs.

As theatre, it had been an adequate performance, but would it be enough? Would Feral leave, or charge up to the nursery and attempt to remove Mannington by force?

If it came to that, she hoped the staff would assist her, though she wasn't sure she could count on them.

To her relief, a few moments later, Mr Feral, his manner distinctly aggrieved, exited the parlour and paced to the front door, trailed closely by Smithers.

Light-headed with a relief that made her dizzy, she sagged back against the door frame. The first skirmish went to her, but she knew that small victory had won her only a brief respite. At worst, after pondering the matter, Mr Feral might well return and try to carry out Blankford's order by force. Even in the best case—Feral electing to leave her alone and return to the Duke for further instructions—within a week or so she'd face a renewed assault.

Surely Fate wouldn't be so cruel as to strip James

from her now, as she was just beginning to know him again! No, she simply must find some way to prevent it.

Blankford would be furious that she hadn't capitulated to his demand, and was sure to summon every tool of law and influence to exact his will in the next round.

If it did come to that, would a Court of Chancery uphold her right to keep James until he went to university? She had no idea what provisions her husband had made for his second son in the event of his death. Although Blankford had received the title, all the entailed land and the bulk of the assets of the estate, there had probably been something left for James, with trustees named to oversee the assets until he came of age. Her legal position would be weaker still if Blankford had been named one of those trustees—though given the bitterness of the break between her husband and his heir, she doubted the Duke would have appointed him as one.

If Blankford were not a trustee, would that make retaining custody of James easier? She scanned her mind, trying to dredge up what little she knew about how the affairs of wealthy minors were settled under law. But she quickly abandoned the effort. A mere woman, she'd never be allowed to argue the case anyway. She'd chosen Bath over London as her refuge not only because she could live here more cheaply, but also because, as a town still frequented by the fashionable, she might find a solicitor skilled and clever enough to outwit a duke.

The unexpected appearance of Alastair Ransleigh had deflected her from setting out to find such a person as soon as they had settled in. She'd have to begin the search at once, and to hire the best, she'd need additional funds.

However, much as she'd tried to prepare herself for this eventuality, she couldn't repress a shiver as she assessed the odds against her.

You really think you can defeat the Duke? a mocking little voice whispered in her ear. The panic she'd controlled during the interview with the lawyer bubbled up, threatening to escape.

She gave herself a mental shake. No, she would not think about losing James…Graveston's son, yes, but *hers*, too. That way lay madness. With a control perfected through long bitter years, she forced her mind instead back to planning.

She'd obtain funds, consult a lawyer of her own, and find some way to block the Duke's access to James. Thank heavens, tonight she would see Alastair. Perhaps the peace she'd found in his arms last night might ease, for a few hours at least, the fear that still tightened her chest and laboured her breathing.

She simply couldn't give in to it. Once again, she had someone to protect. Whatever it took, she intended that this time, the Duke of Graveston would not have his way.

Meanwhile, Alastair had spent most of the day at Green Park Buildings. After Diana's departure, he'd silently trailed her as she traversed empty dawn streets just stirring to life. Satisfied that she'd made it safely back to her lodgings, he'd returned to the little townhouse ravenous, downed a hefty breakfast of sirloin and ale, then retreated back to the bedchamber they'd shared to refresh himself after a night of great delight and little sleep.

Dust motes danced in the afternoon sunlight when he awoke later. An enormous sense of wellbeing pervading him, he stretched lazily, running through his mind several of the delicious episodes from last night's loving.

Diana moving under him, over him, pulling his face to her breasts, crying out as he thrust into her, had been intoxicating beyond his wildest imagining. As he'd sensed the first time he touched her, the woman she'd become more than fulfilled the promise of passion in the girl he'd once loved.

Perhaps desire would diminish over time, but thus far, each meeting with her left him more enchanted. The mere thought of touching her, kissing her, tasting her was so arousing he could scarcely wait until evening. Already he was hard and aching, needy and impatient.

But it was more than just the rapture of the physical. When she awakened beside him, rosy with sleep and satisfaction, the unguarded expression of joy and wonder as she recognised him had pierced the barrier he'd erected to armour himself against her and gone straight to the heart. The awe and tenderness with which she'd traced his face and whispered his name had weakened still further the barricades restraining the tender feelings for her that, unable to fully exterminate, he'd buried deep.

She'd gazed at him as if he were her most precious dream.

As she had once been his.

His euphoria dimmed a bit. Allowing her to touch his emotions again wasn't wise and could end badly. He'd entered this affair to purge himself of her, not to fall under the spell of a woman much more complex than the straightforward lass he'd loved. The mere thought of the devastation he'd suffered when she'd abandoned him all those years ago made him suck in a painful breath.

Well, it wouldn't come to that—not this time. He might want to penetrate all her secrets, but he'd not risk his heart imagining they had a future.

And what of her secrets? 'I'm not the girl I once was,' she had told him.

That much was certainly true. She was instead a woman who had, he was reluctantly beginning to believe, suffered isolation, hardship and abuse. If he fully accepted the truth of her account, she'd endured all that to protect her father—and him.

He recalled how frantic she'd become at the thought of the danger their being together placed him in, before he convinced her that her husband was dead.

Then there was that odd ritual at the mirror, during which, she fought her way from distress back to calm.

Alone.

So you had no one, the comment came back to him—a statement she'd neither affirmed nor denied. He recalled Lady Randolph's description of how she'd been isolated from all her former friends.

Isolated, abused—but defiant.

Pity and admiration filled him in equal measure. And despite the danger of letting her touch his emotions, he couldn't beat back the warmth he'd felt at seeing her glow of contentment when she'd awakened in his arms. Couldn't help the need building within him to penetrate the impassive mask and bring that expression to her face again, in the full light of day.

He couldn't give her back the eight years she'd lost, erase the suffering she'd endured, or resurrect the innocent, carefree girl she'd once been. But before they parted, he vowed to do whatever he could to convince her she was truly free to take up all the activities she'd been denied—painting, reading, music—and embrace life fully.

As he thought of that future, a small voice deep within whispered that she must share that new life with *him*.

Ruthlessly, he silenced it.

He was no longer a starry-eyed young man, confident that the future would arrange itself as he wished. In the dangerous matter of Diana, he would move one cautious step at a time, holding the reins on his feelings with as tight a grip as he could manage.

He'd need that knack immediately, for it was past time for him to return to Jane's. Though he had the run of his sister's house and might come and go as he pleased, his absence for an entire day would not have gone unnoticed. The all-too-observant Jane would be curious where he'd been, and he'd have to manufacture an unreadable expression to prevent her from teasing out of him that he was seeing Diana again.

The mere thought of the storm of scolding and possible hysterics that admission would unleash made him shudder.

It would be more prudent to time his return for when his sister was occupied with other matters. Though he did appreciate her genuine concern for his welfare, the matter of Diana was too complicated—and Jane's animosity towards Diana too deep—to be quickly and easily explained.

He hadn't yet brought Jane a hostess gift. Perhaps he'd stop by the jewellers and pick up a trinket to surprise her—and hopefully distract her from any pointed questioning over the curious absences of her brother.

Chapter Ten

Accordingly, an hour later, after a brief stop to bathe and change at the Crescent, Alastair was strolling down Bond Street, bound for the jeweller recommended by his sister's butler. Jane loved flowers; an intricate silver vase or epergne for her table should delight her enough to give him a few days' grace from scrutiny.

Just as he turned the corner, a woman exited the shop. The black cape that swathed her, hiding her face under the overhanging hood, instantly recalled Diana and the delights they had recently shared. He was smiling at the memory when, an instant later, something about the retreating figure made him realise the woman was, in fact, Diana.

A shockingly intense gladness filling him, Alastair set off after her. But by the time he reached the corner, the lady had disappeared. With a disappointed sigh, he turned back towards the shop.

Just as well he'd missed her. Anything he said or did with her on a public street would set tongues wagging. Though he didn't think he was known to any of the pedestrians now passing by him, he'd not noticed any acquaintances in the park the first day he met Diana, either, and word of that encounter had begun circulating immediately.

Besides, he'd rather savour seeing her tonight, when he could undress her, caress by caress. Warmed by that thought, he entered the jeweller's establishment.

Taking one look at him, the junior clerk who greeted him sent at once for the owner. Though he tried to extinguish his curiosity, after that gentleman had shown him several fine silver pieces, one of which he selected for his sister, he couldn't help asking casually whether the lady who'd just left the shop had purchased something similar, so beautifully wrought were the vases.

'I'm afraid she was selling, rather than buying,' the owner replied with a sigh—before his eyes lit. 'I bought from her a particularly nice pearl necklace. Truly, the piece is so fine, I don't think I'll have it for long. A vase is a charming gift, but ladies often prefer a more…personal item. Might your sister be interested in such a necklace?'

Jane might not, but Alastair certainly was. 'Please, do show it to me,' he replied, his curiosity tweaked even further.

Why would Diana be selling jewellery? Whatever the reason, he knew at once he would buy the necklace back.

Beaming, the jeweller disappeared, returning a moment later with a long double-twisted strand of perfectly matched pearls.

For a moment, shock displaced curiosity, as Alastair recognised the necklace. One of the few mementos Diana had of her mother, who'd died giving her birth, the pearls had been a gift to her from her father on her sixteenth birthday. She'd mentioned several times how special it was to her. He couldn't imagine why she would part with it.

Glad he'd encountered the jeweller before the piece had been shown to some other customer, he said, 'You are right. It's exquisite. I shall take that, too.'

Purchases completed, he picked up the wrapped parcel containing the vase and tucked the velvet case with the pearls in his pocket. He'd give Jane the vase just before guests arrived for dinner, leaving them only a short time for conversation, then slip away when her party left for the theatre.

Already impatient to see Diana again, he was now even more eager for the day to fade into evening. He'd present her with the pearls immediately—and try to discover what circumstance could possibly have induced her to part with something that held such dear memories of her long-dead mother.

Alastair arrived at the rendezvous even earlier than the previous nights, then paced the parlour until Diana arrived. Though he'd intended to return the pearls to her immediately, the intensity of the kiss she gave him in greeting fired his simmering desire at once to irresistible need. Almost ravenous enough to take her right then and there, he restrained himself, barely, hurrying her to the bedchamber moments after she stepped in the door.

She seemed as ravenous as he was, kissing him urgently while she tugged at his neckcloth and made short work of the buttons of his trouser flap. Pushing him back to sit on the bed, she lifted her skirts and straddled him, guided him deep and rocked against him, driving them both to their peak within moments.

The next loving was nearly as swift, clothing scattered as it was removed in haste. Then after another, languid cherishing they both drifted into the sleep of the satiated.

* * *

Awaking sometime later with Diana tucked in his arms, Alastair smiled as he surveyed the chamber: candles burned low in their sconces, her gown tossed on the back of a chair, her stockings on the bedside table, his neckcloth flung into a corner. Sated for now, he knew that after they consumed the cold collation he'd had set out for them, he'd want her again.

He couldn't seem to get enough of her. Underlying desire, this odd sense of impending loss throbbed in his head like a ticking clock, as if the hours they had together would be limited this time, as they had been before, by some malevolent fate.

Nonsense, he told himself, shaking off the feeling. Eight years ago, they had both been young, still susceptible to the demands of Society and dependent upon others for their support. With him the master of his own estate, she a widow, they now controlled their own destinies, alone and together.

At that encouraging thought, Diana stirred in his arms. Waking, she opened sleepy blue eyes—those beautiful, mesmerising, intense blue eyes—and smiled at him.

Ignoring the wise intention to proceed with caution, his heart leapt with gladness.

Placing a kiss on her forehead, he eased her up

against the pillows. 'I'm famished. There's refreshment in the next room.'

He wrapped her in his banyan, donned another, and escorted her to the sitting room, where a fire glowed on the hearth and a simple meal awaited. Though she sipped her wine and accepted bread and cheese, something in the set of her body and the guarded expression of her face suggested an underlying tension.

In a rush, he remembered the necklace. She might well be troubled by whatever had made her part with that once-cherished memento.

'I've got something for you,' he said, hopping up to find his breeches and extract the velvet pouch from the pocket.

'What, more gifts? You really don't have to get me things.'

'I like to get you things—especially when you have such delightful ways of appreciating them.'

'Ever calculating,' she said with a smile. 'Ingenious Alastair.'

His mouth dried and for a moment, he couldn't speak. *Ingenious Alastair...* Diana had coined the nickname, and taken up by his cousins, it had stuck.

It was only one of those she'd devised, her favourite in the game they played, he praising her in verse, she describing him in different moods and circumstances: Adulating Alastair, Adamant Alastair, Eccentric Alastair. He'd joked that she would run out of adjectives, and she'd assured him she had an endless trove of them, enough to last all the years they'd spend together.

He refocused his gaze on Diana. From the stark expression on her face, he knew she was remembering, too—the lost years, the unrealised promise.

'I've brought you something,' he repeated, breaking the mood. He held out the pouch.

Uncertain—the wounded look still in her eyes—she took it from him and extracted the pearls. Colour came and went in her cheeks before she looked back up at him. 'How did you get these?'

'I happened to stop by the jeweller right after he purchased them. Thinking me a likely customer, he showed them to me. I knew at once they must be yours, and bought them back. Why on earth would you sell your mother's pearls?'

The subtle agitation he'd noticed in her earlier intensified. At first he thought she'd simply refuse to answer, but after obvious struggle, she said, 'I was short of funds. I must consult a solicitor about a matter I'd hoped to delay until…until later, but changing circumstances make the need to settle it urgent.'

'Short of funds?' he tossed back, his tone sharpened by a bitterness he'd not quite mastered. 'I find it hard to believe a duke's widow would be less than amply provided for. Graveston was exceedingly wealthy. I should think the settlements would have left you very well off.'

She shook her head. 'In the haste of the wedding, I don't believe settlements were ever drawn up.'

Alastair frowned. 'It would have been exceedingly careless of your father to neglect doing that.'

'You must remember, the Duke possessed a large number of my father's vowels. If the Duke assured him settlements were unnecessary, he was not in a position to press the issue.'

'In the absence of settlements, you're still entitled to the dower. Though much of the estate, like my own, is probably tied up in land, your right to a third of it should provide more than sufficient funds to meet whatever needs you have.'

'Perhaps. Except for the fact that the new Duke despises me. Any claims I might make against the estate, whether entitled to them or not, he would do his utmost to disapprove or delay. And I can't afford to delay.'

'What is it you must do that is so imperative, you would sell your mother's pearls to accomplish it?'

She opened her lips, closed them. With short, jerky movements, she set down her wine glass and leapt up. 'I…I must go. It's late, and I cannot stay the night this time.'

Everything about her radiated distress. His concern intensifying, Alastair caught her arm. 'What is it, Diana? You can tell me. Surely you know I wouldn't break a confidence.'

Eyes wide, she stared up at him, her breathing quickening, then cast a glance through the open door, towards the dressing table.

'Talk to me,' Alastair urged, following the direction of her gaze. 'I think I can be at least as much help as a mirror.'

She snapped her gaze back to him and pulled her arm free. 'You don't understand! I…I can't talk to you. I can't confide in anyone. I don't know how any more.'

'We used to talk easily, about everything. We can do so again. Won't you trust me?'

The urgency of her expression became tinged with sadness. 'Even if I could, you won't be here for long. Why should you? This…trouble has nothing to do with you. I'll have to face it alone. I should prepare for it alone. After all, I've had years of practice.'

For a moment, he had nothing to reply. She was right; he hadn't planned for this to be more than a temporary liaison, initially one restricted only to the physical. He'd not yet resolved the conflicting desires pulling at him to embrace her, or to escape before she drew him in more deeply.

'That may be so,' he said at last. 'But you're no longer forced to be alone. You can fashion a life for yourself now, the life *you* want, with friends and allies and advocates. There's no danger to them any more for helping you. If you're going to be confronting the Duke, you'll need allies.'

In her face, he could read the hesitation, the conflict between the urge to speak and the habit of withdrawal. Pressing, he continued, 'If there's something threatening you, a friend would want to help.'

Her eyes widened, and he knew he'd scored a hit.

'A threat. Yes.' She took a shuddering breath. 'You are right. When battling a duke, one should enlist all the allies one can muster.'

'So tell me.'

To his intense satisfaction, at length, she nodded. 'Very well. There is a threat—but not to me.'

Anxious to have her begin before she changed her mind and fled, he urged her back to her seat. 'What sort of threat?' he prompted, pouring more wine and handing it to her.

'Blankford's—the new Duke's—solicitor called on me today. I'm not sure how he traced me so quickly, but I anticipated the demand. He wants to take my son back to live at Graveston Court.'

'Were you not planning to return at some point to the Dower House at Graveston anyway?'

A look of revulsion passing over her face, she shook her head. 'I'll never willingly set foot on the estate again. Nor do I want my son there. I've told you how the Duke coerced me into wedding him. His heir was raised with the same beliefs— that he possesses ultimate power and the right to do whatever he pleases with it, heedless of the desires of anyone else. Even if I didn't fear for James, I wouldn't want my son reared under the influence of such a man.'

Alastair raised an eyebrow. 'Fear for him? Is he frail?'

'No, but he might be in danger. You may remember I told you that when Graveston—the late Duke—first paid me attention, his wife was still living. Before I could become too uncomfortable with his unusual regard, it ceased, and he struck up a friendship with Papa. Guileless as he was, Papa welcomed anyone who seemed interested in the botanical studies that consumed him. Within the year, the Duke's wife died and, using the debts Papa had accumulated, he forced me to wed him.'

A frown on her forehead, Diana leapt up and

began to pace, as if the agitation within was too strong for her to remain still. 'I was…rather oblivious of my surroundings after being brought to Graveston Court, only dimly aware of the quarrels between my husband and his heir. Blankford had not previously acknowledged my existence or exchanged a word with me, but the day he broke with his father and left Graveston for good, he tracked me down in the garden. He accused me of having bewitched the Duke, obsessing him so that he drove his first wife to her death and lost interest in his only son and heir. He warned me that he'd outlive his father, and when he inherited, he would exact vengeance for himself and his mother.'

'Troubling words, but he was younger then, hotheaded as young men often are. Are you sure he still bears such enmity?'

'He is his father's son. In the coldness of his absolute will, Graveston spent almost a year setting up the trap to force me to wed. Blankford would be fully capable of nurturing his hatred for five years. He wants to deny me access to James to punish me, of course. But why would he have any interest in nurturing the son of the woman he holds responsible for the death of his mother and the break with his father? I cannot trust his intentions.'

'You really believe he might harm the boy? I have to say, that seems…excessive.'

'So was Graveston's poisoning my dog and threatening to ruin my father,' she flashed back. 'For men of their stamp, the lives of others are of no importance. Only their will matters.'

Alastair still thought it highly unlikely the new Duke, however arrogant and wilful, would go so far as to harm a child. But quite obviously, *Diana* believed it. And that was enough for him.

'I sold the pearls, the most valuable of the jewels I possess, to obtain funds to hire the best solicitor I can find,' she continued. 'One who can build a case for retaining custody of James that will prevail against the Duke's claim in a Court of Chancery.'

'Preparing such a case is likely to be a lengthy endeavour—which will cost you far more than the value of a string of pearls. I already have an excellent solicitor on retainer. Why not let him look into it? As you already admitted, if you contest the Duke on this, he'll likely do everything legally possible to delay or tie up whatever you're entitled to as dower, so you need to conserve the assets you have with you. Unless you have substantial cash reserves on hand?'

'I wouldn't have sold the necklace if that were so,' she admitted.

'Then let me find out what I can,' he urged.

She frowned. 'As much as I appreciate your offer, I...I really ought not to accept it. The battle will likely be ugly as well as expensive. The Duke will not forgive anyone who takes my part, and I don't want you dragged into it.'

'I'm not a callow collegian any more, Diana. I can hold my own. Besides, you need to utilise every resource you can muster to protect your son.'

'To protect James,' she repeated with a sigh. 'Very well, let your solicitor look into it. I've been a poor enough mother thus far, I cannot afford to turn away help, hard as it is to accept.'

'You, a poor mother? That, I can't imagine.'

She laughed shortly. 'Do you remember the paints? The books? The music? Everything that might affect me was utilised by the Duke to try to force a reaction or keep me under control. A child was just one more tool. The only way to protect him was to be indifferent to him...whatever the Duke said or threatened.'

Her voice faded. 'To my shame, as the years went on, I didn't have to struggle so hard to be indifferent. Not nearly as hard as I should have. Every time I looked at James, I saw...his father.'

'Truly? I knew the first time *I* saw him that he must be *your* son. He has your eyes.'

Startled, Diana looked back up at him. 'You think he has…something of me?'

'Absolutely! Have you never noticed?'

She shook her head. 'I am trying to do better, now that I can. But after years forcing down and bottling up and restraining emotion, I…I'm afraid I'll never find my way back to loving him.'

Alastair thought of how he doted upon his nephew, how easy and affectionate the relationship was between Robbie and Jane. A pang of compassion shook him, that the honest, open, loving Diana he'd known could have been brought to shut out her own son.

The late Duke of Graveston had much to answer for.

'Just let him love you,' he said, thinking of how Robbie had inveigled himself into Alastair's heart. 'In time, you will find yourself responding.'

Diana smiled sadly. 'I hope so. Now I really must go. How long do you think it will take for your solicitor to have an answer? If Feral—Graveston's man—left Bath today, he could reach the Court by week's end. Which means Graveston could make some new demand within a fortnight, if not sooner.'

'I could summon Reynolds, but it would be faster for me to call upon him in London. If I leave tomorrow, I should be able to return with some word in six or seven days, so you have time to prepare before the Duke can make another move.'

She nodded. 'I would like that.' Swallowing hard, she said softly, 'How can I thank you? Or ever repay you?'

'Protecting a child is payment enough. As for thanks…' He gave her a wicked grin. 'When I return from London, I'm sure I can think of something.'

She managed a wan smile. While normally he would have tried to persuade her to stay longer, now that he was aware of the worry consuming her over the safety of her son, he made no attempt to seduce as he helped her track down and slip on her garments. When she was clothed again, her hair tidied as best they could manage and the concealing cloak in place, he pulled her close. To his delight, after a moment of hesitation, she clung to him.

Though he didn't regret his offer to go to London, it meant probably a week or more until he would see her again. Already he felt bereft, and with her pressed against him, his body protested the abstinence about to be forced upon it.

'Try not to worry too much,' he told her as he released her at last.

'I'll try. I'll try with James, too.'

He kissed the tip of her nose, still reluctant to let her go. 'I'll miss you,' he admitted.

'Then come back quickly.'

With that, she walked from the room.

Alastair followed her through the bedchamber to the stairs, listening to the soft footfalls as she descended and the murmur of voices in the entry below where Marston, as previously arranged, waited to engage a chair to carry her safely home.

Once the last echoes faded, he returned to the sitting room, threw himself in a chair, poured another glass of wine, and reviewed what he'd just committed himself to doing.

It did not represent him easing the reins restraining his feelings, he assured the cautious voice in his head. Any man of honour would step in to assure the safety of a child.

It did indicate, however, that sometime over the course of their renewed association, he had come to accept as true the explanation she'd given him for breaking their engagement to marry the Duke.

Drawing back from considering the full implications of that transformation, he turned his mind instead to considering what Diana had told him about her relationship with the new Duke and her fears for her son's safety.

Though he still thought Diana's long, bitter association with her husband and his heir caused her to exaggerate the son's ruthlessness and enmity, he had to admit he was curious how well she'd been provided for. If there truly were no settlements outlining the exact arrangements for her support if widowed, it represented a grievous failure of his responsibilities on the part of her father.

But it was also true that the professor had been a completely unworldly man, a scholar absorbed in his studies. If he had come to view the Duke as a friend and colleague, he might well have been satisfied with just a verbal assurance that his daughter would be well taken care of in the event of her husband's demise. Particularly as, in the absence of some formal agreement, she would have the dower to a very wealthy estate.

He'd have to confer with his solicitor on this matter, but he didn't see how the new Duke could deny rights guaranteed under English law. He had to admit, though, that being entitled to something and effectively claiming it could be quite different matters, especially if a personage with the power and resources of a duke set his mind to making it as time-consuming and difficult as possible.

But all of that was for his legal counsel to discover. What warmed him now, as much as the satisfaction of his well-pleasured body, was the fact that he'd managed to persuade Diana to confide in him.

Since encountering her again, he'd been accumulating evidence in mites and snippets of what her married life had been: her at first rejected account of her marriage, the episodes described by Lady Randolph, the information he'd teased out of her about the removal of her paints and books. But aside from that single moment upon awakening yesterday, when she'd looked at him with awe and tenderness, she'd maintained emotionally aloof.

Regrettable as it was that she'd found herself in such a vulnerable position, Alastair had to admit he was almost—glad of it. Without such an imminent threat to her son, she might have continued keeping him at arm's length indefinitely.

Instead, with some persistence, tonight he'd managed to breach the wall of impassivity she'd erected to disguise her thoughts and feelings, giving him the clearest-yet glimpse into her life. It wrung his heart to realise how difficult it had been for her to force herself to reach out to him, emphasising even further how isolated and alone she'd become.

Still, the concern, independence and initiative she'd exhibited in seeking to shelter her child not only called out his strongest protective instincts, they also gave him enticing glimpses of the girl he'd once known, now more mature, stronger and seasoned by the loss and suffering she'd survived.

Having disarmed her defences to the point of eliciting those revelations, he was more determined than ever to complete the job. To release the Diana still not free of the mask, persuade her it was now safe to step out of isolation and encourage her to claim the life that awaited her.

Only after he'd arranged for her and her son's protection and coaxed her out of the shadows, would he turn his attention to their possible future. And decide whether to try winning her anew, or let her go before it was too late for him to walk away.

Chapter Eleven

Several days after Alastair's departure, Diana restlessly paced her parlour. Rain had kept her from a walk with James this morning, and with the resulting mud and wet, it was probably best not to attempt to walk this afternoon.

She was finding it harder and harder to force down her worry, bottle up concern over the future, and present an impassive face to the staff. Even sessions before the mirror were failing her.

Would talking with Alastair again help? She'd felt calmer after returning from their last rendezvous. She told herself it was not missing him that further complicated her tangle of thoughts.

He certainly had been effective at stirring up her feelings. Which meant it would be better to avoid him, once he ended their bargain. Since she'd started seeing him, dribs and drabs of emotion had been leaching out, each leak further weakening the dykes she'd erected to contain them.

Perhaps one day she would be able to ease those restraints, release the anguish and the memories in slow, manageable bits and at length, be free of them.

But now was not that time.

She'd thought if she relaxed just enough to permit Alastair to reach her physically, she'd be able to distract him with passion and escape more intense scrutiny.

Instead, after only two meetings, he'd managed to unearth her most shameful secret and her deepest worry.

In her defence, only the imperative to do whatever she could to protect James had pushed her to reveal the situation. In the wake of that confession, she'd careened from horror that she'd divulged the dilemma to him, shame over admitting her failings with her son, and relief that she would not have to contest the Duke alone. Embracing Alastair without reservation before she left him, she'd felt...safe. That concerned her.

It had been wise to elicit the aid of anyone willing to help her in her battle with the Duke—that much she owed to James. But to assume that Alastair Ransleigh or anyone else would stand by her was foolish. Not only foolish, it put James's safety at risk to depend upon support that could disappear as unexpectedly as the whim to offer it.

Alastair hadn't denied it when she'd stated that he'd only be around a short time. He'd pledged to have a solicitor spell out the legal parameters of the threat she faced. She could not expect him, nor had he offered, to involve himself beyond that point. She must prepare herself to enter the struggle and deal with its consequences alone.

She began to consider what she would do if the solicitor returned an unfavourable assessment of her ability to retain custody of James.

Allowing him to go to Graveston was out of the question. She would flee England before she'd permit that. With the war finally over, they might be able to settle in some small rural village in France. Her French was impeccable—Papa had seen to that; she could give lessons in English, piano, watercolours.

Except how was she to obtain a position without references? The amounts she could obtain from selling her few remaining jewels would support them for a time, but even in the depressed economy of a war-ravaged area, they wouldn't be able to live on them for ever.

She had no other assets besides that small store

of jewellery, inherited from her father's mother. Not grand enough that the Duke had permitted her to wear any of it, nor valuable enough for him to bother selling the pieces, she'd been able to secrete them away. She'd left all of the ornate and valuable jewels presented to her by the Duke at Graveston Court, wanting nothing that reminded her of her life as Graveston's Duchess.

What would she do if they exhausted her small store of assets?

Coming up with no answers, exasperated with pacing, she decided to go visit James. She felt a slight smile curving her lips. As Alastair had predicted, her son was always glad to see her.

'Let him love you,' Alastair had advised. She'd been trying that, not forcing her emotions, simply chatting with him, asking about his interests and responding to his answers.

He particularly loved getting outdoors, but that wasn't wise today. Suddenly, she remembered something else she might try. The morning after Alastair had given her back the pearls, a package arrived containing the box of watercolours and the sketchbook she'd told him to return. Not knowing from which establishment he'd obtained them, she had kept them.

On impulse, she gathered the supplies from her wardrobe and continued to the nursery.

As she entered, James was listlessly pushing a soldier around on the floor before the hearth, a picture of boredom. When he turned to see her, his small face lit up and he jumped to his feet. At that expression of gladness, Diana felt herself warm.

'Mama! Can we go to the park? It's not raining any more.'

'That's true, but I fear it is still very wet.' Giving the nursemaid a nod, she walked over to seat herself at the table before the fire, setting down the package. James hurried over to perch on the bench beside her. 'Just think how cross Minnie would be if she had to soak out of your breeches all the dirt you would surely get on them, jumping in and out of puddles.'

His face fell. 'I promise I won't go in puddles.'

He looked so earnest, she had to laugh. 'I know you would try to be good, but heavens, how could anyone resist discovering how deep the puddles are, or seeing how high the water splashes when one jumps in them? I know I cannot, and Annie would be even crosser than Minnie if she had to press the mud out of my skirts. No, I've brought something else for us.'

His crestfallen look dissolved in curiosity. 'In that package? May I open it?'

'You may.'

He made quick work of the wrappings, unlatched the box and drew out a brush. 'How soft it is!' he exclaimed, drawing the bristles across his hand. 'It's awfully little for scrubbing, though.'

'It's not for scrubbing. It's for painting. Those little dishes contain watercolours. Minnie, would you pour some water in that bowl and get James something he can use as a smock? A nightshirt will do.'

Though it had been years since she'd prepared paints, she fell back into the familiar pattern immediately, blending into the dishes some of the paint with water from the bowl brought by the nursery maid. By the time the girl had James's nightshirt over his head to protect his clothing, Diana had half-a-dozen colours prepared for his inspection.

'Which colours do you like the best?'

'Red and blue,' he pointed out promptly. 'What do we do now?'

'We decide what we want to paint.'

James looked around quickly. 'My soldier!'

'Good choice. Let's sit him on the table so we can see him better. First, we'll make an outline of his body, then fill in with the colours.'

She showed James how to dip his brush in the

paint, then stroke the brush across the sketchpad. She expected that after a few minutes of meticulous work he would get bored with the process, but he did not, continuing with rapt attention under her direction and suggestions until he'd completed a creditable soldier in a bright-red coat and blue trousers.

'That's very good!' she said approvingly, surprised that it was true. Even more surprised that, with his head bent and a rapt expression on his face, James reminded her of her father, recording in deft brushstrokes the details of one of the plants he'd discovered.

Another wash of heat warmed her within. Perhaps Alastair was right. Perhaps there was more of her—and her father—in the boy than she'd thought.

Vastly pleased with his work, James was delighted when she set it above the mantel. 'There, you'll be able to see it from your bed and admire it as you eat your supper.'

'Look at my painting, Minnie!' he cried to the nurse, who, to Diana's mild amusement, hovered nearby whenever Diana visited her son. Though the girl seemed to have somewhat relaxed her vigilance, Diana sensed Minnie still didn't entirely trust her mistress's sudden, unprecedented interest in her charge.

'That's wonderful fine, young master,' the maid

answered, a deep affection in her tone. 'A right handsome soldier you've drawn.'

'Mama, will you make one, too?'

'If it would please you.'

'Oh, yes! I'd love having something from you, something to keep.'

The artless words pricked her again, reminding her how little she'd offered her son since she'd forced herself to turn away from him as a toddler. True, she'd had a compelling reason for withdrawing from him—but no more. Silently she renewed her vow to do better.

'What kind of picture do you want?'

'Another soldier.'

'Very well.' Taking the brush from him, she deftly created a replica of the toy soldier. James looked over her shoulder as she painted, seeming entirely absorbed.

When she finished, he gave a little sigh of awe. 'Oh, Mama, that's wonderful! He looks just like my soldier. Will you put him on the mantel next to mine, so they can keep each other company?'

'Of course.'

After she'd arranged the two pictures side by side and stepped back, James clapped his hands with delight. 'It's like having more soldiers for my army!

Only maybe better, 'cause you and me made them together. Thank you, Mama!'

Jumping up, he ran over and wrapped his arms around her.

Still not accustomed to hugs, she started—then slowly wrapped her arms around him as well. From deep within, an impulse welled up to pull him nearer, hold him tighter.

Immediately she resisted it…until she realised that she didn't have to restrain herself any longer.

Let him love you. You'll find yourself responding.

Hearing Alastair's words echo in her ears, she hugged James tighter, pressing her face against his soft dark hair. An aching warmth curled around her heart.

As much as she owed Alastair Ransleigh for his efforts to keep her son safe, she owed him even more for this.

Meanwhile, in the London office of his solicitor, Mr Reynolds, Alastair explained his need for some information regarding settlements.

A smile creased the older man's face. 'Dare I hope that means you expect a momentous occasion in the near future? Let me offer my congratulations!'

Startled at first, Alastair had to laugh. 'I'm afraid not. A close family friend was recently widowed.

Her father is now deceased, and she is not aware if settlements were ever drawn up.'

'Are the circumstances not specified in her late husband's will?'

'The circumstances are rather...complicated. What would normally be set up?'

'Normally, the dowry or portion brought into the marriage by the bride is guaranteed to her as an annuity in the event of the husband's death. If a specific sum is not mentioned, usually she is deeded some property as her jointure, the income and rents from which are intended to support her after the husband's death, when his estate passes to his heir.'

'In the absence of settlements, she would be entitled to a dower?'

'Yes, to one-third of the property and assets of the estate. Which, for a wealthy man, could be quite considerable, hence the desire for settlements to simplify the process and limit the annuity to a specific sum.'

'If dower rights were invoked, how would the widow obtain the assets?'

'The local sheriff's court would have the handling of it.'

That was what Alastair had feared. 'And if there were...ill feelings between the heir and the widow?'

Mr Reynolds sent him a questioning look. 'Would this heir be a man of high rank?'

'The highest.'

The solicitor gave him a thin smile. 'Then obtaining her due could be difficult. The local sheriff would, understandably, be reluctant to antagonise a man of wealth and influence in the community. Your widow would require a strong solicitor and a prominent advocate to ensure the heir was compelled to recognise her rights.'

Alastair nodded. 'Thank you, Mr Reynolds. I appreciate your expertise.'

'If I can assist you further, please let me know. The poor widow is entitled to her due.'

'She is indeed,' Alastair agreed. 'I will certainly call upon you again if circumstances require it.'

'Always a pleasure to serve you,' Mr Reynolds said with another smile as he ushered Alastair to the door.

As he paced the street to summon a hackney, Alastair mulled over what he should do next.

Would the new Duke really make problems for Diana? How much of her suspicion and foreboding were the results of her miserable existence as his father's wife? Would the mature Blankford have outgrown his youthful resentment?

There was only one sure way to find out.

He'd just have to make a trip to Graveston Court.

Chapter Twelve

Several days later, Alastair passed through the entry gates and rode down a long, tree-bordered lane. Around one bend, set like a jewel against the hill behind it, its long columned facade reflected by a symmetrical pond before it, stood the huge Palladian mansion that was Graveston Court.

After turning his mount over to a waiting lackey, he was admitted by a grim-faced butler, ushered through the marbled entrance down a corridor flanked with what appeared to be Grecian antiquities, and shown into a beautifully appointed parlour. The Duke would be informed of his arrival, the butler intoned before bowing himself out.

So this was the prison in which Diana had been trapped for so many years, Alastair thought. He paced the room, whose arched windows, flanked by gold brocade drapery, echoed the Palladian influences evident in the mansion's facade. More antiquities—vases embellished with Greek battle scenes, Roman busts and bas-relief carvings—were set on pedestals or artfully arranged on shelves.

The scale was oppressively overwhelming, everything about the room and its opulent furnishings designed to dazzle the visitor and intimidate him with a sense of his insignificance, compared to the wealth and rank of his host.

At length, losing interest in examining the various treasures, Alastair took a seat on the lavishly embellished gold sofa, and waited. And waited. And waited some more, his anger beginning to smoulder.

Of course, he had arrived without notice and the new Duke would have many pressing matters to attend to, taking over the reins of such a large estate. However, leaving him tapping his fingers this long, without an offer of refreshment or any other courtesy, was, Alastair felt sure, a deliberate insult.

Any deference to rank Alastair might once have felt had long since been dissipated by the refusal of his uncle, the Earl of Swynford, to support his younger son, Alastair's cousin and best friend, after the scandal that had embroiled Max at the Congress of Vienna. A deference already worn thin by his army service, where experience and ability was worth far more in battle than rank or title, and his own previous dealings with a Duke of Graveston.

So he was not feeling particularly amiable when the Duke finally deigned to make an appearance.

After exchanging the obligatory bows and greetings, the Duke said, 'So, Mr Ransleigh, to what do I owe the honour of this visit?''

The sly smile accompanying those words gave Alastair the distinct impression that the Duke knew exactly who he was and why he was here.

Which shouldn't come as a surprise. In order for Graveston's solicitor to have found Diana so quickly, the new Duke must have had his own spies hidden among the household at Graveston, some of whom had trailed her when she fled to Bath after her husband's death. If those informers remained in the city to watch her, they would have already sent word to the Duke about his relationship with the widow.

If the Duke wished to be coy, not revealing what he already knew, he could play along, thought Alastair, his irritation building. 'As a friend of the Dowager Duchess, I wished to approach you about a family matter. Gentleman to gentleman, without recourse to involving the sheriff or the courts.'

'Gentleman to gentleman,' the Duke repeated, raising an ironic eyebrow. 'Do proceed.'

'The Dowager, naturally distraught over the death of her husband, needed time away to compose herself. She seemed to doubt that you would agree to provide her with the support and assistance to which she is entitled as your father's widow.'

The Duke's smirk of a smile compressed to a thin line. 'I'm surprised the doxy is intelligent enough to understand that. Support *her*?' His raised voice had a derisive ring. 'She left Graveston Court voluntarily; let her support herself. I'm sure she wheedled enough baubles out of my father to keep herself in furs, gowns and sweetmeats for the rest of her life.'

'Nonetheless,' Alastair countered, holding on to his temper, 'she's still entitled to her dower.'

The Duke's eyebrows lifted again. 'She can certainly apply for it. Any claims submitted on that account will be referred to my solicitor.'

'She was your late father's legal wife. Your man might obstruct, harass and delay such a petition, but in the end, the law will see she gets what she's entitled to.'

The Duke laughed outright. 'Oh, I certainly hope she gets what she deserves! My father's legal wife—ha! Only think, he set aside my mother, who lived only to please him, for *her*. And what an ideal duchess she made! Incapable of running the household. Contradicting my father in front of his guests.

Disputing the gentlemen's opinions and ignoring the ladies, to whose company she should have directed her attention and remarks. Well, he had little enough joy of her. Just the one brat, after eight years of marriage.'

While Alastair bottled up his mounting ire and disgust, Graveston continued. 'Ah yes, the brat. I shall very much enjoy helping him discover what it's like being the son of a displaced mother!' He smiled, anger glittering in his eyes. 'I'll enjoy even more having *her* know he's experiencing that delight, and she's responsible.'

Diana had warned him, but he hadn't believed it. 'You would punish a child?' Alastair asked incredulously, revolted.

Graveston shrugged. 'Not punish. Just…instil in him a proper recognition of his place. He'll survive. I did. It will make a man of him.'

A man like you? he thought. *No wonder Diana wants to keep her son away.*

'He's a Mannington brat, for all that, even if he is half *hers*. Perhaps we can beat that out of him. One can try.' He smiled again, as if relishing the prospect. 'He will need to be trained to his role— to serve my son and heir. Which brings me back to a matter more important than the spurious claims of my father's former *wife*. Since you seem to be on such good terms with her, perhaps you'll inform her if she does not return the boy voluntarily, and soon, I shall have the Court of Chancery order it.'

'She would appeal such a demand. You can't know for sure they would rule in your favour.'

'Can I not? When the head of an ancient, venerable family of vast resources magnanimously offers to support a half-brother, even though he's the spawn of a nobody? Worse than a nobody, a woman whose odd and irregular behaviour forced her husband to banish her from Society. Who fled her home before her husband's body was scarcely cold, instead of remaining to greet the heir and see proper tribute paid to her late master. Not to mention, as any number of witnesses can testify, a mother who paid practically no attention to her son from his early years until his father's demise. Do you really think she has any chance to hang on to him? If you're such a *friend*, you should advise her to spare herself the embarrassment of having her conduct censured before the Court, and send the brat back now.'

So Diana was right; the miserable little muckworm did intend to exact his revenge on her son. His fighting instincts fully aroused, he said coldly, 'I certainly couldn't advise that.'

His eyes narrowing, the Duke examined Alastair's

face. 'So that's the way it is, eh? I suspected as much. Though she has a pretty enough face, I suppose, and the same charms as any trollop, I still find it hard to understand how she entices men, but take some friendly advice. Have your fill of her and get out. She's about to face the consequences of her infamy, and it would grieve me to see a *gentleman* get dragged in it.'

'I think she has suffered quite enough already at the hands of the Dukes of Graveston.'

'Do you, now? Then let me assure you, the retribution she so justly deserves is only beginning. The investigation is in its early stages, but it's highly likely that she, ah, *assisted* my father's departure from this earth. It's common knowledge that she and the Duke did not get along, as every servant in this house would swear under oath. If this investigation bears fruit, I intend to have her brought up on charges of murder. So you'd be well advised to make your exit before she entangles you any further.'

Alastair first thought the Duke must be joking, but by the end of that incredible speech, realised Graveston was entirely serious. 'Bring her up on murder charges! That's preposterous! I advise *you* to consider your position before making such a ridiculous charge. It's more likely you, not the widow, who would appear reprehensible if Society learned that, not only had you no intention of honouring your obligations towards a woman who, despite your dislike of her, is still a dowager duchess, you are persecuting her with baseless and slanderous charges.'

'And I advise you again to consider your own reputation! How do you think Society will react to learning that, within days of the suspicious death of her husband, his widow hurried off to Bath to meet her former lover, with whom she is now conducting an illicit affair? Perhaps also the man who incited her to dispose of the husband he'd always hated for winning the woman he loved?'

Hot words hovered on his tongue to challenge the Duke then and there. But the man would probably welcome a confrontation—such behaviour would give credence to the absurd scenario of illicit passion and revenge the Duke was constructing.

Besides, Alastair was quite certain a man intent on exacting revenge against a defenceless woman was likely too much a coward ever to meet him; bullies preferred to attack weaker beings rather than confront a man equal to them in vigour and influence. Better for him to take his leave now, before Graveston could provoke him into losing his temper, then plan in the coldness of reason how to counter this threat.

Accordingly, he raised his eyes and fixed the Duke with a glare that had made many an errant subordinate quake. 'If it weren't beneath me to soil my blade with the blood of such a scoundrel,' he said softly, 'I'd call you out for such slander. I can promise you, I won't forget it, and there will be a reckoning.'

Keeping his temper in check with some difficulty, Alastair rose. 'Since it has become quite plain you are unwilling to recognise your responsibilities towards the widow, there is nothing to be gained from prolonging this interview.' He sketched the briefest of bows. 'I will no longer keep you, as you doubtless have many pressing duties,' he finished, with a last jab at the wait forced on him.

'Indeed I do, Mr Ransleigh.' The Duke nodded, looking very pleased with himself.

Alastair found it even more infuriating that the Duke appeared so supremely confident of his own power, so dismissive of the possibility that Alastair might devise some way to check him, that he gave no credence to Alastair's threat. His heart smouldering, he knew in that moment that even if Diana's welfare were not involved, he would have to bring the man down. He also knew he would do everything in his power to prevent the Duke from getting his hands on Diana's son.

The Duke accorded him a brief nod of dismissal. Fuming, Alastair stalked out of the salon.

Just outside in the hall, he encountered a tall, thin, hawk-nosed woman with housekeeper's keys hanging at her waist. She stared at him boldly as he paced by her, a thin smile on her face.

We'll see who laughs last, he vowed under his breath as the imperious butler shut the entry door behind him.

Several days' hard riding later, before returning to his sister's lodgings on Royal Crescent, Alastair rode instead to the townhouse at Green Park Buildings. He knew he owed his sister some attention after decamping with hardly a word, but he also knew Diana would be anxious, waiting to learn what he had discovered. He wished he had a better report, but the bad news wouldn't improve by putting off the telling.

He'd debated calling on her in Laura Place—if the Duke knew of their relationship, how many others were aware?—but on the chance that it had not yet been discovered by half of Bath, opted instead for discretion, sending her a note asking her to meet him at their usual rendezvous, as soon as she was able to get away that evening.

He would have to figure out how much to tell Jane, since, with his frequent absences in the evening and recent unexplained travels out of town, his needle-witted sister was certain to suspect something. But first, he needed to consult Diana.

Since he had no idea how early Diana might get away, he ordered a bath and an early dinner. As afternoon faded into evening, unable to distract himself with a book, he took to pacing.

At last, he heard her light step on the stairway, and leapt up to meet her as Marston ushered her in. She gave him her hands and lifted her face for his kiss, worry etched on every feature.

'I'm glad you returned safely. What did you discover?'

He swept her to a chair and poured her some wine. 'You're certainly entitled to something, probably a handsome something, whether from dower or as income from whatever jointure might have been established in your late husband's will. That is the good news. The bad news, although, is that if it involves dower, the local sheriff's court must oversee the administration. It's very possible a local man could be too intimidated to vigorously pursue his duty, if the Duke or his representatives resist the process at every turn.'

'As he certainly would. But I'm not so much concerned about jointures or dower. What about James?'

'The legality in that case is less clear.' Alastair paused, recalling the gloating expression on the Duke's face. 'I now fully understand and support your intention not to let the current Duke of Graveston gain control over your son.'

Diana gave a grimace of distaste. 'Has he already made himself so infamous that even your solicitor knows of him?'

She must have seen something in his face, for without giving him time to respond, she cried, 'Oh, Alastair—you didn't seek him out, did you? Tell me you did not!'

There seemed no point hiding it. 'I called on him at Graveston Court,' he admitted. 'I have to confess, I thought you were exaggerating the vengefulness of his character, but after talking with him myself, I'm forced to concede you were not.'

She sprang up and took an agitated turn about the room before halting abruptly before him. 'I should never have confided in you! Don't you see? Not just James is at risk now—you've placed yourself in harm's way as well!'

All too aware that he had been threatened, he said, 'I doubt there is much Graveston can do to me. But I fear I have complicated matters.'

She shook her head. 'You'd better tell me the whole.'

She seated herself again and remained silent through his recitation: the aggravating discourtesy of being made to wait, the Duke's sly baiting, his disparaging words about Diana, his demand that James be returned to Graveston Court, his certainty that Chancery would uphold his request for guardianship. Finally, reluctantly, he revealed the Duke's infamous design to have her brought up on murder charges.

Though her eyes widened at the mention of murder, she said nothing until he revealed the Duke had threatened to involve him, too, as a motive for the crime, unless he ceased to support her.

'Infamous!' she exclaimed. 'And how very like him!'

'Infamous indeed, but I must say, after repeating it to you here in prosaic candlelight, I find it difficult to credit. Making ungrounded accusations is a serious matter that could severely damage his own reputation. More probably, it was the ranting of the boy who never outgrew his rancour towards you for displacing his mother. He's a grown man now. When, in the coolness of reason, he considers the repercussions of making such accusations, I cannot see any rational man moving forward with such a project, nor any solicitor or adviser agreeing to assist—'

'You are wrong,' Diana interrupted, clutching his hand. 'Blankford is quite capable of moving forward in defiance of all reason, equally capable of doing whatever is necessary to discredit and destroy anyone who gets in the way. Only remember whose son he is!'

Tossing down his hand, she took another agitated turn about the room. 'How gleeful he must be at how cleverly we've played into his hands!' she said bitterly, turning back to face him. 'Had I withdrawn and lived quietly at the Dower House after Graveston's death, it would have been more difficult to hurl such accusations, though I suspect in his hatred, he would have done so anyway. But now—a widow fleeing her home to take up with an old lover with her late husband's body hardly settled in its grave—the bare facts of which we cannot deny? Only think how London's penny broadsides will love it!'

'It does look bad,' he had to admit. 'But I've no intention of abandoning you, so you needn't fear that.'

'On the contrary, that's exactly what you must do.'

Her reply was so unexpected, for a moment he thought he couldn't have heard her correctly. 'You think I *should* abandon you?'

She nodded. 'I learned long ago to take the Duke's threats seriously. My husband would have destroyed you then; the son will destroy you now, if you don't walk away. Even if he can't manufacture enough witnesses to convince the assizes to bind me over for trial, only think of the scandal! "Former lover helps unfaithful wife murder her husband!" Imagine the scurrilous cartoons in the print shops! The embarrassment to your sister, to your mother, the stain on your family name. No, it's unthinkable. You must sever all relations with me at once.'

Nodding to herself in final conviction, she backed away, as if preparing to leave.

'Wait a minute!' he exclaimed, jumping up to catch her hand again. 'Have I no say in this? Have you so little confidence in my abilities—this time, too?'

'You don't understand what you're facing. He will stop at nothing to obtain what he wants, just like his father!'

'No, I don't know what I'm facing,' he snapped back, anger over that long-ago episode resurfacing. 'You never told me, just made the decision for both of us. I understand the threat to your father was serious enough to prompt you to action, but I don't understand why you didn't trust me to help. I was no paragon, but I'd done nothing that could have given Graveston cause to ruin me. I can't imagine how he convinced you otherwise.'

'Can you not?' When he gave a derisive shake of the head, she sighed. 'Very well. Even now, it's difficult for me to utter the words, but I suppose you have a right to know what Graveston had designed for you.'

Seating herself beside him, she said quietly, 'At that time, you were not yet known as a valiant soldier, the hero of many battles, but had instead built quite a reputation as poet. You're surely aware it's often whispered that poets are...unmanly. Graveston warned if I told you anything of what he planned, he'd produce witnesses to testify that you'd forced them into...unnatural congress. Can you only imagine how such an accusation would have humiliated your family and destroyed your reputation, even if he couldn't produce enough witnesses to make the charges stick? And if he could— sodomy is a capital crime! You would have been forced to flee England. I couldn't risk it.'

Astounded, Alastair could think of nothing to say. He'd considered a few minor debts, some petty pranks played at university that might have been held against him. But nothing of that magnitude. 'That's…unbelievable.'

'Believe it. And believe the son just as capable of carrying out his threats as his father. Please, Alastair! What good is the sacrifice I made all those years ago, if I bring down destruction upon you now? Blankford would do it. And enjoy doing it.'

Recovering his wits, he countered, 'So, having persuaded you into an affair and gifted your persecutor with more ammunition to blast your character before a Court of Chancery, you expect me to slink away and leave you to suffer the consequences alone? What a fine fellow you must think me!'

'You *are* a fine fellow. I want your reputation to remain unblemished in the eyes of the world. I'm not prepared to let a venal man destroy your good name because of his vendetta against me.'

'It seems we are at an impasse, then, because I'm not prepared to let the threats of a venal man chase me away, so he may harass with impunity a woman already once victimised by his family. Besides, have you anyone else who could help you keep your son from his clutches?'

At once, the fire faded from her eyes. 'No,' she said in a small voice. 'Papa was an only son, as you know. All his near relations are dead, and the earldom to which his family is connected passed some years ago to a distant cousin I've never met. But if it comes to disaster, I do have a plan.'

'Running away again?' he guessed. 'Living the rest of your life looking over your shoulder? No, Diana. It's past time for confronting a bully and calling his dare.'

She shook her head wonderingly, tears pooling in her eyes. 'My brave, honourable, foolish Alastair. What can you do against the power of a duke?'

It pierced his heart to see her in such anguish— and hardened his resolve that this time, whatever was required, this Duke of Graveston would not have his way. This time, Diana would be freed of his menace, able to live her own life—whether she chose to keep him in it or not.

He pulled her into his arms, and to his immense satisfaction, she clung to him. 'Never underestimate the ingenuity of a rogue,' he whispered in her ear. 'I must go make peace with my sister, but I'll return later tonight, to plan what we should do next. Will you wait here for me?'

For a moment, she looked hesitant. As his mind scurried about, hunting up more arguments to persuade her, she nodded.

'Very well, I'll wait. If only so I can convince you tonight we must part for good.'

'You'll never convince me of that,' he said, giving her a kiss. 'I'll be back as soon as I can.'

And with that, he paced from the room, leaving her staring pensively after him.

Chapter Thirteen

Alastair hoped to catch his sister at home, preparing for dinner and whatever entertainment she'd chosen to attend that night. To his relief, Simms informed him as he took Alastair's hat and cane that his mistress was still at her toilette.

Alastair went immediately to his sister's room and rapped at the door. 'Jane, it's Alastair. May I come in and have a word before you head off to dinner?'

A moment later, his sister's maid opened the door. 'Please do come in, Alastair,' Jane called from her seat at her dressing table, where she was latching a necklace of pearls and diamonds about her neck. 'That will be all, Waters. I'll ring for you when I return; I shan't be late tonight.'

After the maid curtsied and went out, Alastair walked to his sister. 'I owe you an apology, Jane. I've neglected you dreadfully.'

She turned towards him as he approached, but when he bent to kiss her cheek, she gave him a roundhouse jab to the ribs. 'Oh, Alastair, how could you?' she exclaimed, and burst into tears.

'Damn and blast!' he muttered, certain he knew the cause of her distress. For all his attempts at discretion, he might just have well have had the town crier stroll the streets, proclaiming the affair.

Still cursing silently, he held her at arm's length as, weeping, she tried to pummel him with her fists. 'Merciful heavens, Jane, get hold of yourself!'

Prevented from striking any further blows, she soon subsided. Pushing him away, she looked up at him accusingly, her lashes glistening with tears.

'I couldn't believe it when Hetty Greenlow whispered that you'd leased a house in Green Park Buildings. There could be only one reason for that. Oh, Alastair, how could you let yourself be drawn back into that evil woman's web?'

'Am I permitted to speak before you've condemned me utterly?'

'Say what you will. There's nothing that could reconcile me to the disaster of a renewed association with That Woman.'

'The circumstances surrounding Diana's marriage were more complicated than any of us could have imagined. I'd ask you to withhold any further judgement until I've acquainted you with the facts.'

And so he related the story Diana had told him of the Duke's machinations, her submission to them, something of the hardship of her life as the wife of a violent, controlling man, and her difficulties now with the new Duke, who wanted to deny her dower and take away her son. Jane sat stone-faced throughout.

'I don't blame you for being sceptical,' he coaxed. 'I didn't believe the story myself, at first. But as I've learned more, I've come to realise that she truly was coerced into the marriage to protect her father.' With his sister's expression still so sceptical, he left out the fantastical threat the former Duke had made against him, as well as the current Duke's threat, if he were to support Diana against him.

'She may have convinced you to believe that fairy tale, but I don't,' Jane said with a sniff. 'The only pressure upon her was her desire to be a duchess, and when she'd landed her prize, she broke your heart without a qualm. She deserves whatever she gets! And if, in her scheming, she wasn't clever enough to secure her financial future after her husband's death, that's her own fault. Hasn't she injured you enough? I cannot believe you would let her draw you into a tawdry fight over guardian-ship and dower! Her well-being and that of any off-spring ceased to be of any importance to you the day she severed your engagement in front of half of London.'

'Jane, you can't believe I could, with honour, stand by and let any woman be bullied, threatened, and dispossessed.'

'I could readily agree to it, if the woman involved is Diana.'

The mantel clock chimed. 'Drat,' she muttered, looking over at the timepiece. 'I must leave at once, or I shall be late for dinner at the Weatherfords'.'

As she rose from the bench and went to the ward-robe for her wrap, Alastair said quietly, 'Would you like me to leave?'

She halted and looked back over her shoulder. 'No! No, I want you to stay here. Away from her. Far away from her.' Her eyes glazing with tears again, her lip trembling, she said softly, 'I can't bear the thought of you being hurt again. And I'm terrified that the Dowager Duchess of Graveston still has the power to hurt you.'

He went over and drew her into a hug, which this time, she did not resist. 'I don't want to be hurt again either. I admit, there is still…something be-tween us. However, whatever it is, whatever it might

become, will have to wait until I've seen her protected from a family that has already treated her
cruelly.'

'Just…be careful, Alastair,' Jane said, disengag-
ing from his embrace. 'Promise me you'll be very
cautious and very careful.'

'I can certainly promise that,' he said, before,
smoothing her hair and catching up her shawl, Jane
hurried from the room.

Alastair watched her go. Though sorry to have
distressed his devoted sister, he was not about to be
deterred from the course of action he'd already determined to be essential. Despite the danger that his
involvement might draw him ever closer to Diana,
a woman whose emotions he might never be able
to touch, inviting a heartbreak that could decimate
him.

Well, he'd not worry about that now. A small
boy's safety was far more important than the risk
to his heart. Telling himself he'd try again later to
persuade Jane, after she'd had time to take in all
he'd told her, he walked out of the bedchamber.

In the hall, he encountered a delighted Robbie.
Anxious as he was to return to Diana, there was
nothing for it but to return to the nursery with his
nephew for a quick session with his soldiers until
the nursemaid bore the boy off to bed.

* * *

By the time Alastair was able to quit the town-house on Royal Crescent, it was already late. Would Diana still be waiting for him? Or, thinking it too late, would she have given up on him and returned to Laura Place. Even worse, might she think she'd convinced him that abandoning her was the best course?

Driven by his anxiety to see Diana again, Alastair was too impatient to wait for a sedan chair, deciding instead to cover the distance on foot.

He was still disappointed that Diana had had the same reaction as Graveston, discounting his ability to successfully counter the power and influence of a duke. Much as he appreciated her desire to protect him, her fatalistic acceptance that the only way to do that was for him to abandon her made him worry she might take her son and flee before he had the chance to convince her otherwise.

When he skidded over the threshold to be told by Marston that the lady still awaited him in the parlour, the sense of relief left him light-headed.

After ordering refreshments, he went at once.

Diana looked up as he entered, then ran to him. From the fierceness of her hug and the bleakness in her eyes as he leaned down to kiss her, he suspected she'd only waited in order to bid him a final goodbye.

He'd just have to persuade her that wasn't going to happen.

Marsden brought in wine and food. Not until after he'd coaxed her to sit and take some nourishment, did he finally return to the matter at hand.

'Thank you for waiting for me. I'm still not convinced Graveston is foolish enough to proceed with his ridiculous vendetta, but it would be best for us to make plans in case he does.'

She gave him a sad smile. 'I've already told you what we need to do. I would have returned to my lodgings when you went out, so I might begin my preparations—but I left you once without a word. This time, I wanted to give you at least the courtesy of a goodbye.'

'I thought as much. Thank you for giving me the opportunity to speak before proceeding alone. First, although it may not mean as much to you as it does to me, I consider that my honour is at stake in this matter. It was, after all, *my* suggestion that we began this liaison. Of course, I had no idea that an affair which should have remained a private matter would end up furnishing the Duke with ammunition to use against you. But so it has proven. I couldn't possibly abandon you to face the consequences alone and still call myself a gentle-man—or a man.'

'You should not consider this in any way touch-ing on your honour,' she countered.

'Shouldn't I? Were the circumstances reversed, and you had initiated something that caused me harm, would you walk away and do nothing to rec-tify the situation?'

She opened her lips—but remained silent, as he knew she would, for he had her there. 'I hardly think so,' he concluded. 'Else you would never have made such an enormous sacrifice eight years ago. I appreciate your continuing desire to protect my name and reputation. But I'm no longer a callow youth just out of university. I own a lucrative es-tate, my uncle is an earl and I, too, have power-ful friends. After surviving dozens of battles, I've also learned a little about confronting a treacher-ous enemy.'

He could see the conflict in her face, the long-ing to believe him and accept his help warring with the long-ingrained habit of independence and her own sense of honour that drove her to spare him involvement, whatever the cost to herself.

Before she could speak, he pressed on. 'Besides, it is not just your safety at stake—I'm doing this to protect your son. With the stakes so high, don't you want to at least hear how I propose to counter Graveston's threat?'

At the reminder of her son's danger, she sighed. 'Very well, I'll hear you out.'

'Good,' he replied, relieved to have passed the first hurdle. Diana was shrewd, determined, and brave. Alastair knew if he could just get her to listen, he could convince her to fight instead of flee. Unless…she feared what he'd demand from her if she let him help her.

Better reassure her on that score immediately.

'I would hope you know this, but let me say it anyway. I assure you that when we win this battle, I will not press on you any…association you do not want. You'll be free to walk away. Your safety and that of your son is all the recompense I want.'

She smiled, relieving his mind and warming his heart. 'I do know that.'

'Very well, then. Let's begin with a rule of battle: the best response to attack is a well-designed counter-attack.'

'Counter-attack,' she repeated, light sparking in eyes that had looked tired and discouraged. 'I like the sound of that.'

Encouraged, he continued. 'First, we need to assess how strong a case Graveston could devise against you. Who might testify?'

She frowned, her gaze losing focus, as if she were running through a mental list in her mind. 'It could be anyone. As I told you, the staff at Graveston Court was loyal to the master—or more accurately, to Graveston's first wife, who had the running of the household for fifteen years before I was installed there. The former housekeeper in particular despised me. Since the staff didn't dare display hostility towards the Duke for his treatment of his first wife, they transferred that enmity to me.'

'Is the housekeeper a tall, thin, hawk-nosed woman?'

'No, Mrs Forbes is a rather rotund—' Her eyes widened. 'The current housekeeper is not, but the former one, the one who disliked me so, Mrs Heathson, is exactly that. You saw a woman of that description with the household keys?'

'I did. Blankford had obviously been informed of who I was and my connection to you before he came in to meet me. I had the impression that this housekeeper knew as well, and understood that anyone intervening on your behalf would be threatened with retribution. As I passed her in the hallway, she looked as pleased about the prospect as the Duke was.'

'I'm not surprised, if it was Heathson. She was fanatically devoted to her former mistress, doted on her son, and certainly would have been ranged on his side when he broke with his father. She'd been…retired; Blankford must have brought her back. With so many of the staff loyal to his mother, he could easily have recruited some of them to be his spies in the household after he left. He probably also instructed some to follow me to Bath after Graveston's interment.'

'So I concluded,' Alastair said, nodding. 'But what of his accusation? Are there any possible grounds for considering your husband's death suspicious?'

Diana stared into distance, frowning, before shaking her head with a sigh. 'I'm afraid I can't be of much help, since I avoided Graveston as much as possible. Thinking back, he did look somewhat pale. His hand trembled when he reached for the wine glass at dinner. I didn't think much of it; he went to work in his study every day as usual— a Duke of Graveston does not neglect business because of some trifling ailment, nor summon a physician to quack him. I suppose the estate agent did call at the manor more frequently than usual those last few months, rather than Graveston riding out with him.' She shrugged. 'I don't know— one might be able to make a case for some sort of slow poisoning.'

'Were you surprised when he died?'

She was silent for a long time. 'I never considered whether it was sudden or timely,' she said at last. 'After living for so long pressed down by a weight so heavy I could hardly breathe, once it was removed, all I felt was…relief. My sole thought, when his valet informed me of his death, was to get away before anyone could stop me. As soon as the coroner, after consulting Graveston's physician, declared that he had died of natural causes and authorised the burial—which by custom I would not have attended in any event—I left Graveston Court.'

'That's a point in your favour,' Alastair said, relieved. 'If the coroner did not suspect foul play, it seems unlikely Blankford will be able to turn up anything.'

'Perhaps. Perhaps not. The threat of prosecution might simply be a ploy to try to distress and intimidate me. But I don't think so. Blankford hates me enough to make accusations, even if he cannot unearth enough evidence to force a trial.'

Her description of determining to flee upon Graveston's death recalled to him the one detail of her account that still pricked at him.

'You lost your father less than two years after you wed the Duke. You were still childless, and I was with Wellington in the Peninsula, beyond his reach. Why did you not leave him then?'

'Oh, but I did leave him.'

He frowned. 'I don't understand.'

She rose and began to pace, a habit Alastair had noticed she often resorted to when distressed. 'Papa had been gone nearly a month when Graveston finally informed me of his death—and even then, he did so indirectly, by summoning me to his study to turn over some family jewellery. I recognised the pieces immediately as belonging to Papa's mother, and knew the only way he would have got them was if Papa had died.'

Alastair was struck by how unfeeling the Duke had been. 'I'm so sorry. You were always so attached to your father. It must have been terribly difficult.'

She shook her head. 'After the wedding, I distanced myself from Papa. Partly for his protection, but mostly because it would have been impossible to hide from him for long that I had not, as I assured him when he questioned me, thrown you over so I might become a duchess. Had he worked out the truth, it would have tortured him, and I didn't want that. But you asked about my leaving Graveston.'

She halted before the mantel and gazed into the

flames, while he waited for her to begin, a sick feeling in his gut about what she was about to reveal.

'I left the same night I learned of Papa's death,' she said at last. 'Slipped out through the kitchen wing after all the servants were abed, taking only a portmanteau with a few old gowns and my family's jewellery. I made it through the village and almost to the posting inn on the mail-coach route before his men caught me. They dragged me, screaming and fighting, into a carriage and drove me back to Graveston Court.'

Shocked, he simply stared at her as she continued. 'It was, of course, unthinkable for the Duchess of Graveston to abandon her husband. He had me locked in my rooms, but he must have known I would try again, claw the wood out of the window frames if necessary, for he had me drugged. Downing the nourishment brought to me to keep up my strength to escape, I didn't notice until it was too late.'

'For how long?' Alastair asked, appalled.

'I don't know exactly. A long time. Once I had figured out what was happening, I tried keeping back some of the drugged wine, intending to drink it all together and escape that way.' She shook her head. 'Apparently Mrs Heathson—still the housekeeper then—figured out what I planned, and was quite willing to let me secrete away enough laudanum to carry me off. But for some reason, despite how often I'd displeased him, my husband wasn't. When I recovered from the overdose, Mrs Heathson had been "retired". And I discovered I was pregnant.'

She turned from the hearth to look at him. 'I didn't care what happened to me, but much as I hated bearing the son of such a man, I couldn't cause the death of an innocent child. Then, after his treatment of James, I couldn't flee and leave him at the mercy of a father like Graveston.'

Unable to restrain himself, Alastair went to Diana and pulled her into an embrace. She clung to him, her head pressed to his chest, shaking with tears she would not shed.

At length, she straightened and pushed against him. Knowing how cruelly she'd been imprisoned, he at once loosened his grip.

'I'm so sorry,' he said, running a fingertip down her cheek as he let her go. 'But you're free now, you and the boy. I won't let Graveston hurt you ever again. I promise, on my sacred honour.'

'My noble Alastair,' she whispered, squeezing his fingers. 'But even if you risk your reputation by getting involved, I don't know how you could prevent that.'

'Have a little faith, sweeting! First, I'll need to consult the solicitor again. I'm not an expert on the courts; I have no idea what evidence would be needed to persuade a coroner to open an inquiry into the death of a man already buried, with no suspicion of foul play. More than vague testimony from witnesses produced by a man well known to harbour a hatred of the woman he's accusing, I would think.'

'Even if that man is a duke, owner of nearly all the land in four parishes, employer of hundreds on the estate and in the adjoining villages, patron or supporter of most of the businesses, trade associations, and churches in the county?'

Alastair grimaced. 'True, with that much influence, Blankford could probably manage to get an inquest begun on his insistence alone. But an inquest is a far cry from convincing the assizes to convene a trial, and even further from a conviction. I'm confident it won't come to that.'

'You can't be sure. He'll pay for testimony, if necessary. There are always poor wretches ready to swear to anything, if the reward is rich enough.'

Payment for testimony was all too common, and frequently distorted the findings of a court. 'Perhaps,' Alastair allowed, 'but this isn't the matter of a thief-taker pointing the finger at some poor clerk in order to collect the reward offered for solving a burglary. Nor would the case be settled by a local magistrate, where a high-ranking lord could influence the outcome. For the possible murder of a duke and accusations against a duchess, a trial, if it came to that, would be held in the House of Lords. A chamber my uncle has run for years. Which is why I still believe, once he's recovered from his fit of petulance and thought it over carefully, Blankford will not push for a trial.'

She gave him a sad smile. 'To win, he doesn't have to. Accusations made against me in the county would be enough to poison the local officials against me and make it difficult to obtain any assets from the estate on which to raise my son. Enough to convince the Court of Chancery to take him away, even though he is still a minor child. Enough to create a scandal that would savage your reputation. I still see only one way to prevent all this.'

'Taking James and trying to disappear,' he summarised. 'Don't you see, Diana, doing that would give Graveston the ultimate victory? He'll have made you a fugitive and forced you to raise your son in obscurity, denying him the education, the comfort, the status to which his birth entitles him. Moreover, I'd be astonished if your husband hadn't made some provision for James in his will; disappearing so that legacy goes unclaimed—what a fitting revenge for the neglect Blankford feels you made him suffer! And as a final coup, a Duke of Graveston will once again have been able to drive us apart.'

She raised her face to him, frustration and fury in her gaze, and he knew he'd finally reached her. 'How do we prevent all that?'

We, she'd said, he noted, a thrill blazing through his heart. Stifling it before the gladness could distract him, he continued. 'We gather our own evidence, enough to convince Graveston it would be better not to make any public accusations—and I know just the rascal to do it. In the meantime, we need to move you and James some place safer, where a well-placed bribe won't risk tempting a low-moralled rogue to breach the security of your house and carry off the boy. There's only one place I can guarantee to be that safe—Barton Abbey.'

She looked at him incredulously. 'You propose to carry us to Barton Abbey? You can't be serious!'

'I'm completely serious. I doubt even the delusional Graveston would attempt to touch you there. Were he foolish enough to try, you'd have a small army of staff and retainers loyal to *me* to protect you. Who would turn away representatives from Chancery, if it came to that.'

'But would not my being at your house immedi-ately bring down upon you just the scandal I wish to avoid?'

'There's nothing scandalous about my mother in-viting a widow who was once a close family friend to spend part of her mourning period in the se-clusion of Barton Abbey. Indeed, having you and James at my family home, under my mother's care, would further diminish the credibility of there being some clandestine plot between us. I assure you, no one in Society would believe Mrs Grace Ransleigh would be a party to something as dis-honourable as that!'

'Quite true. Which is why your mother would most likely forbid me to enter the premises.'

'Leave Mother to me. Can you think of any place in England that would be safer? Your first duty, after all, is to protect your son.'

She looked up at him, her expression anguished. 'You know how much I want to keep you out of this. But…but you are right; my first duty is to James, and I cannot think of any place where I could be sure of protecting him, alone.'

'You would both be secure at Barton Abbey.'

Pensive, she turned once again towards the flames in the hearth, as if ultimate wisdom might be found in their dancing light—before abruptly whirling to face him. 'If I did agree to accompany you to Barton Abbey, and your mother did not turn us away, I—I could no longer come to you. Not in your mother's own house!' she finished, her cheeks flushing.

She looked so scandalised, Alastair had to laugh. 'My reputation is bad, I admit, but even I wouldn't embarrass my mother by conducting an affair under her roof. Once past the gatehouse, the agreement between us would be in abeyance, until Graveston is no longer a threat.'

'If all the trouble I envisage comes to pass, you will be thoroughly tired of me by then,' she said, reminding him of the terms he'd specified for ending their agreement.

'I will never tire of you…but you will still be free to do as you wish.'

She looked away and paced several more circuits around the room. Alastair waited, sure he was right, not wanting to coerce her, but hoping that after she'd considered all the possibilities, her own good sense would convince her his plan was the best course of action.

Hoping, though he knew it wasn't prudent, that accepting him as an ally would bring her even closer to him.

At last, she halted and turned to him. 'When do you propose to leave for Barton Abbey?'

'As soon as you can be ready,' he said, relief—and steely resolve—filling him.

This time, he would protect her and her son.

This time, the Duke's will would not prevail.

This time, they would defeat Graveston—together. And then, at last, find out whether or not they had a future.

She nodded. 'Tomorrow it is. Then we had best make the most of tonight.'

He held his breath, but she added nothing further—no admissions of affection, no confession that she had enjoyed their time together so much, she didn't wish it to end.

As closely guarded as she kept her emotions, he couldn't reasonably expect such a declaration—but he was still disappointed.

'We can both agree on that,' he said at last. Taking her hand, he led her up the stairs.

Much later, as they lay together in the aftermath of loving, still bone of bone and flesh of flesh, he whispered, 'Promise me you won't take the boy and run. Promise me this time, you'll trust me.'

She opened heavy-lidded eyes. 'I promise,' she said, and kissed him.

Chapter Fourteen

As arranged when they had parted late the previous night, shortly after daybreak, Alastair downed a quick breakfast and prepared to leave his sister's house at the Royal Crescent. His few belongings packed, he settled for penning Jane a note; he regretted parting from her on such unhappy terms without even a goodbye, but as she'd already been abed when he returned, and since leaving Bath early was imperative, it was the best he could do.

After hiring a post-chaise, he set off for Laura Place. A grim smile creased his lips as, for the first time, he knocked at her front door. At least now, there would be no more need for subterfuge.

Admitted within, he found Diana ready. The nursemaid had her sleepy son bundled up, and the small staff was busy closing up the house. A short time later, he ushered them to the coach.

'I still can't believe you talked me into going

to Barton Abbey,' Diana murmured to Alastair, steadying the maid as Minnie carried her sleeping son up the step.

'You trust me to keep you safe, don't you?' he asked as he handed her in.

'If I didn't trust you to keep my son safe, I wouldn't have agreed to go.'

Tacitly accepting, for the moment, her slight change of emphasis, he followed her into the vehicle.

Soon, the coachman negotiated his way through Bath's busy streets and on to the road south towards Devon. Despite the jolting of the carriage, after a late night and an early rising, both the maid and Diana drifted off to sleep. Alastair sat watching them, savouring the feel of Diana's head nestled on his shoulder.

Finally, an end to shadow-boxing the family that had so drastically altered his life eight years ago. He couldn't wait to confront the Duke in open combat, drive home a victory, and free the two of them to explore their future.

Would Diana, compelled by extreme circumstance to rely upon him, continue to reveal herself after this episode was successfully concluded? Or would she close back in upon herself, refusing to admit him any further? So manipulated and constrained had she been, he knew he couldn't force or even cajole her to warm towards him.

Ah, but how he ached to help her further along the road to recapturing the joy, optimism and confidence she'd once possessed in such abundance.

Even if it meant, in the end, she took her revitalised spirit into a new life without him.

Initially too shy to speak, James soon overcame his reserve and proved an amazingly resilient traveller, eagerly watching the countryside and peppering Alastair and his mother with questions about the towns and vehicles they passed, the fields and workers observed out the windows. He'd also been delighted with the novelty of dining at public houses and spending the night at a busy coaching inn.

Forced to concede the necessity for it, Alastair had ordered two rooms, one for himself and a second for Diana, Minnie and James—and lain awake for hours each night, acutely conscious that Diana slept close by. Knowing that a period of enforced abstinence lay before them at Barton Abbey, its duration impossible to predict, he was sorely tempted to urge Diana to slip into his room after the others fell asleep.

But it wouldn't be wise. James's maid Minnie, Diana told him, had been informed they were travelling to visit an old family friend, who had sent her son to escort them. Alastair didn't know whether Diana's staff knew where—or with whom—she had spent her evening 'entertainments'. If the boy's nurse was aware that he was a more intimate acquaintance, she'd given no indication of it, and Alastair wished it to stay that way.

Who knew whether Graveston might summon the maid to testify against her mistress? Alastair meant to ensure the girl would have as little to say as possible.

After several long days on the road, even the curious six-year-old was tired of being cooped up in a coach, begging Alastair, who hired a horse to ride each day, to take him up in the saddle. Denied that treat, he and the rest of the party were increasingly impatient to reach their destination.

Finally, the longed-for moment arrived. Eschewing a mount for this last phase of the journey, familiar with every hill and turning from the last posting inn to his front door, Alastair joined the company in the coach. Eagerness, anticipation—and a touch of unease over the reaction of his mother to the guests he was about to foist on her—kept him on the edge of his seat.

'The entry gate's just ahead,' Alastair told James, who immediately thrust his small shoulders out of the window, impatient to get a look.

'It's not so big as the gatehouse at Graveston Court,' he pronounced as the carriage bowled through.

'Probably just as old, though, and full of nooks for boys to explore, as my cousins and I did when we were your age.'

The boy's eyes brightened. 'Could you take me exploring, too?'

Alastair smiled at the boy's artless assumption that he would still consider that a treat. 'When we have a chance.'

Diana, however, did not lean towards the window to get a glimpse of the estate of which she'd once expected to become mistress. Displaying none of James's excitement, she remained quietly in her seat, her impassive expression impossible to read.

Once, he'd anticipated bringing her here as his bride, envisaging her delight at seeing her new home for the first time. A sharp pain pierced his chest at the contrast between that old dream and the prosaic present.

They could never go back, he reminded himself. For now, it was enough that he'd persuaded her to come here, where he could keep her and her son safe. He'd content himself with that—and despite finally sheltering her under his roof, resist the deceptive illusion that the dreams he'd once cherished might still come true.

Despite that sober reminder, he couldn't seem to make himself stop watching her. Though her serene exterior gave no hint that she harboured any anxiety about what awaited them, he could read the small signs—the hands tightly gripping the seat, the rigid set of her shoulders—that said she was not as calm as she appeared.

He'd carefully refrained from any gesture of affection during their enforced closeness in the coach, with her son and his nursemaid always watching, but now, he leaned over to squeeze her hand. 'It will be all right. Trust me,' he murmured.

A short time later, the driver pulled the team up before the front entrance. As always, Alastair felt a surge of gladness at returning to the manor that had been his home since birth. Not even the uncertainty of his mother's reaction could dim that delight.

Then a footman was trotting over to let down the stairs. 'Mr Ransleigh!' he exclaimed, stopping short in the act of handing Diana from the coach. 'Welcome home, sir! But we weren't expecting you.'

'Nor any company,' he agreed with a smile. 'My

mother shall certainly take me to task for that. Would you see that the baggage is carried upstairs?'

'Certainly, sir.'

Firmly taking Diana's elbow, he escorted the party up the stairs and into the hall, where the butler was hurrying to meet them. 'Wendell, you're looking well.'

Like the footman, the butler stopped short for a moment before giving him a bow. 'Master Alastair! What a pleasure to have you home, and your guests.'

'Would you have refreshment sent to the blue parlour, and let my mother know we're here?'

'Certainly.'

Once within the cosy blue chamber, Diana was invited to have a seat, while Minnie took James to the window to inspect the vista of the distant hills.

'Better not have the footman carry our bags too far,' Diana murmured when the maid was out of earshot.

'Nonsense. Mother would never be so discourteous as to ask someone I invited to my home to leave.'

Diana raised an eyebrow and made no reply. But her fingers twisted together even tighter, Alastair noted.

He truly did not worry that his mother would turn her away. To be sure, she would cloak her initial reaction to Diana's presence in politeness, and probably give him a furious earful once the guests were sent off to settle into their rooms. But he was convinced, once apprised of the truth of Diana's past actions and present circumstances, she would never turn away a woman and child in need.

If he were wrong, and she remained as opposed to his championship of Diana as Jane, she would simply have to take herself off to visit his sister. Barton Abbey belonged to him, and he would house there whomever he chose.

He hoped it wouldn't come to that. He would soon find out.

A few moments later, he heard his mother's quick step outside, and went to intercept her at the door.

In a graceful sway of skirts and a hint of rose perfume, she walked in, a delighted smile on her face. 'My darling Alastair! How wonderful to have you home again—even if unannounced, you naughty boy! And you've brought guests. How lovely!'

After hugging him, as she turned to greet those guests, her eyes widened and the smile fled from her face. 'Miss Northcot?'

'The Dowager Duchess of Graveston now, just recently widowed,' Alastair interposed smoothly. 'This is her son, Lord James Mannington, and his nurse, Minnie.'

The ladies curtsied. 'An unexpected honour, Duchess,' his mother said, an edge of irony in her voice. 'You and your son must be fatigued after your journey. I'll have Wendell show you to your rooms at once, so you may rest yourselves before dinner.'

At that moment, the butler returned, bearing a tray. 'Wendell, our guests are worn out from their travels. We should allow them to retire to their rooms at once. Escort them upstairs, please, and have John carry some refreshments to their chambers. I'm sure they will enjoy it much more after they are able to wash off the dust of the road.'

'As you wish, ma'am,' Wendell said, bowing. 'Ladies and young gent, if you would follow me?'

His mother waited only until the door had shut behind the visitors before rounding on him, incredulous fury on her face. 'Alastair, have you taken leave of your senses? How *could* you expect me to play hostess to the woman who put you and everyone who loved you through such agony? Jane wrote me that you were seeing her again! I've been praying ever since that if you didn't have the good sense to avoid her, you'd at least get your fill of her quickly and be done with it. How *dare* you bring her here?'

Not at all deterred by her reaction, he said, 'I dare, Mama, because it was the right thing to do. Please, calm yourself and hear me out! Once I've acquainted you with the facts, I believe you will agree with my decision.'

'That's highly doubtful,' his mother said with a sniff.

'But you are fair-minded enough to listen before making a judgement.'

'Wretch!' His mother gave him an exasperated look. 'When you put it that way, what can I do but listen?'

He waved her to a chair and pointed to the tray Wendell had left. 'Shall we have tea?'

'Probably wise. I've a feeling I'm going to need something to steady my nerves.'

She poured them each a cup and seated herself beside him on the sofa. 'So, tell me the whole.'

He took his time, and his mother did not interrupt, sipping her tea thoughtfully while he related the circumstances leading to Diana's marriage, gave an account of her life after, and concluded with the present difficulties with the heir and the need to protect her son. After he finished, she remained silent for some time, while he held his breath.

'You believe the boy to be in danger?' she said at last.

'Diana certainly does. After my conversation with the Duke, I do believe he would mistreat him, exacting revenge upon the poor boy for an alienation of his father's affection that he blames upon Diana. He wants the boy to "suffer as he did", I believe he put it.'

'He actually said that?' His mother gasped. When he nodded, she grimaced. 'Peer or no, he seems thoroughly reprehensible.'

'So you understand why I felt it necessary to intervene, even though the child in question is Diana's.'

'I do, much as I wish the mother were anyone but Diana! Now, what else are you not telling me?'

A little startled, Alastair hedged. 'What makes you think there is more?'

'My dear son, you may be a man grown, and harder to read than you were as a child, but I have known you since the cradle. There's something else going on, isn't there?'

Alastair gave a rueful smile. 'I never could hide anything from you, could I?'

She smiled. 'As you got older, you didn't always confide in me, but I could still tell when there was something wrong. What is it this time?'

'I intended to tell you the whole, once I had your agreement to shelter the boy. Bringing him here may mitigate the accusations somewhat, but I'm afraid it's quite possible that by helping Diana, I shall be dragged into a rather ugly scandal. If, once I've related the circumstances, you'd prefer to take refuge with Jane until the storm blows over, I'll understand.'

With a sigh, she rose and poured them each another cup. 'I'm not likely to abandon either a helpless child or my son, but perhaps you'd best lay it all out.'

'Jane was correct when she told you that I'd…become involved with Diana again. I thought if I…could claim her for a time,' he said, his ears reddening at the thought of confessing this to his mother, 'I might finally rid myself of the lingering attachment that, try to deny it as I might, I never truly succeeded in stamping out.'

'But once she poured out to you the reasons for breaking your engagement, described how shabbily she was treated during her marriage, and threw herself upon your compassion, you felt you must become her champion?'

He gave a negative shake of the head. 'She made no such appeal. Oh, she told me why she had jilted me, of course, but that was all. The rest—what her life was like after her marriage, the threats against her son—I discovered only gradually, after inadvertent comments prompted me to make more pointed enquiries. She never could tell a lie, you know.'

'Nor even a convincing evasion,' his mother agreed, looking troubled. 'I do remember.'

'I know the story must seem fantastical to you. At first, I didn't believe her account either. But as I spent time with her, dredging out the facts bit by bit, I gradually came to accept it was true. Oh, Mama, can you imagine—Diana without paints, without books, without music? It makes my heart ache to envisage it. And so isolated. Alone, with no one to call upon for sympathy or protection.'

'So how does this lead to that great scandal you mentioned?'

'I told you that, wanting to get a sense of whether there was in fact a danger to the boy or not, I decided to call upon the Duke. At the conclusion of a rather unpleasant conversation, during which he refused to acknowledge that Diana, as his father's widow, was entitled to support from the estate and expressed his desire to punish her son, he boasted that he intends to accuse Diana of hastening his father's death. If I persist in championing her, he threatened to allege that I encouraged Diana to do away with her husband, in revenge for his father stealing her away from me years ago.'

'What?' His mother gasped again. 'But that's outrageous!'

'True. But since she did come to Bath immediately after his death, and we did…establish a relationship, the bare facts make such an accusation plausible.'

'But it's absurd! No one who knows you would believe such a calumny. I may hold Diana responsible for many sins, but murder? Surely Graveston isn't seriously going to try to implicate her in his father's death!'

'Diana seems to think he will at least make the attempt. Pointing the finger of suspicion upon her, as she well understands, would do enough damage to her reputation that she will have more difficulty accessing the funds due her from the estate, and would almost certainly induce the Court of Chancery to take away her son.'

'Being implicated as a widow's lover who persuaded her to murder won't do much for your reputation either,' his mother noted tartly.

'Which is why you might want to decamp to Jane's.'

'Surely you don't intend to let the wretch get away with this!' she said indignantly.

Alastair's face hardened. 'When it comes to Diana, I think the Dukes of Graveston have got

away with quite enough already. The enmity between her and her late husband might have been
well known, but so was the break between the former Duke and his heir. Fortunately, Will is back
from Paris. I'm going to ask him to slink around
Graveston Court and see what he can dig up. I'm
betting he can gather enough counter-testimony that
I can persuade Blankford to refrain from making
any accusations, honour the estate's responsibilities
to Diana and leave the boy where he is.'

His mother chuckled. 'If anyone can do so, Will
can, the rascal. And love it, I'll wager. Last time
he and Elodie visited, he admitted that all that re-
spectability, as a trader and Crown representative,
was getting a bit dull.'

'So he told me as well,' Alastair agreed, smiling. 'In the meantime, I want Diana and James
here, where the Duke cannot bully or intimidate
them. Frankly, it would be helpful to our cause
if you would remain, so we can put it about that
you invited Diana, an old family friend, to spend
some time at Barton Abbey during her mourning
period. Society would never believe *you* would
countenance a murder plot, nor that I would dare
to install a mistress under your roof.'

His mother raised an eyebrow. 'Are you trying to
install a mistress under my roof?'

Alastair felt his face flush again. 'Whatever our relations might have been elsewhere, I would never insult you by attempting such a thing here.'

'Good,' his mother said, then surprised him by adding, 'Whatever my opinion of Diana, she deserves better.'

'Still, I have to warn you that though I am hopeful of resolving this without scandal, it might come to that. If you'd rather distance yourself, I'll understand. As long as you understand that, regardless of what happens, I will not desert Diana.'

'What, let my son oppose a child-threatening autocrat alone? I'm not such a pudding-heart!'

Love and gratitude warmed Alastair like the blaze of a welcoming fire after a long winter journey. He leaned over to give his mother a fierce hug, rattling her teacup in the process.

'Thank you, Mama. I knew I could count on you.'

'I should hope so. Heavens, if you can't trust in your mother's support, who can you trust? Just promise me, Alastair, you'll be…careful. I cannot bear to think of you suffering again as you suffered before.'

'Almost Jane's words,' he said ruefully. 'I've no desire to suffer either, so I'll do my best.'

His mother had paused, watching him. When he remained silent, she said, 'Very well. I'll put it about to my friends that I've…reconciled with Diana and offered her my support. I shall even do my best to be civil to her. As for the child, it's not been all that long since you and your cousins ran wild here. I think I can remember how to entertain a little boy.'

'Bless you, Mama. What would I do without you?'

She smiled and tapped him on the nose. 'You'd be desolate. Now, off with you. I must confer with Cook and the housekeeper and make sure we have something to tempt a child's sweet tooth.'

Giving her another hug, Alastair rose and walked out. He knew she'd hoped to have him confess what his intentions were towards Diana after the battle with Graveston was over. Fortunately, she didn't press him, because he wasn't sure himself.

The more time he spent with Diana, the less he could envisage letting her go. Perhaps, once she was safe, he'd feel differently. Perhaps, with her able to pursue a normal life again, like Napoleon on St Helena setting the world at peace, the momentous chapter of his life labelled 'Diana' would close, letting him finally move forward.

And perhaps Diana would go her own way.

The mere thought of her leaving made his heart squeeze in protest. Stilling it, he set his jaw. Winning her again—or not winning her—would have to wait. First, he had to protect her.

Chapter Fifteen

That night, as soon as the household retired to bed, Diana slipped along the darkened hallway to her hostess's room.

Mrs Ransleigh had been surprisingly cordial at dinner. Still, Diana knew it must chafe her extremely to be forced to house the woman who had so wronged her son.

Hopefully, that distress would be relieved after this interview.

Arriving at her destination, she tapped on the door. 'Mrs Ransleigh!' she called out softly. 'It's Diana…Northcot. May I talk with you for a moment?'

Her enquiry was met by a silence that lasted so long, she was debating how to proceed if her hostess refused her admittance, when suddenly the door opened. In gown and robe, with a frilly cap tied over her curls, Mrs Ransleigh stood on the threshold.

She looked Diana up and down, her expression wary, like someone approaching an unfamiliar dog, not sure if it would wag or bite. 'I suppose I shall have to hear you out sometime, so you might as well come in now.'

'Thank you.' Diana followed her hostess through the bedchamber into the blue-and-rose sitting room beyond.

'Take the wing chair by the hearth,' Mrs Ransleigh directed as she reposed herself on the sofa. 'The fire's been banked, but there's still some warmth.'

As Diana hoped there would be, from this woman she'd once thought to embrace as her mother-in-law, for the child that might have been her grandson. Surely, regardless of her feelings for Diana, she would have pity on James!

'I wanted to thank you first for admitting us to your home. I'm sure Alastair pressed you, but, quite frankly, I wasn't at all sure you wouldn't refuse to take us in.'

As her hostess made no reply, merely nodding, Diana continued. 'I imagine you feel nothing but loathing for me and scorn for the dilemma in which I find myself. Let me assure you, I do not intend to impose upon your forbearance for very long.'

'Indeed?' Mrs Ransleigh responded, raising her

eyebrows. 'Has my son exaggerated the menace Graveston poses to your son?'

'No! Not exaggerated. Or rather, as long as he sees my son as a means to make me suffer, James is in danger. But it's me upon whom he truly wants revenge. I believe that if he can obtain that, and James is protected by friends powerful enough to make proceeding against him difficult, he will content himself with me and leave James alone.'

Mrs Ransleigh frowned. 'What do you intend?'

'I once caused Alastair, and indeed your entire family, great suffering and embarrassment—quite enough for one lifetime, I think! I shall do whatever I can now to ensure that none of you is harmed by Graveston's anger towards me. I wouldn't have agreed to come here at all, except I knew Alastair would never bring James without me. But I plan to leave tonight, return to Graveston Court, and confront Blankford.'

'Return to Graveston Court!' her hostess echoed, obviously surprised. 'Are you sure you should do that? Would you not be placing yourself at Blankford's mercy?'

Diana shook her head. 'That doesn't matter. If Blankford wishes to order up an inquiry, or have me bound over to the assizes, let him do so. So long as James is safe, and Alastair's reputation protected.

Before I go, though, may I beg of you one final, but most important favour?'

Mrs Ransleigh paused, opening her lips as if to speak, then closing them. 'What is that?' she said at last.

'I know it's a great deal to ask, but would you watch over my son? I've…not been much of a mother to him, but despite all he has been deprived of, he is a warm-hearted little boy, so anxious for and deserving of love. I couldn't imagine anyone more capable than you of guiding him to becoming a strong, intelligent, honourable man. A man like Alastair. Can you pity James, an innocent in all this, and forgive me enough to care for him?'

As Mrs Ransleigh stared at her, probably astounded by her audacity in demanding such an enormous boon, Diana held her gaze and prayed that compassion would triumph over dislike. Alastair would do whatever was necessary to protect James—but to become the man she'd want him to be he would need the kindness, wisdom and guidance of a mother. If she could assure that for him, she could return to face Blankford with an easy heart.

To her relief and joy, Mrs Ransleigh's eyes welled up with tears. 'Yes, I will watch over him.'

Overwhelmed, Diana went over to kneel at her

hostess's feet. 'Thank you,' she whispered, humbled. 'I don't deserve such a favour, but he does.'

Now to put the rest of her plan in action. Rising once more, she curtsied to her hostess. 'I shall be gone by morning, so I'll bid you farewell. Would you convey my…goodbyes and my thanks to Alastair?'

'Shouldn't you do that yourself?'

Diana stifled the pang of longing before it could escape. 'No, it's best if I don't see him. Excuse me again for disturbing your rest, and may the Lord bless you for your mercy.'

This might even be a better solution, she thought, her anxiety lessening as she walked from the room. She might never become the mother James needed—but now she was turning him over to a woman who already was. With James safe, what difference did it make what happened to her?

As for the tantalising possibility of a future with Alastair—that was an illusion so cruel she should have crushed it the moment it whispered in her brain. Her emotions crippled and her heart stunted by years of living under Graveston's tyranny, she was as unsuitable a partner for a man like Alastair as she was unfit to be James's mother.

She hurried into her pelisse. The small portmanteau was already packed; a nearly full moon would illuminate the track to the village, several hours' walk away. Next morning, she could find a ride with some market-bound farmer to the posting inn on the main road and by midday, obtain a seat on a mail coach that would take her towards Graveston Court.

She couldn't bear to see Alastair—who would, in any event, try to dissuade her from a course of action of which he was certain to disapprove—but before she left, she would visit her son one last time.

Silently, she ascended the stairs and entered the nursery, setting the portmanteau by the door. Though unused for some years, she'd noted when she'd escorted James there earlier this evening that it was a cheerful place, its large windows overlooking the garden and bathing the room in light for lessons or play. Ranks of toy soldiers, tops, balls and a few precious books were arranged on shelves and a well-used rocking horse stood in the corner. Warm and inviting, it was as different as one could imagine from the formal, artefact-filled room her son had occupied at Graveston Court.

She hoped before long, Mrs Ransleigh would develop a fondness for James. He was a handsome boy with charming manners, who had already re-animated her deadened heart enough that she felt a real sorrow at having to leave him, just as she was finally beginning to know and appreciate him.

Tiptoeing past the sleeping Minnie, she eased herself on to the edge of his bed, careful not to disturb him. For a long moment, she gazed down on his face, cherubic in the moonlight.

'Be safe, my son,' she whispered. 'I know you will wonder why I left you, but some day, when you are old enough to compare Alastair's character to the Duke's, you will understand.'

She rose to leave before, driven by a compulsion beyond reason, she hesitated. Cautiously, as though attempting the forbidden, she leaned down to kiss James's forehead. From deep within, love long repressed and denied seeped up, bringing tears to her eyes.

He murmured and stirred, and she drew back. 'Goodbye, my dear son,' she mouthed silently, then picked up the portmanteau, and slipped out of the room.

Down in the darkened kitchen, Alastair paced, hoping his mother's warning had not brought him here too late. He'd checked Diana's bedchamber immediately and found it empty; he'd wait here by the hearth a few more minutes, but if Diana did not appear, he would set out after her. On foot, in the dark, she couldn't proceed with much speed, but though the home woods should not pose too many dangers for someone who kept to the road, he couldn't be easy about her being out there alone, undefended, in the middle of the night.

He exhaled an impatient breath, aggravated at her headstrong decision to confront Graveston without him. Not that he'd been truly shocked when his mother rushed to tell him what Diana intended. After years of being forced to rely on no one but herself, he had suspected that once her son was safe, she might set off independently.

Determined to confront her enemy alone, to spare him and his family.

Damn Graveston! He spat out a few well-chosen oaths. And foolish girl! When would he convince her that she no longer had to fight her battles unaided?

A few minutes later, he heard the soft shuffle of slippers on the stairway. Drawing back into the shadows, he watched as, carrying a small trunk, Diana appeared in the moonlit room.

'Just where do you think you are going?' he demanded, unable to keep a note of exasperation from his voice.

'Alastair!' she gasped, whirling to face him.

'Not the headless horseman. Though you deserve to confront a bogeyman, sneaking out like an ill-chosen guest absconding with the hostess's jewels.' His tone softening, he said, 'How could you think I would let you go off to face Graveston alone?'

In the stillness, he heard a little sigh that twisted his heart. 'I thought after I was gone, when you thought carefully about it, you would realise that was the best course. But how did you know I was leaving?'

'Mama told me. Quite in a rush she was, urging me to hurry so I could intercept you before you escaped.'

'Your mother?' she echoed, clearly astounded.

'Yes, though her warning didn't take me completely by surprise. I remember an account of a girl, freed of her obligations, sneaking out through the kitchens in the dead of night. I just hadn't anticipated it happening this soon.'

'I can't imagine why she would warn you,' Diana murmured.

'Here, give me that,' he said, taking the portmanteau from her slackened grip. 'Come up to the library and we'll discuss it.'

Realising how peremptory he sounded, and remembering how often she'd been coerced, he added in a softer tone, 'Please, Diana? I promise I will not force you to take any action with which you disagree. But let's discuss this again before you throw yourself headlong into danger.'

'Very well,' she said in a little voice, sounding tired and discouraged.

Heartened, he took her elbow and guided her from the room. Not that his assistance was really needed, but after envisaging Graveston dragging her before a magistrate, Graveston hurling accusations against her at the assizes...Graveston striking her, he needed the reassuring feel of her warm flesh under his fingers.

Once in the library, he rummaged up some wine and waved her into a chair.

'I still don't understand why your mother didn't just let me go. I would have thought she'd be relieved to be shed of me.'

'She hasn't quite forgiven you yet for what happened; the tale is a bit much to swallow all at once. But she believed enough of it to warn me—which is enough for now.'

He handed her a glass, noting how her fingers trembled as she sipped from it. He stemmed an overwhelming urge to gather her in his arms, to let his warmth and proximity reinforce the message she seemed so reluctant to believe—that he would stand by her, no matter the outcome. But she still radiated a brittle fragility, seeming half-glad he'd intervened, half-angry that he'd circumvented her will. He wouldn't risk pushing her too hard.

'I thought we'd agreed to face Graveston together,' he said instead. 'I thought you were going to trust me.'

'And I thought you understood I would rather die than destroy your happiness and reputation a second time.'

'Ah, Diana, do you truly think I could be happy, knowing you were going to sacrifice yourself for me? Perhaps if I tell you in more detail what I plan, I can convince you that proceeding together is the better way. You remember my cousin Will?'

A wisp of a smile touched her lips. 'Wagering Will? He went into the army too, didn't he? I suppose he tricked his way to general?'

'Not quite,' he said, momentarily diverted by the image of his reprobate cousin in a staff officer's uniform. 'Though I've no doubt he could have contrived it, had he wanted to. The army did use his skills in several clandestine ways on the Peninsula—who better to creep around and turn things up than Will? He also managed to find himself a wife while setting to rights the debacle with Max.'

Her eyes widened. 'Debacle with Max?'

'You didn't hear? It was quite the scandal.'

'I was exiled in the country the last few years,' she reminded him drily.

'While accompanying Wellington to the Congress of Vienna, he befriended a widow, hostess to a member of the French delegation who later plotted an assassination attempt against Wellington. Max's innocent association with the widow dragged him into it, ruining his political prospects. You remember how Will credits Max with saving him from the streets. He was so incensed by the affair—during which our uncle, the Earl of Swynford, made no attempt to assist his son—he set off to Vienna to find the woman and bring her back to clear Max's name. Succeeded so well, he ended up marrying her—and getting himself a post as a trader in Paris, while also representing the Crown on economic matters.'

'How can an economic envoy in Paris help us?'

'Will's back in England—and still possessed of those, uh, particular skills for gaming and subterfuge Max never succeeded in beating out of him. I intend to send him, in whatever guise he thinks most useful, to the village near Graveston Court and let him investigate the circumstances of your husband's death. We'll see whether he can turn up some counter-testimony to persuade the Duke it would be better not to make public his accusations. Given the enmity between father and son, I'm nearly certain we could find witnesses to support some counter-accusations.'

She sat silent for a moment, obviously considering the possibilities. 'Like his father, Blankford is supremely confident of forcing whatever outcome he wills. Anything Will "turned up" would have to be pretty convincing.'

'Will's a skilful rogue. Trust him. As I hope you'll trust me.'

He came over to take her hand and gazed into her eyes, willing her to believe him. 'I'm no longer an impetuous boy, ready to give up without a fight and slink off to nurse my wounded sensibilities. If I'd listened to the instincts that said you'd never willingly abandon me, pushed past the servant who said you wouldn't receive me and insisted on speaking with you eight years ago, how much misery and anguish would I have saved us both? You gave up your life to save mine then. Now I intend to fight to save yours.'

'But if you cannot convince Graveston to cry off,

only think of the scandal! It is not just you who would suffer, Alastair. What of your mama, your sisters? How embarrassing it could be for them!'

He shrugged. 'I have thought about it. No one would believe ill of Mama, who made her choice to support us when she alerted me to stop you. Jane and Lissa are both married into important families with husbands who can protect them. Try as he might, Blankford would never find enough evidence to convict you in a court of law, so creating a scandal is all he could ultimately achieve. We can face it down together. Besides, neither of us cares a fig about whether we're received in Society or not.'

'You might become "Infamous Alastair" in truth,' she said with a flicker of a smile.

'And never look back. But I really don't think it will come to that. Won't you try this my way?'

He hesitated, wanting to say so much more. That neither honour nor affection would permit him to let her sacrifice herself a second time. That logic and reason demanded she choose his alternative. That he intended to keep her here and implement his plan whether she agreed or not.

But after all she had suffered, any attempt to coerce would probably trigger an instinctive resistance that would make her deaf to logic or reason. Holding her by force would only result in her trying to slip through his grasp again at the first opportunity.

So he waited, every nerve tensed for her answer.

At last, she gave a heavy sigh. 'Perhaps you are right. Maybe Will can find something.' She gave him a rueful smile. 'I can always give myself up in the end.'

She turned to look up into his face. 'Maybe I should have trusted you more, eight years ago. Maybe Graveston would not have carried out his threats. All he needed, however, was for me to *believe* he would. A man of his rank, one who had imposed his will on others practically from birth...' She shook her head. 'What match was a girl of eighteen, with no experience of the world, against a man like that?'

'So this time, you'll trust me to keep James safe, to keep you safe. Trust *us*, working together?'

She squeezed his hand and nodded. 'I'll trust us.'

Overwhelming relief swept through him like a storm wind over the moors. Seizing both her hands, he kissed them.

'Thank you. I appreciate how hard it is for you to share control over your safety and James's with anyone,' he told her, both pleased and humbled by her trust. 'So, no more running away into the night! We'll stand and face Graveston, stare him in the eye, if necessary, in the full light of day. Fight, not flee.'

Taking a shaky breath, she nodded. 'Fight, not flee.'

He released her hands and motioned to her glass. 'Finish your wine, then, and get some rest. I'm off tomorrow to find Will—I could send a message and ask him to Barton Abbey, but it would be faster to seek him out. I'd like him to head to Graveston Court as soon as possible.'

Obediently, she sipped the last and rose to leave. As he escorted her out, she paused at the doorway to look up at him. 'Thank you, too. For protecting us.'

She lifted her face. He pulled her to him, and she clung to him through a lingering kiss that set every part of him throbbing with the need for fulfilment.

Oh, that he could make her his—truly his! But that couldn't happen here and now, so he'd better disentangle himself.

Heeding Jane and his mother's warnings, he'd better maintain a little more emotional distance, too.

Reluctant despite those cautioning thoughts, he

released her. 'I only wish there had been some other, equally safe place to bring you. I'm already missing Green Park Buildings.'

She sighed as well. 'So am I.'

Chapter Sixteen

The next morning, Diana woke with a start. Her heart pounded through a moment of panic before she recalled where she was, in a pretty guest bedchamber at Barton Abbey, with James safe in the nursery on the floor above.

Safe.

It had been so long since she'd experienced the condition, she found it still difficult to believe. Like an injured soldier testing a wound, she prodded the edges of her anxiety, feeling for tender places where such concern was justified.

She and James were safe for the moment, but the confrontation had hardly begun. Still, Alastair had an ally who could probe into the circumstances of her husband's death and produce testimony to validate her innocence. Something she could never have managed on her own.

She leaned back against the pillows. Alastair was

right: he was far more than the charming, impetuous young man she'd once loved. If he could face down a charge of French cuirassiers, facing down the Duke or a court of inquiry would hardly faze him. A battle-tested soldier of ingenuity, strength and courage, he would protect her and his family.

Her struggle with Graveston...might even end well.

And if their plan were successful...what then?

She couldn't summon up a single image of a future beyond that. Despite her confidence in Alastair's abilities, the confrontation still to come loomed so large, her mind could not yet envisage anything beyond the yawning abyss of Graveston's threats.

However, until Alastair returned—and his cousin, if Will were amenable to assisting them, completed his work—there was nothing to be accomplished by worrying over the matter any further.

She should instead go down to breakfast and express her thanks to a hostess who, amazingly, had prevented her from departing in the middle of the night and taking her tawdry problems with her.

Hopping out of bed, she crossed to the bell pull. She was inspecting her meagre selection of gowns when a knock at the door heralded the arrival of an apple-cheeked maid.

'I'm Meg, Your Grace,' the girl said, bobbing a curtsy. 'Mrs Ransleigh says I am to attend you while you're here. I pressed and hung up the gowns; I hope I done it how you like them.'

'Thank you, Meg, they look quite fine. Is your mistress at breakfast now?'

'She should be, or if not, she'll be with the house-keeper. Shall I find her for you?'

'No, I'm sure I shall see her there, or later.'

Diana let the maid help her into a modest yellow day gown, then direct her to the breakfast room. She'd seek out her hostess, express her thanks, and go see James.

Having agreed to Alastair's plan, while he pursued the matter of testimony to dissuade the Duke from persecuting her, she'd have more time to get to know her son, she thought, her heart warming with gratitude. And perhaps while they sheltered at Barton Abbey, she might take some lessons from Mrs Ransleigh in how to become a proper mama.

A few moments later, after only a single wrong turn, she arrived at the breakfast room, to find Mrs Ransleigh still sitting over her cup of coffee. As Diana entered, her hostess rose and gave her a curtsy. 'Good morning, Duchess.'

Returning the curtsy, Diana grimaced. 'Please,

Mrs Ransleigh, I should so much prefer that you not use the title. Could you not call me "Diana", as you once did?'

Mrs Ransleigh inclined her head. 'It's certainly not proper. But if you truly prefer it…'

'I would consider it a great favour.' She managed a slim smile. 'Anything that helps me put the last eight years behind me is preferable.'

'Very well…Diana. I hope you slept well—once you slept,' she added with a lift of an eyebrow.

Diana felt her face warm. 'I did sleep well, thank you. Though I cannot imagine why you didn't let me leave.'

'Can you not? I admit, I did not believe the circumstances of your marriage when Alastair first apprised me of them, but as I considered them again after you spoke with me, I changed my mind. Your testimony reminded me that when I knew you before, you never could lie—truth always rang in your voice and illumined every expression of your face.'

A lump rose in her throat. Convincing Alastair had been a gift—she'd never expected to regain the respect of his mother.

'Please, fill your plate!' her hostess urged her. 'Then we can chat.'

Marvelling that, if she'd followed her own plans, she'd now be riding in some farmer's cart towards her reckoning with Graveston, rather than sharing breakfast with the mother of the man she'd wronged, Diana served herself and took a seat.

Once the footman had poured her coffee and withdrawn, Mrs Ransleigh said, 'I liked you immediately when Alastair introduced us years ago, you know, and happily anticipated welcoming you to Barton Court as my daughter. Of course, I was appalled when you jilted Alastair. Incredulous, too,' she added with a smile. 'What girl of sense would give up my son for a mere title?'

Diana had to return it. 'What girl indeed!'

'I've been fortunate,' Mrs Ransleigh continued, 'I was allowed to marry a wonderful man for whom I cared deeply, to bear three children who returned a thousandfold in pride and pleasure for any trials experienced in raising them. But I know many women are not as lucky. Men have their land, or their skills or trade; they can choose how to earn their bread, settle in the community where they were born, or leave it to find new adventures—or to forget disappointments. Whereas most of *our* lives are dictated by others—fathers, husbands, brothers. But within the narrow range of our choices, I believe we women can display bravery and endurance equal to that of any soldier upon a battlefield. "Greater love hath no man than this, that he lay down his life for a friend." *As you did. But one sacrifice was enough, Diana. This time, Alastair will fight to protect you, and I'll do all I can to assist.'*

Diana's hard-won control seemed to be unravelling, for she felt tears prick her eyes. Once again, from deep within where she'd shut away all memories of that long-ago affair, a recollection slipped out: how much she, who'd never known her own mother, had eagerly anticipated sharing Alastair's. The flush of warmth—and longing—that followed in its wake, she made no attempt to suppress. 'Thank you for believing me,' she whispered.

'It's a travesty that you were distanced from loving your son! To have been forced to miss his first six years! Fortunately, you have several more before he's old enough to prefer friends to his mama. You need to make the most of them.'

'I know,' she replied, brought back to her first, most pressing concern. 'But I'm not sure how.'

'Having already met the young lad, I think I can with confidence advise you just to spend time with him and let him be himself. He can't fail to delight you.'

Diana smiled faintly. 'Alastair gave me the same advice.'

Mrs Ransleigh laughed. 'That's how he was beguiled by my rascal of a grandson! Robbie reminds me so much of Alastair. Watching your son grow is a joy you must experience. And now, you shall.'

Oh, how much she wanted to create for James the sort of loving home that had produced an Alastair! 'Will you...help me?'

His mother's face softened. 'I don't think you will need much help, once you are truly convinced you may love him openly without danger, but of course I will. By the way, the two of you may stay here as long as you wish. Treat Barton Abbey as the home we once hoped it would be.'

She'd hardly dared expect forgiveness from Mrs Ransleigh—and never imagined she would be treated with such generosity and compassion.

'There are no words to express how much I appreciate your kindness, to me and to James. How can I repay you?'

'Be happy, for Alastair.'

Be happy. Could she ever discover how to do that—to thaw out the frozen lump of emotions still trapped within, let go of fear and restraint, finally allow herself to *feel* again freely?

'He still cares for you deeply. But you must not worry Alastair will try to push you into anything you do not want, once this is all over,' her hostess added quickly. 'Nor would I let him. You've been coerced quite enough.'

'He's already promised to respect my wishes, and I believe him.'

'Good,' Mrs Ransleigh said with a nod. 'What *do* you wish for, once this is all over? If I may ask—I don't wish to pry.'

'I really don't know,' Diana admitted. 'I lived a virtual prisoner for so many years, with no hope of escape, I ceased to imagine a life beyond the walls of the estate. I'm not even sure where to begin.'

'You might start by taking up activities you used to enjoy. We've a fine library; make use of it. There's a pianoforte at your disposal. Supplies for painting, sketching and needlework. You're welcome to borrow my mare, Firefly, if you'd like to ride. Join me for tea, for dinner, cards and conversation after if you like, or dine alone, if you prefer.'

Gently she took hand Diana's hand, and to her own surprise, Diana did not instinctively flinch away. 'You've been hurt and battered for too many years. Give yourself time to heal. And don't worry. Alastair will make sure no one harms you ever again.'

'I know he will try.'

'He will succeed,' his mother said firmly. 'Alone, my warrior son is a formidable force, but with Will by his side? Invincible! You will see.'

'I certainly hope so.'

'Never doubt it. You can relax and focus on your son—and regaining your life.'

Regaining her life... What would that life look like? Completely absorbed since her husband's death with protecting James—and dealing with Alastair—she hadn't begun to consider. Even now, it seemed somehow to be tempting fate to dare envisage anything beyond the end of Graveston's looming menace.

After taking a final sip, Mrs Ransleigh set down her cup. 'I enjoyed our chat, dear, but I must get to work.'

'Is there anything I can do to help?'

'It's a fine day, with the autumn flowers in the garden in brilliant hue. Perhaps you could gather some?'

Swift as a darting lark, a memory swooped back. Papa had delighted in having fresh greenery nearby as he worked, so she'd made a ritual of seeking the most unusual plants and flowers to arrange in every room.

A faint flicker of what she realised was anticipation stirred. 'I could arrange cuttings for the house, if you like.'

'I would like that.'

To Diana's surprise, her hostess leaned over to give her a hug. 'Life will be better. You'll see. Why not take that young scamp into the garden with you? Teach him about the plants his grandfather loved. I also seem to remember the coachman mentioning that one of the dogs had pupped. I wager James would love to have a dog of his own.'

A walk through a brilliant autumn garden, blooms to gather and arrange—and time with her son. From within a tender warmth welled up, like the small brilliance of the first yellow crocus emerging from the snow.

'Thank you, I'd like that.' After hesitating a moment, she allowed herself to voice the other concern that had occupied her thoughts. 'Has Alastair gone yet, do you know?'

'Yes, he left at first light this morning.'

She felt a flash of disappointment, quickly squelched. Having settled everything last night, there was no reason he should have come to see her before he left.

As if privy to her thoughts, Mrs Ransleigh said, 'He asked me to pass along his good wishes. He would have delivered them in person, but he didn't want to disturb your sleep. More than anything, he wants you to rest—and heal.'

Diana nodded. 'He's been very good to me. As have you. Far better than I deserve, though I'm grateful for James's sake to have found such strong champions.' Foreboding about what that might cost Alastair swept through her.

'You mustn't worry about him,' Mrs Ransleigh said, seeming to sense Diana's concern. 'It's hard not to worry when you care for someone, as I know only too well. After Alastair's break with you, he was in such despair, I feared he might throw his life away in some great battle.'

Feeling the words as a reproach, Diana said quietly, 'I'm so sorry.'

'No point repining,' Mrs Ransleigh said. 'You had good reason for your actions, as I now know. In any event, I was so relieved when he returned from the war unharmed! But the man who came back brought me new worries. Harder, more distant, and cynical about everyone but his immediate family, he seemed to think females served only one purpose—and not one he would discuss with his mama! I could understand at first why he kept that distance, not wishing to risk a heart once so severely wounded. But as time went on, my worry deepened, for neither his many mistresses nor the proper young ladies to whom Jane tried to introduce him—whom he scrupulously avoided, I might add—seemed able to touch him. I have to admit, when Jane told me he was seeing you, I hoped the experience might break through the wall he'd erected around his heart. It has certainly done that. Whatever happens next, for that, and for the sacrifice you made for him earlier, I will always be grateful.'

Along with teasing out threads from the skein of memory Diana had kept so tightly wound within, Mrs Ransleigh seemed to be able to evoke long-repressed emotions. Once more near tears, Diana said, 'I never wished to harm him. I pray every night these new troubles will not.'

Mrs Ransleigh smiled. 'Prayer is always valuable. I'd best get along now, before Mrs Andrews sends a maid looking for me. We dine early, but if you wish something before then, nuncheon is available. Just ring. Shall I see you at dinner, or would you prefer a tray?'

Having not been given that choice for years, Diana hesitated. She could visit the library, choose a book, sit over her dinner reading.

But she didn't have to hurry off—she might choose a book at leisure, and read whenever she chose, for as long as she liked. The idea seemed strange—and wonderful.

But for the first time since she'd left her father and Alastair, Diana felt an inclination for company. To get to know better the remarkable woman who'd raised such a remarkable son—and forgiven her for hurting him. To learn all she could from her, to better raise her own son. 'I'd like to join you, if you don't mind.'

'I should be delighted. I'll look forward to those flower arrangements as well.' Giving Diana's hand another squeeze, she rose from the table. 'Try to enjoy the day, my dear. I'll see you at dinner.'

As her hostess walked out, Diana sipped her coffee. *Enjoy the day.* A whole day, for nothing but her pleasure.

The notion seemed almost impossible.

For all pleasures but one, she amended, remembering last night's single kiss. Her body aflame, she'd regretted as keenly as Alastair the need for the celibacy now imposed upon them. She hadn't expected to miss their intimacy quite so dreadfully.

Would Alastair wish to resume their relationship, once the confrontation with the Duke was over?

This last battle might be the end of the episode for him, the denouement that allowed him to finally close the chapter of his life labelled 'Diana'. Distress, a tangled mix of anxiety and sadness, arose at that possibility.

She would have to accept that, of course. The Alastair she'd known, the Alastair she was coming to know again, would support the cause he believed in and fight to the end. If that end was scandal and disgrace, he would see her comfortably established before moving on.

But what if he were not ready to move on? It required but a moment to conclude she'd welcome him back as a lover. More than that, she couldn't yet envisage. Would he be content for long with such a restricted offering? A man who should command not just the passion, but the unrestrained love of any woman lucky enough to be chosen by him?

She wouldn't think about that now.

Though slowly coming to believe she was truly freed of her prison, she hadn't yet untangled the twisted threads of her thoughts, desires and still-repressed emotions to figure out who she might become—whether it would ever be possible for her to love again with the passionate intensity she'd been capable of before Graveston. She hadn't the energy to contemplate her life beyond tomorrow. All she could manage at the moment was to begin working on dismantling the automatic ban she'd imposed over things which gave her pleasure, lest the Duke take them away.

The most important barrier to dismantle, before she could consider what might develop between herself and Alastair, was the one she'd been forced to erect between herself and the small boy whose emotional future depended upon her. With that thought, she set off for the nursery.

Chapter Seventeen

Diana found James rearranging the soldiers staged on shelves in the nursery. A delighted smile sprang to his face when she walked in. 'Mama, see what wonderful soldiers Minnie found for me! There's twice as many as my army!'

'So I see. Do you want to play with them, or go into the garden with me?'

James set down the soldiers at once. 'I should like to go outside, if you please.'

'Then outside we shall go. Minnie, if you'll get his jacket while I fetch my cloak?'

Diana hurried back to her bedchamber, gathering up a warm hooded cloak and her heaviest gloves. When she arrived back at the nursery, she noted approvingly that James was also warmly attired.

'You needn't go with us, if you'd prefer to remain inside,' she told the maid. 'I promise I won't get him too untidy.'

For a moment, the girl hesitated. 'Very well, ma'am, I'll stay here and catch up on my mending.'

Diana felt a little glow of satisfaction, as if she'd passed some sort of test. In the few short weeks since she'd begun making overtures to her son, this would be the first time she would spend time with the boy without Minnie hovering nearby.

'Are we going to a park?' her son's piping voice interrupted.

'To a garden,' she answered as she ushered him out and down the hallway. 'We're going to hunt plants.'

'Plant hunting? Is that like the fox hunting Papa used to do?'

Her jaw automatically tightened at the mention of his father. *He can't touch you any longer*, she told herself, pushing aside the reaction. 'No, it's the sort of hunting your grandfather, my papa, used to do.'

'The papa who taught you to paint?'

'The very one. We're going to find some flowers for Mrs Ransleigh's tables—giving flowers to your hostess is a very good idea, even if the flowers come from her own garden—and we'll look for some of the little plants my papa used to paint, too. I'll show you how later, or perhaps you'd like to make a portrait of some of your new soldiers.'

'Can I do both? I like painting.'

'And you are quite good at it, too.'

The child glowed at the compliment, and Diana felt a stab of regret. Her father had been lavish with his praise, whether complimenting her skill at reading and letters, or offering encouragement and advice as she began to experiment with paint and brush. James needed appreciation, too, and from more than just his doting nursemaid.

After asking direction of a footman, they set out for the cutting garden behind the kitchen garden. As Mrs Ransleigh had promised, the autumn flowers were reaching full bloom: chrysanthemums in rust and orange, asters in lavenders and whites, and Bourbon roses in the final flush of beauty.

After obtaining scissors and a trug from one of the gardeners, Diana let James carry the basket and helped him cut an assortment of the vivid blooms. They then returned to the kitchen garden, where she wandered among the rows to add sprays of mint, tansy, and rue to add a variety of green hues and a piquant aroma to the bouquet.

In between cutting the flowers, she allowed James to hopscotch down the flagstones of the back terrace, toss some pebbles from the gravel walk surrounding the herb beds into puddles left from the previous night's rain, and make friends with one of the kitchen cats sunning itself on a bench.

When at last the trug was full, she said, 'We'll arrange the flowers and greenery into vases when we go back to the house.'

His smiling face sobered. 'Must we go in already?'

She smiled at his disappointment. 'It's a lovely day, isn't it? No, I don't suppose we must return to the house yet. Would you like to walk some more?'

'Oh, yes! I can see woods from the schoolroom window. Could we walk there?'

'It might be too far away, but we can walk in that direction.'

So they set off, James full of curiosity, commenting on every wall, bench and tree, noting its similarities or differences from those in the gardens at Graveston Court.

'Why aren't there any stone people, Mama?' he asked suddenly.

She suppressed a smile at her son's description of the valuable antiques her husband had placed along the series of descending terraces that led away from the house at Graveston Court, where visitors could see them and be suitably impressed. 'Not everyone likes a very formal garden with statues,' she replied.

He nodded. 'Some of them were scary. I like this garden better.'

Smiling as she recalled some of the classical themes—the Rape of the Sabine Women, for one, which could in no way be considered appropriate viewing for an impressionable young boy—she said, 'I prefer just plants, too.'

Around a turn bordered by a wall of boxwood, they reached the end of the gravel walk. Beyond a wide expanse of grass stood a field of wheat, the long tassels nodding in the breeze, and at a good distance beyond that, the woods James had seen from his windows.

'Mama, it's so pretty—the tall grass that's all gold!'

'Part of that pretty grass is ground into flour to make your bread,' she told him.

'Really? Can I go see it?'

She tensed, wondering whether the watchers would allow them to cross the lawn to the edge of the estate's working fields. A second later she remembered: there were no watchers, ready to herd her back to the house—or drag her there, if need be—if she strayed too far.

A heady sense of freedom filled her, made her feel as light as if she were floating above the earth in one of those new Montgolfier balloons. 'Yes, let's go see the wheat.'

James set off at a trot, and she kept pace beside

him. After a moment, tentatively, she reached for his hand. Eagerly, he grasped her fingers and together, they skipped over the uneven surface towards the golden sheaves beckoning in the distance.

Arriving, James realised the stalks blocking their path to the far-away tree line were nearly as tall as he was. 'Look, Mama, it's like the maze in the park we went to in the city.'

The Sydney Gardens maze had fascinated James and his friend Robbie, who had been taken there by kindly Uncle Alastair.

'Can we walk through it?'

'It's not cut in a pattern like the one in the city,' she explained. 'But I suppose we could walk down some of the rows, as long as we're careful not to harm the plants. This part...' she pulled a stalk closer and showed the kernels to James '...is ground into flour for bread.'

'Come, Mama, you walk down that row and I'll walk down this one.'

Amused by his imagination in turning a common farm planting into a playground, Diana agreed. For a few moments they walked parallel, before with a giggle, James darted several rows away. 'Come find me, Mama!' he shouted.

Warmed by the afternoon sun and her son's innocent enthusiasm, Diana walked along, peering through the sheaves and calling his name, pretending she couldn't find him, then bounding across the few rows separating them to seize him. His shrieks of laughter as she caught and released him made her laugh, too.

'Again, Mama!' he pleaded.

For a surprisingly enjoyable interval, Diana searched and pounced as James ran about, hiding among the wheat. When at last she told him they must return to the house, so they might arrange the flowers they'd picked into vases before they wilted, he'd protested.

She'd given him no more than a warning look before he instantly capitulated. 'Don't get angry, Mama. I'll go back. Minnie says I mustn't tease you, and I don't mean to.'

Another pang of sorrow for time and circumstance lost went through her. She couldn't ever remember worrying about 'teasing' her father with her questions or her presence—he had always had time for her. How many years had the nursemaid been protecting her son from the seemingly harsh scrutiny of his parents?

But time and circumstance were different now, and she meant for James to benefit from it.

'I know you weren't trying to tease me. There's

a treat for you before we go back to the house, too. Shall we go see what it is?'

He brightened instantly. 'A treat! Is it ices?'

'No, but something I think you'll like even better.'

'I don't know,' he said solemnly. 'There's practically nothing as good as ices.'

As she had suspected, once they arrived at the stables, ices were forgotten in his delight with the mother dog and her pups.

'Mrs Ransleigh said you may choose one of the puppies to be your dog for our visit,' she told him.

'Can I? A dog for my very own?'

She nodded. 'You won't be able to bring it to the nursery; he or she is too young yet and must stay with the mama. Which one would you like?'

James took his time, his little face serious as, with a grinning groom's assistance, he held and examined each spaniel—until a brown-and-white-spotted puppy with fly-away ears stretched up to lick him on the nose. Drawing away at first in alarm, he then leaned forward to get another lick. 'I think this one is choosing me!'

'I believe you are right. What shall you name him?'

'How about Pebbles? He has little brown spots just like the pebbles I threw in the puddles.'

'Very well. You must say goodbye to Pebbles now, but we can visit him again tomorrow.'

Before setting the dog down, James lowered his face for another enthusiastic round of puppy kisses. 'He likes me, Mama!' James exclaimed with a giggle. 'I like living here. Can we stay for ever?'

Diana opened her lips, then closed them, the worry over their future that always hovered just out of mind surfacing at that remark. She didn't want to spoil her son's enjoyment by correcting his innocent assumption that Barton Abbey was now their home.

'Mrs Ransleigh is a very kind lady, isn't she?' she evaded.

'Oh, yes! She came to the nursery after Minnie found the soldiers and showed us where to get more. And she brought some teacakes Cook had just made. They were almost as good as ices.'

'I hope you thanked her politely.'

'Oh, I did! I told her she could bring me cakes any time.'

Diana grinned at his artless self-confidence. Oh, that she might share it about their future!

She wasn't sure where their eventual home would be, though it almost certainly wouldn't be Barton Abbey. As long as it was somewhere they could be together, beyond the Duke's reach, she would be content. She trusted Alastair to strike as good a bargain as he could for them; he'd also promised she would no longer have to be afraid—and she was trying to believe him.

But for now, until that eventual fate revealed itself, she vowed to be more like James, pushing aside worry about what the future held—with or without Alastair—and enjoying the respite he and his mother had given her. To breathe free and run through the fields, to get to know her son better, to read books, make conversation, paint and reacquaint herself with the pianoforte.

Her son was not the only one who was finding Barton Abbey a wonderful refuge, she thought as she followed him into the house.

A week later, after a futile stop in London, Alastair finally tracked his cousin down at Salmford House, the small estate Will had purchased in Sussex. Arriving in mid-afternoon, he was shown to the library, where the butler told him the master was going over the estate books.

'Alastair!' Will exclaimed with delight as the butler announced him. 'What an unexpected pleasure! Tate, would you bring some wine and see if Cook can scare up some meat and cheese? If I know my cousin, after the ride in, he'll be famished.'

Turning back to Alastair as the butler bowed himself out, he said, 'I didn't think we'd see you until we returned to London. Much as she loves Paris, Elodie needed some time here in her gardens before heading back to the city.'

'I did look for you there first, but no matter. A trip to Salmford is always a pleasure. Everything is well, I trust?'

Will nodded. 'It's always better when Elodie can bring Philippe to England with her. She's had her son back such a short time, she's never truly easy when he's out of her sight. Luckily, she was able to persuade the *comtesse* to let him accompany us on this trip. What brings you here?'

'Have you heard nothing?'

'About you? No. What have you got yourself into this time? Max didn't mention a word when we stopped to see him in Kent.' He shook his head. 'It seems I need to add to my network of informants. What is it?'

Well aware of Will's dislike of the woman who'd broken their engagement, he warned, 'Before I tell you, you must promise to reserve judgement until you've heard the whole.'

Will's grin faded. 'Must be serious indeed, if you're issuing such a warning to me, the most affable of men. Forget the wine, this calls for brandy.' Motioning Alastair to a chair, he walked to the decanter on the desk and poured them each a glass.

Seating himself again, he faced his cousin. 'Very well, begin.'

Alastair did. Though some thundercloud expressions darkened Will's face during the recitation, he honoured his promise and made no comment as Alastair related once again the reasons behind Diana's rejection of his suit, her ongoing battle of her marriage, and the new fight with her husband's heir.

Will's silence continued for some time after Alastair finished his account. Knowing he would not win approval by pressing Will, Alastair stifled his impatience and sipped his brandy, waiting while his cousin reflected on all he'd been told—and mentally trying to construct an alternate plan for thwarting the Duke, if Will refused to help him.

At long last, Will sighed. 'The tale is spectacularly unbelievable—which, I suppose, is the strongest recommendation for its truth. In any event, since I ended up marrying the woman I swore to drag back to England, to the gallows, if that proved necessary to vindicate Max, I suppose I don't have room to object to your championing the lady who injured you.'

'The story is hard to accept, I admit. Swallow

that whole for a moment, and while it digests, let's move on to what we need to do now. Something I think you'll find much more palatable.'

'Something has to be done?' Will said with a grin. 'That does sound promising.'

'I called on Graveston to try to impress on him his responsibilities to his father's widow. Far from being convinced, he announced his intent to broadcast his suspicion that his father did not die of natural causes; he intends to accuse Diana of his murder.'

Will's eyebrows flew up. 'Has he any grounds?'

'Beyond his wish to punish her, not really. It's a ridiculous accusation that, were he anyone else, would probably be laughed at by local authorities. But because of his rank, he would probably be able to force an investigation. He seems certain he can find witnesses to support his version of events.'

'Or buy some?' Will interjected drily.

'I see you have as much confidence in the reliability of our legal system's evidence-gathering methods as I do,' Alastair replied acerbically. 'Now that I've had time to think about it, having his father buried already probably works in his favour. The coroner may well conclude there would be no purpose in exhuming the body, as it would be too late to find any evidence.'

'Either to prove—or more importantly, to disprove the charges,' Will said, shaking his head. 'I saw evidence enough during my years on the streets of how the law supports the mighty,' he added, his tone turning bitter. 'Boys transported because a shop owner claimed they stole bread, innocent men imprisoned over evidence from thief-takers intent upon winning a reward. So, what do we do to defend your lady?'

'Since I am too well known to be of much use, what *you* can do is more important. I'd like you to go to Wickham's End, the village nearest Graveston Court, and hang about. See what you can nose out from the locals about the old Duke's death, his relationship with his heir—anything of interest you can find. Anything we could use to persuade the heir not to drag Diana into a sordid public battle.'

'If it comes to that, we could buy witnesses of our own,' Will pointed out.

Alastair laughed. 'Yes, that's the rogue I need! I knew I could count on your expertise. But I'd prefer it not come to a trial.'

Will nodded. 'So you want me to poke about, see what I can find that might persuade His High-and-Mightiness not to move forward with charges? Excellent! I have to admit, though the give and take of bargaining on wine lots is exciting, much of the negotiation over trading rights between the Crown and our new French allies is damnably dull. I shall relish a bit of an adventure.'

'There's probably one more thing I should tell you.'

Will raised an eyebrow. 'Why is there always one more thing?'

'The Duke also threatened me. He had Diana watched, and so discovered that, very soon after she fled Graveston Court for Bath, we...began a relationship. He advised me to keep my distance, warning that if I intervened to help her, he would drag me into this, claiming that I'd encouraged her to do away with her husband so she might take up with the man who'd once been her lover.'

'The cad!' Will exploded. 'There'd be immense satisfaction in thwarting him just because he's a duke—but now, it's personal. No one can get away with threatening one of the Rogues. But devil's teeth, Alastair,' he added in exasperated tones, 'you certainly led straight into the Duke's trump suit with that play!'

'Well, I wouldn't have, had either of us any idea there was a game on. Or maybe not,' he admitted. 'Once I saw her again, once she approached me, the...need to be with her, to try to finish what had been between us, would have been too strong to resist, whatever the danger.'

Will studied him for a moment. 'Am I allowed to ask whether this *will* end once and for all what was between you?'

'You can ask,' Alastair said with a sigh. 'I just don't have an answer yet—and not because I'm trying to fob you off. It's impossible, of course, to recapture the innocence of the passion we shared eight years ago. Too much has happened, to both of us. This business with the Duke interfered before I'd been with her long enough to decide whether this was the bittersweet epilogue to something ended long ago, or the start of…something new. Either way…she's still in my blood. But all I mean to concentrate on right now is seeing her safe from his bullying—she and her son, whom, by the way, the Duke is also trying to take away from her so he may make the boy suffer. I'll worry about what happens next afterward.'

'He'd vent his pique on a child?' Will said in disgust. 'He truly is a piece of work! You do realise if the Duke continues to be unreasonable about this, there is no way, short of kidnapping and transportation—which I might be induced to attempt on a man vile enough to prey upon a defenceless woman and an innocent child—to prevent him from making the accusations public, however groundless they may be. You know how London loves a scandal. The demise of a duke, accusations against the widow, an illicit affair with a former lover when the earth has scarcely settled over her late husband's grave—the penny press would make a fortune! Not that anyone who knows you would credit your being involved in such a scheme, but the hullabaloo might seriously damage your reputation. You are sure you want to do this?'

Alastair looked at his cousin incredulously. 'You don't truly think I'd turn tail and abandon a woman—any woman—to face slander and intimidation alone, after walking her into it?'

'If you did, we'd have to ceremonially break your sword and drum you out of the Rogues,' Will agreed. 'I just wondered if, in your zeal to right this wrong, you fully understood the risk.'

Alastair shrugged. 'If we fail, and scandal is the result, so be it. After years of snubbing virtuous young maidens in favour of actresses, widows and matrons of dubious character, my reputation isn't that shiny-bright anyway. Whether the Duke's vendetta succeeds or fails, if he convinces the Court of Chancery to give him custody of the boy, I'll take them abroad. But I have a high regard for your powers of discernment and invention. If anyone can figure a way to pressure Graveston into reconsidering his attack, it's you.'

Will made a bow. 'Many thanks for the vote of confidence. Have you thought of speaking to our uncle? In case the Duke does manage to intimidate the local authorities into pressing forward to a trial?'

'I don't imagine the Earl would receive me with much enthusiasm. Last time we spoke, I left him in a cold fury for not defending Max—though I wasn't bold enough to take him to task for not supporting his son during the scandal.'

'Then you'll be happy to know Max and his father have reconciled,' Will informed him. 'Max told me when we stopped at Denby Lodge on our way from Paris. Not that the Earl admitted he'd been wrong not to embrace Max's cause, but he did apologise.'

'He apologised?' Alastair echoed incredulously. 'Wish I could have heard that! Maybe he's mellowing, now that Max has produced a grandson.'

Alastair fell silent, thinking furiously. He'd not meant to approach his uncle unless absolutely necessary—but if the Earl had belatedly developed some family feeling, perhaps he should rethink that decision. Someone of the Earl's wide-ranging influence could be tremendously helpful in squelching whatever scandal the Duke could dredge up.

'Maybe I will consult him. I'd like his support, but even if he won't offer that, if yet another Ransleigh cousin is about to stir up a hornet's nest of trouble that might come buzzing into the Lords, I should give him a warning before he gets stung.'

'A good precaution. About your lady... I don't think any man can offer truly useful advice on a matter so individual but...let me just say this. Regardless of the scandal that might ensue, if you can't envisage life without her, don't give her up. The Earl's displeasure, the censure of those who know your name but not the man, the vast titillation you'd provide for Society's tattle-mongers—none of that matters a pin. To build a life with Elodie, I was willing to risk a break with everyone—even the Rogues, and you know how much all of you mean to me. If what you feel for Diana is that strong, the Rogues will stand by you—regardless of our initial doubts about the lady. And if she must flee England to keep her son, bring her to us in Paris.

'But enough of melodrama,' Will pronounced before Alastair could get past the lump in his throat to thank him. 'Let me pour you another glass while I put my reprobate brain to formulating a plan for evidence-gathering. I shall also have to think of an excuse to put off Elodie, lest she try to come along and keep a watchful eye over me.'

'You think she might be induced to visit Barton Abbey instead?' Alastair asked, taking another sip of his brandy. 'Mama would enjoy seeing her, and Diana's son is of an age with Philippe. James, I'm sure, would love to have another boy to explore with.' He gave a short laugh. 'Though Mama's come round to supporting Diana, I don't think my sister Jane has yet forgiven me enough for taking back up with her to lend me Robbie.'

'If I can convince Elodie I don't need her to guard my back, you could probably persuade her to visit. Our being safe and together, like her recovering Philippe, is still so new, we're hesitant to be apart. Though she was a full participant during our adventures on the road from Vienna to Paris, I think she views disguise and subterfuge as unfortunate necessities, rather than tricks that add spice to the game.'

'Still the same Wagering Will,' Alastair observed with a grin. 'Your journey being a continuation of the sleight-of-hand spectacles you organised at Eton to earn pennies? No, don't tell me—I'm probably better off not knowing. I always thought, though, you enjoyed the thrill of besting the other boys—and the risk of punishment if you were discovered—more than the meat pasties you bought with your earnings.'

'Spoken like a true privileged son, who's never known what it is to be hungry!' Will shot back, though Alastair noted he did not disagree. 'Elodie is looking for activities to amuse Philippe, so he will be as eager to accompany us on our trips back to England as she is to have him with us. I'm sure she'd be delighted for Philippe to make an acquaintance he can look forward to renewing each time we return.'

'Beginning a new generation of Ransleigh Rogue cousins?'

'Something like,' Will agreed. 'You can ask her yourself at dinner. You will stay a few days, won't you?'

'Just the night. Diana will be anxious,' he explained to Will's murmur of disapproval. 'I want to reassure her you will soon be in place, with our plan under way, and I think I'll take your advice and consult our uncle in London before I return to Barton Abbey.'

Will whistled. 'Your case must be serious indeed, if you'd rather face our censorious uncle than go rousting about with me.'

'If I thought I could be useful slinking about Wickham's End with you, I'd go without hesitation. But as someone once pointedly informed me that I look and act too much like a "privileged son

of wealth" to pass unnoticed, I'd better leave subterfuge to the master.'

'Probably wise. I do understand the need to do
everything you can for someone you've pledged
to protect, so I'll not tease you any further. You'll
want to change out of the dust of the road before
dinner; Susan will show you to a bedchamber. Did
you bring your valet?'

'No, I hired horses and brought only a portmanteau. Despite the awful paces of some of the job
nags, it was the fastest way.'

'I'll send Maurice up; he'll fit you out in something of mine—we're enough of a size.' Will shook
his head, a rueful smile on his face. 'Oh, the necessities of presenting a proper appearance in official
circles! Cor, if any of me mates from Seven Dials
could see me now—a regular toff, with a French
valet!'

Chuckling, Alastair downed the rest of his brandy.
'I'll see you at dinner, then.'

'At dinner. And then, as quickly as I can run to
ground the situation at Graveston Court, I'll report
to you back at Barton Abbey.'

Following the maid towards the guest bedchamber, Alastair took a deep breath. Had Will not
agreed to help him, he would have come up with

some other way to pressure the Duke into dropping his plans for revenge. But he couldn't deny the vast uplift to his spirits, knowing that his ingenious—and if necessary, ruthless—cousin would be working for them.

He was nearly certain, given the long estrangement between Blankford and his sire, there was some animosity that could be turned to their advantage. With Will to sniff it out, he was more confident than ever their plan would prevail.

Then, with Diana safe, he could return to figuring out what the future might hold for them.

Chapter Eighteen

Four days later, on a late autumn afternoon whose crisp wind gave a foretaste of the winter to come, Diana stood at her easel in one of the north-facing parlours, a bowl of blooms set out on the table before her. For years, she'd only observed the colours of nature, barred by her defiance of Graveston from access to the supplies that would let her reproduce them on canvas. Now that she'd got a brush back in her hands, she found herself increasingly fascinated by the play of light over the vivid petals—rust and amber and coral, fading to ochre and chocolate in the shadows. At least twice daily, while morning and afternoon light lit the room to its brightest, she left James to his soldiers in the nursery and returned to her canvas.

'Beautiful hues—I like it.'

Her pulses leapt at the sound of Alastair's voice. Setting down the brush, she whirled around to find him standing in the doorway, smiling at her. Without further thought, she ran to him, leaning into his embrace as he took her in his arms.

'I've missed you,' he murmured into her hair.

'I've missed you, too,' she acknowledged, knowing as she said the words what an understatement they represented. Oh, how she'd missed him! His physical presence, his companionship—even the support she didn't wish to depend on but, from prudence and necessity, had accepted in order to prevail in the second-greatest challenge of her life.

With seeming reluctance, he set her at arm's length. 'I don't want to interrupt your work, but I did want you to know I was back. I expect you are anxious to know what transpired with Will.'

'I am. Can you tell me now?'

'I've estate business to tend, but it can wait until later. I'll have Wendell bring us some tea.'

He dispatched a hovering footman, then returned to take a seat beside her on the sofa. An almost tangible fire sparking between them, Diana found herself intensely aware of him.

A rapid series of images flashed through her mind—his mouth on her; his hands on her body; riding him, borne away on a tidal wave of pleasure. Heat flushed her face, spiralled through her body.

She looked up to see him watching her, an answering passion glittering in his eyes. With a little murmur, she angled her face up, her eyes drifting closed.

His kiss began gently, but rapidly turned hungry. Just as famished, she opened her mouth to him, her tongue urgent against his, then cupped his face and dragged him closer. Not until she almost succumbed to the impulse to work loose the buttons of his trouser flap so she might straddle him, right here in the parlour, did her brain manage to loosen the hold of her senses. Trembling, she broke the kiss.

She would have been embarrassed by her lack of control, if Alastair's breathing had not been as erratic as her own. 'How I miss Bath!' he said on a groan.

'Despite the necessity for it, I'm discovering that chastity is a good deal harder than I thought it would be,' she admitted. Shackled to a husband who neither aroused nor attempted to incite her desire, she hadn't realised, when she'd tumbled into an affair, how compelling and addictive passion could be.

'When we began this, I expected it would be of short duration, affecting only the two of us,' Alastair said, setting her gently back against the cushions. 'How wrong I was! But there's nothing for it now; I'll not abuse my mother's hospitality by forgetting myself again.'

'A wise resolution,' she said. 'Despite my reaction to the contrary, I entirely agree. Besides, I'm very concerned to hear what you've discovered.'

'Despite my reaction to the very great distraction you pose,' he said, running a fingertip along her lips, 'I'm very keen to give it.'

She'd closed her eyes on a sigh, savouring his touch, when Wendell arrived back with the tea tray. The ritual of pots, cups and cream gave them further opportunity for passion to cool while they sipped hot tea.

After Wendell bowed himself out, Alastair began. 'I'm happy to report Will has agreed to investigate at Wickham's End and Graveston Court. He'll pose as a pedlar; such a man, he told me, is welcome everywhere and can tease out the most interesting details while mesmerising the unwary with his shiny wares. He should be there by now, poking about to see what he can turn up.' Alastair laughed. 'If he finds no one else suitable, Will promised to hire us some witnesses, if circumstances require it.'

She grimaced. 'I hope it won't come to that—though I'm certain Graveston wouldn't hesitate to hire witnesses if *he* thinks it necessary.'

'There was one other favourable development. On

Will's recommendation, I stopped to see our uncle in London. I'd steeled myself to forewarn the Earl of the scandal that might turn up on his doorstep in the Lords, expecting to receive a proper jobation for getting myself into it. To my astonishment, he welcomed me with an apology for the harsh words we exchanged the last time we met, when I was defending Max's conduct in Vienna.'

'An apology?' Diana raised her eyebrows. 'As I recall, the Earl never apologised.'

Alastair laughed. 'Indeed! I couldn't have been more surprised if the stone dogs on the fireplace had leapt up and bit me. The Earl proceeded to explain that, after holding on by a single vote to the majority he'd ruled over in the Lords for thirty years, he'd realised that his decades of work could be wiped away in a few sessions—and that only what he accomplished with the family he'd ignored for so many years would live on. He said he regretted not having spent more time with us boys while we were growing up, and that he intends to change that now. Then, when I told him of your dilemma, he seemed positively enthusiastic. It appears he did not much like your late husband, and if the matter should make it to the Lords, found the idea of being able to put a spoke in the wheel of Graveston's son very attractive. He also pledged to tap his network of friends, acquaintances, and colleagues, if we have need of them.'

Diana felt a stir of excitement as a new thought occurred. 'Might he know any of the judges from the Court of Chancery?'

'Very possibly. With the Earl volunteering, not just to assist in the Lords, but to do whatever he can to prevent it coming to that, I'm more hopeful than ever that we can convince Graveston to give up his intention to harass or publicly accuse you. By the way, the Earl's last admonition was for me to bring you by to see him after all this is over.'

'Heavens! He has changed! I don't believe he even bothered to have me introduced when we were engaged!'

Alastair's smile faded. 'He was present at that political dinner the night you appeared in front of all of Graveston's guests wearing only your bruises for jewellery.'

She gasped as the memory of that evening's shame and desperation slashed through her like a sabre cut. 'He told you about the dinner?'

'No. Your former friend, Mary Ellington, now Lady Randolph, asked me to call on her in Bath. Not knowing we'd already met, and hoping to blunt any anger I might express if I encountered you, she told me about it. The Earl thought your bravery that night magnificent, as do I. But Heaven forfend, Diana, how could you have risked further angering a man who'd already brutalised you?'

'It wasn't bravery—not at all. Papa was gone, you were lost to me, and I hadn't yet borne James. I no longer cared what happened to me—and I wanted the world to know what kind of man Graveston was. I even taunted him when he came up later, furious.' She smiled grimly at the memory. 'The high-born Duke, who lost control and beat me like some gin-soaked labourer with a two-penny harlot. I'd thought it might incense him enough to finish me for good. Instead, it seemed to smite his pride; he never struck me again after that. Or perhaps it was the knowledge that beating me wouldn't make any difference.'

'Praise the Lord for that mercy, anyway,' Alastair spat out, a look of revulsion on his face. 'It sickens me that you were forced to live under his hand for years afterward. Well, soon you'll no longer need to fear the malice of a Duke of Graveston. With Will's help, and the Earl's if necessary, you will be free of their menace for ever.'

Reluctant as she'd been to reveal her tawdry circumstances, cautious as she knew she must remain about depending on help from anyone else, she couldn't help feeling a wave of relief and gratitude.

'Thank you for all you've done. Even now, it's difficult for me to place reliance on others, though I know you have only my best interests at heart. How can I resist, though, when you are risking your own reputation to protect mine?' she said, marvelling at the depth of his sense of honour and the strength of his resolve.

He gave her a wry smile. 'In a way, I should feel grateful for Blankford's nefarious scheme. If you hadn't needed to marshal every possible resource to protect your son, you'd probably never had confided in me—would you?'

'No,' she admitted, knowing it was true. Only desperation had pushed her to reveal the humiliating truth about her marriage that she would otherwise have carefully hidden.

'You would have pleasured me, held your innermost self aloof, and slipped away.' He shook his head. 'It scares me to think how close I came to losing you again without ever knowing you.'

'If Blankford ends up arm-wrestling you in the mud of a public scandal, you may be less sanguine about my asking for your help,' she retorted.

'Never,' he exclaimed, kissing her hands. 'I'm glad to assist you. Glad that you are allowing me to act for you. I can well imagine, after being forced and coerced and bullied for so long, it's hard to trust anyone but yourself.'

He gazed at her, an oddly expectant look on his face. Was he hoping she would deny it, assert that she was completely comfortable relying on him?

Much as she appreciated his efforts, she could not in honesty tell him that. Uncertain what to reply, she said, 'So now, we wait?'

The hopeful look faded from his eyes—and she feared she'd disappointed him. Tacitly accepting her evasion, however, he confirmed, 'Now, we wait. Will promised to come report as soon as possible. We may also have a visit from his wife, Elodie. The Frenchwoman who, you may remember, embroiled Max in the scandal that ruined his diplomatic career. Somewhere along the way from Vienna back to England, Will fell in love with her.'

'She must be quite a lady to hold Will's interest,' Diana said, grateful that he'd moved the conversation to less personal matters. 'As I recall, women always found him fascinating, and though he returned the favour, he was as fickle as the wind.'

'Yes, it's quite a love story, which I'll let her tell you when she visits. She also has a son a bit younger than James. I thought he'd enjoy having a playmate.'

'I know he would! It's so kind of you to think of him.'

'It's high time someone was kind to you both.'

Diana shook her head ruefully. 'Your mother seems to think so, too. Sometimes I feel I'm living in a dream! Paints and brushes at hand, an excellent pianoforte to play whenever I like, a library full of books to explore. Your mother shall be tossing me out of the house before long because I'm running through so many candles, staying up late to read. I keep thinking that one morning, I'll wake up and all this will vanish.'

'Be assured it will not.' He lifted her chin so she had to meet his gaze. 'The future is yours to determine, Diana. You'll never be constrained again.'

Though she still found it difficult to express her feelings, she made herself say, 'No matter how this turns out, I'll never forget it was you who thought to bring me the first paints I'd touched in seven years. You who lured me back to the piano bench. You who escorted me to the library at Barton Abbey and invited me to sample it.'

He shook his head. 'I still can't believe you existed for years without books, paints, music. How dull it must have been, with nothing to do all day but manage that vast house.'

She laughed shortly as another flood of bitter memories engulfed her. 'I didn't even do that.'

He raised his eyebrows and, flushing, she waved

a dismissive hand, not wanting to admit the painful truth.

'Won't you explain, Diana? I want to understand. And I think, to move beyond the past, you must face it. I want to help. Won't you let me?'

Eight years of instinct pressed her to retreat, fall silent. But after a brief internal struggle, the sympathy in his gaze—and the memory of the sweet peace she'd found after confessing her dilemma about James—overcame her reserve.

Slowly she began. 'The Duke's first wife retained the sympathy of the staff, the housekeeper in particular. I admit, I made no attempt to take over the reins, but it probably would have been very difficult to pry them away, even had I wanted to.'

'Having spoken to Blankford, I can well imagine the hostility of anyone loyal to his mother. How did you occupy your time, then?'

'I was permitted needlework, since I expressed no fondness for it, and making garments for the poor was an approved occupation for the Duchess. I walked around the rooms, the Long Gallery, the garden. I *looked*—at the garden, the woods, the buildings, the tapestries, evaluating their textures and colours, imagining what paints I would blend to reproduce their images, were I ever to paint again. I examined such grounds as I was permitted to stroll, noting plants I'd found with my father, ones he'd illustrated for his books and lectures.'

Once begun, she couldn't seem to halt the flood of words. 'I could sit or stand for hours, no doubt to the puzzlement of whichever menial had been assigned to trail me, listening in my head to Papa's analysis. Or in the house, I'd stare at some object, evaluating its shape in geometric terms, figuring how I would position it for sketching, where to place the lines of shading. Observed it as the light playing over it changed with the advancing hour, watching how it changed those patterns. Sometimes, if I passed by a book I'd enjoyed, I'd try to recall as much of its prose or verse as I could. And I spent a great deal of time training myself not to *feel*, or to at least be able to mask my emotions enough that *he* could not read my countenance and use my reactions against me. Quite an interesting and useful life,' she concluded bitterly.

In the next instant, anxiety seized her. Whatever had induced her to blather on so? Alastair must think her shallow, cowardly, despicable for allowing herself to exist in such a mocking echo of a life.

Wary, she looked up to see him studying her, but rather than disgust and condemnation, she read compassion in his gaze. 'I'm so sorry,' he said, lifting her hand to his lips for a kiss. 'Though I hesitate even to give such facile advice, you must try to leave all that behind you.'

For a moment, the relief that she had not alienated him held her speechless. 'I am trying,' she managed at length. 'After all those years at Graveston Court, Barton Abbey seems a wonderland. Like a starving man invited to a banquet, I hardly know what delight to taste first.'

He smiled. 'I'm so glad you are finding it so. But *are* you allowing yourself to *feel* delight?'

She nodded. 'I am, a little. It's still hard to believe that the things that bring me pleasure won't suddenly disappear again. But…I'm trying to believe it. Or I will, once all this is over.'

'Believe it, and believe also that it *will* soon be over. And then…'

Diana tensed. Would Alastair tell her what he envisaged for their future? Would he gently let her go—or ask her to remain his mistress? If he wanted that and more, could she possibly give him an answer now?

A knock sounded at the door, followed by the entrance of Mrs Ransleigh. 'I'm not disturbing you, I hope? Wendell just let me know you'd returned.'

'Not at all,' Diana told her, not sure whether she was relieved or disappointed by the interruption. She didn't want to think of a future without

Alastair—but she wasn't sure, damaged as she still was, what she could offer him, beyond a temporary passion.

Would that be enough?

Alastair rose to give his mother a hug. 'Diana tells me you've been taking good care of her and James.'

'Indeed she is,' Diana confirmed.

'I'm so much enjoying her stay! James is delightful, and I've been grateful for her companionship. I even compelled her to play for me in the evening. I've missed hearing the pianoforte, with both your sisters now gone.' Mrs Ransleigh gave her a fond look. 'It's almost like having a daughter at home again. I must inform you, I've given her and James the run of house and invited them to stay as long as they like. And once this matter is resolved and it's safe for Diana to establish her own residence, I hope they will return to visit often.'

'Of course I approve.'

'Thank you, Mrs Ransleigh,' Diana said, touched by her kindness. 'It's been a long time since I lived with my father and felt like part of a family. It's something I very much wanted James to experience. I'll be forever grateful for your friendship.'

'As I esteem yours! But now, I must go check on dinner. I'm so glad you're safely home, Alastair. Will I see you both at table?

'Very good,' she said as they both nodded. 'I'll leave you to your chat. No naughtiness, now!' she added with a smile, waving a finger at them.

At the memory of the torrid kiss they'd shared, Diana blushed—and noted that Alastair's face reddened, too. 'I made you a promise, Mama, and I won't break it…no matter how tempting it might be.'

'You'd better figure out how you'll deal with it later,' came the enigmatic reply as with a wave of her fingers, Mrs Ransleigh glided out through the door.

Alastair looked back at her. 'I'd better go change out of my dirt. Mama isn't as much a stickler as my uncle, but she'd still not appreciate me leaving mud on her dining-room carpet.'

He bent to kiss her fingers, sending another sizzle of sensation through her. 'Mama's right. We will have to figure out what to do about this later, you know.'

Both delight and dread made her stomach churn. 'I know.'

'I won't tease you now, though. I'll see you at dinner.'

Diana watched him go. Their physical bond was, without question, as strong as ever. Would that be enough? And how long would it last?

She was trying hard not to depend on support which, once she was safe again, could well be withdrawn. She was trying not to hunger for the company of a man who, after having a husband who did everything possible to control, coerce, and deprive her, made it his task to indulge her, expand her horizons, and give her the freedom to choose her own destiny.

With complete freedom, what would that be?

She simply didn't know. She was, as she'd assured Alastair, just beginning to allow herself to experience happiness, while a love for her son, natural and unforced, seemed to increase with each interlude they spent together.

But she was still a long way from recovering from years of repressing all feeling, nor had she exorcised the demons left from her late husband's abuse. She'd shown she could be a mistress. She was not at all sure she could be more.

Well, she'd not tease herself either. For now, she must wait with what patience she could muster for resolution of the challenge from Graveston. Only then would she figure out what came next.

Chapter Nineteen

Two weeks later, the early morning sun a smouldering suggestion on the eastern horizon, Alastair was grabbing an early breakfast when Diana walked in.

Seeing him, she halted, her face lighting with a smile that made his heart swell in his chest.

'I thought you'd be gone by now. Your mother said last night you were meeting Hutchens today to visit some of the outlying farms.'

'Yes, and to arrange some assistance for one of the tenants. With crops about ready for harvest, the poor fellow fell off his barn roof and broke a leg. Hutchens has already talked with some of neighbours; today we'll arrange a schedule so they can work together to get all the fields harvested.'

'Will you be away the whole day?' she asked as she poured herself some coffee.

Alastair hoped he wasn't imagining the wistfulness in her tone. 'Much of it. What do you have planned?'

'The bouquets in the rooms need refreshing. I'll scour the cutting garden, then take James for a long tromp through the fields and see what plants we can find to augment them.'

Alastair smiled, remembering all the exploring through the woods and fields he'd done with his cousins. 'I'm sure he'll enjoy that. Barton Abbey is a wonderful place for an adventuresome boy.'

She nodded. 'Especially when he can bring his new puppy. I enjoy the walks, too. When we come across some interesting specimen, it recalls to me the particular plant-hunting expedition during which Papa first showed it to me. How he taught me to appreciate the lines and shapes of nature, as well as her colours. It's like getting a small part of myself back.'

'You'll bring your sketchbook?'

'Yes. James reminds me of Papa, too. It's not just a mother's prejudiced eye—he has a real knack for drawing. He seems to enjoy spending the time with me, sketching.' She sighed. 'He's missed out on so many simple things. Thanks to you, I'm beginning to make it up to him.'

'No, it's thanks to you, for thinking of them,' he corrected. 'You are a good mother, Diana.'

'I'm trying to be.' As her gaze traced his face, lingering on his lips, he felt heat rise within him.

She must have felt it, too, for she gave a little sigh. 'I am trying hard to be good—in many ways.'

His thoughts flew immediately to intimacy, and he had to suppress a groan. 'As are we both.' Then he grinned. 'I'd love to be "good" to you in a most different way, but that will be for later.'

'Oh, I hope so! Anticipation makes the heart grow fonder?'

'And other things,' he muttered. He rose and walked to her chair, fighting the urge to kiss her. She placed her hand on top of his, tracing the edge of his palm with her fingertip, setting his senses simmering, sparking his barely banked desire into flame.

'Witch,' he murmured when he could speak again.

'Wizard,' she replied, a little hitch in her voice. 'Sometimes doing the honourable thing is beastly difficult.'

'It won't be for much longer, sweeting. Once you are protected, settled with what is due you and James, we can move forward—to whatever you want.'

To his surprise, rather than looking relieved, her face clouded. 'I hope everything will transpire as you envisage it.'

'I'll never let you be hurt. You believe that, don't you, Diana?' He tilted her face up to gaze at him. 'I know with James in danger, you can't help worrying. But…try to be easy, won't you?'

She sighed. 'I will try. And I do trust you.'

He ought to go…but the desire to spend time with her while he could—and ease her apprehension—made him linger. 'I don't need to meet with Hutchens until later. How about I join you and James on your walk?'

'Do you have the time? I don't wish to pull you from your work.'

'I can spare an hour. And I know a few places an adventurous boy would enjoy visiting.'

To his delight, she chuckled, smoothing the worried creases from her brow. 'I'm sure you do! James would love to have you join us. He told me you've stopped by the nursery and played soldiers with him several times, which has quite won him over. I can't thank you enough for your kindness.'

'I enjoy spending time with him. He reminds me of Robbie.'

'Let me fetch him, then.'

'Finish your breakfast and we'll go up together.'

And so, after she'd nibbled her toast and sipped her coffee, they left the breakfast room and headed towards the nursery. As they climbed the stairs, Alastair felt an odd sense of déjà vu.

So it should have been, he and Diana going up together to fetch their son.

Too late for that, he thought, hauling back on the reins of his fantasy. *And too soon yet*, he reminded himself, *to picture anything for the future.*

As Diana had predicted, James was delighted to add him to their excursion. 'Are we going to explore the gatehouse, like you promised?' James asked after they'd descended the stairs and exited the house.

'We'll save that for a rainy day,' he replied, hoping they would be at Barton Abbey long enough for him to make good on his pledge. 'It's so lovely this morning, I thought we'd go to another special place.'

'Are we going to the woods?' James asked, skipping along beside him. 'Mama took me to the wheat field, but she wouldn't let me go all the way to the trees.'

'The woods are closer if you go this way, through the kitchen gardens,' he told them as he opened a gate into the walled enclosure.

'Mama and I walked here already,' James informed him. 'We picked the plants with smelly leaves.'

'The ones with fragrant leaves,' Diana corrected. 'Lavender, mint and rosemary, to add some scent to the bouquets,' she explained to Alastair.

Within a few moments, they'd traversed the neat arrangement of symmetrical beds filled with herbs and vegetables and reached the gate at the other side. Opening it, Alastair pointed to a path that set off into the woods beyond a border of shrubs. 'We're going that way.'

'What's there?' James asked. 'A treasure?'

'Of a sort,' Alastair replied. 'You'll see.'

'Let's hurry!' James cried, grabbing his hand and urging him forward.

'Steady on, wait for your mama,' Alastair said with a laugh. 'Ladies must walk at a more dignified pace. Their long skirts hinder them, you see.'

'Do they?' Diana said. 'Well, not this lady.' Raising her hem above her ankles, she took off at a trot while James, giggling, sped after her.

Chuckling himself, Alastair followed.

The trail twisted and turned among the trees before, several minutes later, it opened into a clearing. As they approached, the muted gurgle of water over stone announced the presence of a brook at the far side.

James rushed over. 'Mama, how pretty the water is! Can I go in?'

'Not yet,' Alastair said. 'First we need to find the treasure, and you'll frighten it away if you splash.'

Putting a finger to his lips to signal the child to silence, he took his hand and led him along the bank to where the stream broadened into a shallow pool. Along its edges, several frogs swam lazily.

'Have you ever caught a frog?' Alastair whispered.

The boy's eyes widened. 'No. Can you show me how?'

'You have to be quick. Watch.'

Stealthily Alastair approached, careful not to let his shadow fall over the pool. After choosing his target, he crouched down, and with a quick lightning thrust, snatched up the unsuspecting amphibian.

The frog squirmed and wiggled, trying to escape Alastair's grasp. 'Do you want to hold it?' he asked the boy.

'Oh, yes!' James breathed.

Alastair took the boy's hand and wrapped it around the struggling frog. 'Careful, he's slippery. You must hold him firmly, but not too tight.'

'Oooh, he's soft—and squishy!' James exclaimed. 'Mama, look! I have a frog!'

'So I see,' she said with a smile.

'Can I take it back to the nursery?'

'Unlike your puppy, who would love to join you in your bed, the frog prefers his pond,' Alastair said. 'We'll leave him here—so you can catch him again next time.'

'Do you want to catch one, Mama?' James asked, motioning towards the frog's fellows who, while hopping a safe distance away, still remained in the shallows.

'Ladies don't like to get their shoes muddy—or their hands squishy,' Alastair told him.

Diana raised her eyebrows. 'Well, this lady isn't so pudding-hearted. I'll have you know that, on plant-gathering expeditions with my father—your grandpapa,' she told James, 'the one who taught me to draw—I've caught any number of frogs.'

'Really, Mama? You know how?' James asked, awed.

'Really?' Alastair echoed, grinning at her.

She narrowed her eyes at him. 'I think I recognise a challenge when I hear one. Very well. *Attention*, Monsieur Grenouille!' Pushing up the sleeves of her pelisse, she walked to the edge of the pool.

'Don't fall in,' Alastair advised.

Ignoring him, she manoeuvred around a tree stump and crouched behind a big rock, eyeing her prey. Then, with a speed equal to Alastair's, she lunged forward, capturing a fat bullfrog before he could leap away.

'You did it, Mama!' James shrieked, almost dropping his own frog in his excitement.

'Bravo!' Alastair applauded. 'I'm impressed.'

'Would you like to hold it?' Diana asked Alastair in dulcet tones belied by the twinkle in her eye. When he demurred, she said, 'Shall we put them back, James, so they may swim for a while? Being held is very tiring for a frog.'

'Must I?'

'You can chase another one later. Why don't we sit here on the bank and watch them?'

With a sigh, James carefully lowered his frog to the water, where it leapt free and swam away. Diana pulled him to sit in front of her, smoothing his hair.

'Was this like the time you told me about,' he asked, leaning against her, 'when you went looking for plants with your papa and fell in the brook?'

'Yes, it was very like this.' To Alastair's look of enquiry, she explained, 'We'd gone hunting marsh irises. When I found one, I got so excited I slipped and fell in. Papa came to pull me out, scolding—but he slipped and fell in, too.' She smiled. 'We both started laughing, splashed water at each other, and then he wrapped me in his coat and carried me home for tea.'

'Well, if you fall in today, I promise to wrap you in *my* coat and carry you back,' Alastair said.

'Me, too?' James asked.

'Of course, you, too.'

'Good.' James snuggled back against his mother, who handed him a pebble to throw into the stream. 'You're Robbie's Uncle Alastair, aren't you?'

'Yes,' Alastair answered, puzzled by the question. Surely the boy hadn't forgotten him? 'We went for Sally Lunn cakes in Bath, you'll remember.'

'Oh, yes. They were very good. I just wondered, are you anyone's papa, too? 'Cause you'd be the bestest one. You know about cakes and soldiers and frogs and everything.'

Alastair swallowed hard. *I might have been yours.* 'No, I'm not a papa…yet.'

'Mama says my papa's gone to Heaven and I won't see him any more.'

'I know. I'm sorry. I imagine you miss him.'

The boy shrugged. 'I never saw him much. Minnie said he was a great man and had much important business. He didn't have time for soldiers or cakes or frogs.'

'Then he missed something much more important,' Alastair said sharply, his bitterness towards the Duke expanding to include the outrage of a little boy ignored. 'Spending time with you.'

James gazed up at him. 'You think I'm important?'

'Very important.'

The boy's face broke into a smile. 'Good. 'Cause I think you're important, too. Isn't he, Mama?'

Diana looked over at him, her expression tender. 'He is indeed.'

For an instant, the stream, the child, the bird chatter and brook gurgle faded. All Alastair could see, could feel, was Diana, smiling at him, her face no longer tense and guarded, but open, almost innocent. As he remembered it from all those years ago.

'Mama, look!'

Startled out of his reverie, Alastair watched the boy scramble down the bank. 'Is this the plant you found with your papa?' he asked Diana, pointing to a wildflower covered in tiny white blossoms.

'No, marsh irises bloom in the spring. That's a wood aster.'

'It's so pretty! It looks like stars!'

The words seemed to spring from somewhere deep within him. 'All the wonder of a starry sky/ held in two small hands.'

'Lovely,' Diana said. 'Is that from a poem?'

He shrugged. 'Perhaps the beginning of one.'

'I hadn't thought to ask how your writing has gone. Interrupted by the army, I would imagine, but I should think you'd have completed several volumes of verse by now.'

'Actually, I haven't written since... Not for a long time.'

'Well, you should. You're a wonderful poet! If you considered it a travesty that I haven't painted for years, it's even more so for you not to be writing.'

'Can we pick some of the flowers? For the bouquets?' James was asking.

'That would be lovely. Maybe some of those ferns, too.'

As he watched them gather the plants, Diana looking as carefree as he remembered her from long ago, he thought the day could not be more perfect.

A long-forgotten warmth and tenderness expanded his chest until he felt he might burst with the fullness of it. Thick and sweet as honey, it suffused him, seeping into every cold and bitter crevice of his soul.

The intensity of it brought tears to his eyes.

With a sudden shock, he recognised the emotion: joy. Something he had not experienced in all the years since Diana had jilted him to marry Graveston.

In another sweeping flash of insight, with the words to follow the lines he'd quoted churning and bubbling beneath the surface, he realised that he'd not given up poetry because it was juvenile, or had no place in the army. That inclination, like joy, had died when he lost Diana.

Mesmerised, he watched mother and child, awed by the wonder of it, swept away by the power of the emotion gripping him. The sun seemed warmer, the crystalline blue of the sky brighter, the breeze on his forehead softer. As if all his life, from then until now, had been lived under clouds, until Diana returned to dissipate them and bring him once again into full sunlight.

He'd known that Diana's years with Graveston had taught her to lock away her feelings. But he saw now that without her, he, too, had bottled up or suppressed his emotions. The restlessness, the unresolved anger, the fact that in no place and with no other woman had he found fulfilment, were mute testimony to a soul in bondage, waiting for the one catalyst that could set him free.

Diana. In some fashion beyond logic or reason, she…completed him. Made him whole again.

Savouring the joy, he knew in that moment that, whatever it took, however long it took, he had to win her back. He couldn't return to life in the shadows.

To win her, though, he'd have to help her find her

own way back to the light. And once she was free of the ghosts of her past, he couldn't let her go.

In a daze, distracted by his new insights, he took the flowers and ferns the two had gathered, escorted them back to the kitchen garden and found them a trug to hold their bounty, then bid them goodbye and went off to find the estate agent.

He rode about the estate with Hutchens, setting up assistance for the injured farmer, consulting with other tenants about the harvest, but while he said and did what was necessary, his mind hovered around the imperative of saving Diana, loving her, and having her back in his life.

It had been two weeks now; if Will didn't show up soon, he'd break down and go hunting for him.

It would be satisfying to confront Blankford directly. Alastair wished he might invent some pretext for challenging him, so he might get his fists on the man. Though, in his estimation of Blankford's character, the Duke probably didn't possess the physical courage to meet someone truly his match. He'd rather harass defenceless women, Alastair thought with scorn.

Well, Diana was one woman no Duke of Graveston would ever harass again. The sooner that business was done, the sooner he could begin his campaign to woo her back into his life.

Chapter Twenty

Fading daylight was turning the gold of the ripening fields to amber as Alastair rode back to the barns. After turning his mount over to a groom, he walked back to the house, his pace increasing, eager to wash, change, and seek out Diana.

Just thinking about seeing her made his heart leap with anticipation.

As he approached the side entrance, a carriage drove past him towards the stables. Excitement shocked through him. Might Will be back? Changing course, he sped towards the main entry.

To his delight, he did indeed find his cousin and his lovely, dark-haired wife in the hall, where his mother was embracing a little boy who looked a bit younger than James.

'Alastair, only see who Will has brought to visit us!' his mother cried as he ascended the steps. 'Elodie and Philippe! Well, young man,' she addressed the child, 'there's a boy here—and a puppy—who will be most happy to meet you!'

'*C'est ma tante—et mon cousin?*' the boy asked, pointing to Mrs Ransleigh and Alastair.

'*Oui*, Philippe, but you must practise your English now,' his mother said. 'Alastair, how good to see you again.'

'And you, Elodie. You're looking very well! Living in Paris must agree with you.'

'Paris is my heart, but it is my garden at Salmford that refreshes me, as my loving husband knows.'

'Let Wendell show you to your rooms, so you can get settled!' his mother said. 'Perhaps we can meet for wine and light refreshments before dinner, so our two young boys can become acquainted?'

'That would be lovely, Tante Grace,' Elodie replied. 'Philippe, *viens avec Maman.*'

'I'll be up in a moment,' Will said, squeezing his wife's hand before releasing her to ascend the stairs behind Wendell, while the boy trotted after her, gazing about this new dwelling with unselfconscious curiosity.

'I know you've been anxious, but I thought I'd stop long enough to bring Elodie and her son with me. Let the ladies and the boys get acquainted, while I let you know where things stand. Shall we talk now, or later?'

'Now—once I find Diana. I couldn't discuss what concerns her so nearly without her present.'

'She's like Elodie, then,' Will said. 'Not one to put up with men making decisions for her.'

'After what she endured at her husband's hands, one can hardly blame her. Even if she does trust us.'

'As I recall from years ago, she was always lively and spirited, discussing, with the expertise and directness of a man, topics far removed from the normal feminine concerns.' Will shook his head and laughed. 'A horse-breeder, a French exile, a maligned duchess? We Ransleighs do seem to find unusual women.'

'Truly! Let me go fetch this one. Shall I meet you in the library? If she's where I suspect, I'll be back directly.'

He did indeed find Diana at her easel in the north parlour she'd taken over as her studio. As she looked up upon his entry, he said abruptly, 'Will's back.'

Her eyes widened and she gasped. 'Did he tell you—?'

'Not yet. I thought you'd want to be there to hear his account, too.'

'I would, thank you. Shall I come now?'

He nodded. Hastily pulling off the apron that protected her gown, she tossed it beside the easel and walked to him. 'I'll worry about cleaning paint off my fingers later. Did he…give you any hint of what occurred?'

'No. But he tarried long enough to collect his wife and her son. If something were amiss, I think he would have come directly here.'

He held out his hand, and with a shuddering breath, she took it. 'I hope so.'

He gave her fingers a reassuring squeeze. 'Remember, whatever he has to report, I will make sure you and James are safe.' *Safe and with me*, he added silently.

She gave him a slight smile. 'I do trust you. I just don't want to put you at risk—again.'

'You won't. Not this time.'

They found Will in the library, lounging in one of the leather wing chairs, sipping his brandy. He scrambled to his feet as they entered.

And made Diana a deep bow. 'Duchess,' he said, his face unreadable.

A tiny frown came and went on her forehead. 'Never that. Once it was "Will" and "Diana". I'd prefer that, if you please.'

They stared at each other, Diana standing erect and unflinching under Will's hard, assessing gaze. Alastair held his breath, hoping what he'd told Will and what his cousin had learned at Graveston Court would triumph over any anger his cousin still harboured towards Diana for the anguish she'd caused him—and those who cared about him.

After a moment, apparently satisfied, Will nodded. 'Diana, then, if I'm to be Will again.'

'I would like that—if you can bear it.'

'From what I've discovered, it is you who had much to bear.'

'Please proceed, Will,' Alastair said. 'And leave out no detail.'

After motioning them to a seat, Will began. 'I arrived at Wickham's End in my guise as pedlar two days after Alastair left Salmford, bringing along two of my men, posing as horse-traders, in case I needed reinforcement. After taking a bed at the local public house, I proceeded to the taproom and announced, with some boasting about my wares, that I'd be making rounds of any interested households. Of course, they all were.'

'Played a few hands of cards, too, I'd guess,' Alastair interjected.

'Naturally. How else could a poor pedlar afford a room? While I won a little, lost a little, I got to hear all the local gossip. Since the death of a duke and the arrival of his heir were the most significant events to occur in that small village for a decade, talk soon turned to that.'

'What did you learn?' Diana asked.

'They'd heard nothing of the sort immediately after the old Duke's demise, but more recently, someone had been going about, stirring up rumours. Some said the new Duke's man was asking for witnesses, saying the Dowager Duchess might be complicit in her husband's death. Opinion seemed divided over the possibility. Some said she was a cold woman, not properly submissive to her husband. Others denied that, telling of a friend or relation who'd received clothing or baskets of food from her, and argued it was she who'd done the most to share the Duke's wealth with the community. All knew Graveston as a hard, proud, unapproachable man.' Will laughed. 'One said "if his lady done him in, he probably deserved it".'

'And then what?' Alastair asked, impatient to get to the crux of the story.

'I made my rounds in town, then to some of the tenant farmers—where I had my first break. Gossiping while admiring a trinket she couldn't afford, the farm wife said her no-good brother-in-law was boasting of doing some work for new Duke, that was going to set him up right—serving as a witness against the old Duchess, who was for murdering her husband. It was the work of an afternoon to track down this Jamie Peters and invite him to share a pint. A few hands of cards and a great quantity of gin later, he confided he was to testify that he'd bought large amounts of laudanum for the Dowager Duchess, who told him she was going to slip a little more each day into the old Duke's food unnoticed.'

'The scoundrel!' Alastair exploded.

'You see?' Diana cried, grim-faced. 'I knew Blankford would do whatever it took to incriminate me.'

Will held up a hand. 'Calm down—I'm not finished yet. I asked Mr Peters if he was aware of the penalties for perjury. Painted a vivid picture of prison hulks, transportation and hanging. After giving him a moment to digest that, I suggested if he wanted cash, I would give him more than the Duke was offering if he would shut his mouth and resettle in another area of England. After some…encouragement, he was persuaded to take my money and leave.'

'Encouragement?' Alastair repeated, his eyebrows raised.

'Well, I might have suggested my sword could make short work of a man who'd shred a woman's reputation and risk her life for a handful of coins. I had one of my men escort him to Falmouth, so he might take ship and start a new life in the Americas. Farewell, incriminating witness.'

'Bravo!' Alastair cried.

'There's more. I also persuaded Peters to give me the names of the household staff who were supposedly assisting him and the Duke in their nefarious enterprise. During a trip to show off my wares at Graveston Court, I found all those he named owed their positions to the previous housekeeper, a Mrs Heathson, who just happened to be recently reinstated into her former position by the new Duke.'

'Tall, dark-haired, hatchet-faced?' Alastair asked. When Will raised his eyebrows, he explained, 'I encountered her when I called on Graveston.'

'I then paid a visit to Mrs Forbes, the displaced housekeeper, who, by the way, was turned off without a character and no settlement of wages by the new Duke. She'd gone to stay with the retired governess, eking out a living doing hand work. She told me the old Duke had hired her after the previous housekeeper, fanatically loyal to the Duke's first wife, nearly killed the second wife with overdoses of laudanum when the girl was being "sedated for a nervous condition".'

Will looked over at Diana. 'Nervous condition? I never thought you nervous in your life.'

'When you attempt to leave your husband, are dragged back from the posting inn by his minions and locked into your room, it can make you nervous,' she said bitterly.

Will's face hardened. 'I can well imagine. Mrs Forbes said all sorts of rumours flew around among the staff as the Duchess recovered, though none dared say or do anything for fear of losing their position. Some seemed sympathetic to the Duchess. Others, siding with Mrs Heathson, gave her trouble the whole time she remained at Graveston Court. During that time, Mrs Heathson continued to visit Cook and her other friends among the staff, who often spent their off-days with her. Apparently she never sought another position; Mrs Forbes suspected that the heir, Lord Blankford, was paying her. She was convinced Blankford was also paying some of the disaffected staff to spy on the Duchess and the household. In fact, when the Duke was discovered dead, Mrs Forbes had her suspicions that Cook might have been hired—or persuaded—to do to the Duke the laudanum trick Mrs Heathson had tried with his wife. But within hours of the old Duke's death, Mrs Heathson returned to Graveston Court with a letter under Blankford's seal, informing Mrs Forbes she had been discharged and must leave immediately, or the sheriff would eject her.

With no other recourse, she had little choice but to depart.'

'Would she be willing to testify to all of that in court?' Alastair demanded.

'Yes, particularly as she no longer has to fear retribution for her honesty. It seems she very recently received a, um, handsome bequest to keep her comfortably for the next few months—and the offer of a new position at a fine establishment in Sussex.'

'Remind me to reimburse you the bequest and the resettlement money,' Alastair said.

Will gave an airy wave of the hand. 'No need. Happy to be of service to a fellow Rogue.'

'Are there any others who would testify for Diana?'

'Mrs Forbes named three or four, who fear for their positions now that Mrs Heathson has returned—or just don't approve of her actions against the Duchess. They could also assert that all those accusing the Duchess were hostile to her, if not actually in Blankford's employ even before his father's death.'

'So the primary witness against Diana is now missing, and Mrs Forbes can testify to Mrs Heathson's dealings in laudanum and previous attempt against Diana and her involvement with disaffected members of household,' Alastair summarised.

'That's about it,' Will concluded.

'Excellent job, Will! Even if Blankford has the local magistrate in his pocket and can induce him to write out a warrant, the evidence would never stand in a summary trial, much less in the Lords.'

'Our uncle would see to that.'

'As it happens, I had a very surprising interview with the Earl,' Alastair said. 'After confessing to him we might soon be providing a spectacle with more scandalous twists and turns than a penny opera, I braced myself for a tongue-lashing—that never came. He seemed positively…friendly. It was quite unnerving.'

Will laughed. 'Max can hardly believe the change in his father.'

'We have enough evidence now to convince Graveston it would not be wise to proceed,' Alastair concluded, exultant. 'If he's irrational enough to go forward in any event, so be it. Good work, Will.'

'Did you expect anything less?' Will asked with a grin.

'No—I had full confidence.'

'We aim to please. I'll leave the two of you to plot strategy. I'm famished, and I could use a wash. Diana, it's good to have you back from the wilderness.'

Her eyes widened in surprise before she said,

'Thank you, Will. It's not quite the same, but I think I feel some of what you must have felt, transported from the street into the bosom of the Rogues.'

'We're a shifty lot, but loyal. We'll never let you down.'

'So I should have believed years ago, and spared all of you—this.'

Will gave her hand a pat. 'Wouldn't have missed it. We Rogues like nothing so much as a good fight. I'll see you at dinner.'

As Will walked out, Diana, who'd said nothing during Will's recitation beyond her one outburst, looked over to Alastair. 'Do you think it's enough?'

'More than enough for any sane, rational man. Is Graveston sane and rational?' He shrugged. 'Only he knows that. I'll press him hard, and we'll see.'

At her troubled look, he gave her a quick hug. Holding her at arm's length, willing her to share the confidence he now felt, he said, 'One way or the other, we can move forward. Graveston can force a scandal if he chooses, but your final vindication is not in doubt. Regardless, we'll stand by you, me and all my family. James will stay with you, where he belongs, and we'll fight for what is due both of you. You believe that, don't you?'

'Yes. Just…I have no confidence that Graveston

will prove reasonable. I wish it could be settled without a fight—without the danger of scandal for you.'

'You heard Will,' Alastair replied with a smile. 'We Ransleighs relish a scrap.'

She shuddered. 'I'll pray for Graveston to be reasonable. When…will we go?'

'*I'll* go,' he corrected. 'Tomorrow. I've been itching to confront the man again since our previous encounter.'

'I thought we were to confront him together this time.'

'Only if the matter went to court. I think we have enough to break him and keep it from going that far…but if he sees you, it might revive his anger and harden his resolve.'

'I suppose you're right,' she said with a sigh.

'You trust me, don't you?'

'You know I do.'

'Besides, do you really want to go back to Graveston Court?'

She shuddered. 'No. Never.'

'Then let me do this for you. Let me do it for us.'

He didn't think there'd been anything threatening in his tone, but Diana frowned. 'Promise me you won't beat him to death. Then we really would have to flee to Paris.'

'I'll try to restrain myself. Mama will take care of you while I'm gone.'

'She's been very kind. But I can take care of myself too, you know.'

Alastair's smile faded. 'You've had only you to care for you, for too many years. But that's over. You'll never be without friends and allies again.'

'Avenging Alastair.'

'For you, yes. It's time to finish this.' *And move on to so much more.*

Noting she still looked troubled, he added in a lighter tone, 'I'm hoping for a quick resolution— and then a swift end to chastity.'

As he'd hoped, the anxious lines in her face smoothed and she laughed. 'Rogue. I hope to make that end worth your while.'

In a flash, his imagination raced off like a thoroughbred at the starting gun. Battling back images of her smooth naked skin under his hands, he groaned. 'Temptress! I'd better get myself ready for dinner, before I think too much about what I'd rather be getting ready for.'

She smiled that naughty smile that made his breath hitch and his body harden. 'Don't worry. I'll be ready, too.'

Chapter Twenty-One

Next morning, Diana bid Alastair goodbye in the breakfast room—all too formally, under the eye of his mother, when she would have preferred to send him off after a luxurious episode in bed.

Praying earnestly that Blankford would surprise her by being reasonable, and too agitated to concentrate on her painting, Diana set out for the garden. She'd restlessly circled the cutting garden, intent on walking towards the woods, when she encountered Will's wife, Elodie.

'Mrs Ransleigh has lovely gardens,' Elodie said after greeting her.

'I understand you are quite an enthusiastic gardener.'

She nodded. 'I've found such peace in a garden, during some of the most difficult times of my life.' She smiled. 'My Will, he bought Salmford for us because of the gardens. The fields were fallow, the tenants surly and in need of guidance. The seller was surely laughing behind his hand, thinking he'd made a bargain over a city man who didn't know a plough from a potato. But the gardens of the manor were magnificent and now, the fields too have responded to love and care.'

Responded to love and care. 'Like a neglected child,' she murmured, reminded at once of her own situation.

'And men. Will tells me Alastair is protecting your son.'

Diana felt a wave of gratitude. 'My son, and me— though he had no good reason to do so.'

'They act for honour, these Ransleighs. What is life, without your child? You are wise to defy even the greatest to keep him.'

'You give me too much credit. I hardly cherished him for most of his years, but I'm trying to do better.'

Elodie's eyebrows shot up. 'You were estranged from your son?'

'Factors…prevented me from becoming close to him.' At the incomprehension on Elodie's face, she said, 'The situation was…complicated.'

'I know what it is to battle against powerful men. One caused me to lose my son, too, when he was still very small. Every day I missed him, longed for him, cherished all the memories I had of him. And when I finally found him again, Philippe…didn't even recognise me.' Tears welled in her eyes.

How would she feel if James were indifferent to her, rather than eager for his mother's love? Something painful twisted in her chest. Maybe shutting herself off from her son was not the worst thing that could have happened.

'It must have been terrible.'

'Not so much, for him. He had a stepmother with a high position in Society, who lavished him with love. But he is *my* son, and I wanted to be part of his life. Will helped that happen.'

'Does he remember you now?'

'Sometimes, I think he does. But no matter. His stepmother is a good woman. She works with me.' Elodie laughed. 'She must, for if she did not, my rogue of a husband, knowing how much my son means to me, told her he would simply steal him away.'

'Will would protect you at all costs.'

'He would. You ache for all the lost years with your son, no? So did I. But it is coming back, the bond we once shared. It will for you, too.'

Diana sighed. 'If I don't end up on the gallows, or so disgraced that the Court of Chancery takes my son away.'

Elodie shook her head. 'Will would never allow that, nor Alastair. If he must turn up more rogues and reprobates to testify, he would do so. In the meantime, we rebuild, eh? Love is important, the most important thing. For children. For women. Hold on to your Alastair.'

Diana shook her head. 'He's not "my" Alastair.'

'He would be, if you want him. Good men, they are not so easy to find.'

'I'm well aware of that,' Diana said with a wry smile. 'But good men...deserve good women.'

'Then be one.'

'I'm not sure I can. I'm not sure I know how,' she admitted, voicing her deepest anxiety.

'When life has treated you roughly, it is hard to imagine it becoming better. Believe in it fiercely enough, though, and you can make it so. But I'll not tease you any more. Now, shall we return? There are two boys who, I think, will have the nursery destroyed if we do not hurry back.'

Nodding, Diana turned with her, and the talk moved to a discussion of the flowers they were passing. But as they walked back to the house, Diana wondered: could she put the shattered pieces of herself back together to make a woman good enough to deserve a man like Alastair?

And what would the future hold if she couldn't?

* * *

After a week closeted with his solicitor, doing some investigation of his own, Alastair presented himself once again at Graveston Court.

As he was being escorted by the butler to the same imposing salon, he encountered the house-keeper. The expressionless stare he returned to her mock of a curtsy chased the knowing smirk from her lips and sent her retreating in the opposite direction.

Forewarned by his previous visit, he came prepared for the Duke's reception, pulling a small volume of Shakespeare's sonnets from his pocket as soon as he took an armchair near the cold hearth. When the Duke's arrival was announced by the butler a goodly time later, Alastair did not lift his eyes from the page, continuing instead to read for some minutes before at last looking up to greet his host.

'I hope I'm not interrupting?' the Duke said, an edge of irritation in his voice.

'Not at all,' he replied amiably. 'While on campaign with Wellington, I found reading a wonderful diversion to occupy the tedium between battles.'

'Is it to be a battle, then? You will choose to sacrifice your reputation by supporting That Woman in a losing cause? I am grieved to hear it.'

Since neither the Duke's expression nor his tone

carried a hint of sadness, Alastair grinned. 'So I see. I had hoped that, given the time to consider your course of action, you would reconsider.'

The Duke made a scornful sound. 'It sounds like you are still taken in by her. I never understood the spell she seems able to cast on men—even one as disciplined as my father!'

Holding on to his temper, Alastair said evenly, 'Since we'll never agree on the character of the Dowager Duchess, shall we dispense with discussing her? I'm hoping you will see reason in not proceeding with what could only become an ugly scandal, that would have the great name of Mannington gossiped about by every groom, footman, and busybody from here to London.'

'I'm not concerned about that,' Graveston said loftily. 'Only with justice.'

'Indeed? Of course, you may rush ahead like a fool if you choose, but before you embarrass yourself, perhaps even place yourself and your reputation in danger, there are some points you should consider.'

'Place *myself* in danger?' The Duke laughed. 'I hardly think so.'

Not bothering to contest that boast, Alastair continued. 'First, there's the matter of claiming guardianship of your half-brother. If it came to the Court of Chancery, I would feel compelled to repeat for them the threats you made against the boy.'

'Threats?' he exclaimed. 'What nonsense! I told you only that I wanted to have him raised as befits his birth!'

'True. But you also said you wanted the boy to "suffer as you suffered" and "learn to serve your son". Observations I imagine the gentlemen of the court would find most interesting.'

The Duke's eyes narrowed. 'Even if you made such accusations, it would be your word against mine.'

Alastair fixed on him a steely-eyed stare. In a quiet voice, he said, 'I'm sure you don't mean to imply you would question my veracity before the court. Think carefully before you answer, lest you have a need to choose weapons and find a second.'

Alastair almost hoped Graveston would be too ir-rational to step back. His fingers itched for a sword or pistol, to make this man with all the advantages of wealth, position and authority face someone more his equal than a widow whose only resource was the loyalty of her friends.

To his satisfaction, the Duke looked away first. 'Let's not be so hasty.'

'Then you'll agree you have no reason to appeal to Chancery for custody of the boy. Now, on the question of making accusations of foul play against Dowager Duchess, I've made some enquiries on my own, and discovered a number of witnesses who can attest to your hatred for the Dowager, even of threats to harm her when you inherited.'

Graveston stirred uneasily. 'I'm sure I made no such threats.'

'You did so to me. In any event, the Dowager did not stand to gain materially by her husband's death. You, however, did. I understand you've accumulated some debts.'

'How did you—?' the Duke sputtered. Recovering himself, he said, 'Nothing exorbitant.'

'Then there's the former housekeeper, who I understand was dismissed by your father for attempting to poison the Dowager. One would have thought, faced with the enmity of as powerful a man as a duke, she would have taken herself far, far away. Yet she stayed nearby, even coming and going to this house to visit members of the staff, all who were known to be loyal to you. If your father *was* poisoned, this woman, who had attempted it once before, who was discharged by your father and thus had a motive to wish him ill, had both access and expertise to do so. A woman who, I believe, you have reinstated in her former position as housekeeper. How much did you intend to pay her for her work, once all this was settled?'

'Pay her for—?' he echoed incredulously. 'You can't seriously contend that *I* had anything to do with my father's death!'

Continuing as if he'd not heard, Alastair said, 'The court might wish to have your father exhumed, though I understand coroners disagree on whether poison would leave any trace in someone this long buried. The court would certainly want to know more about your relationship with Mrs Heathson and why you reinstated a woman accused of attempting to murder your stepmother. And then there's the matter of your mistress. Very expensive, I'm told, with a rapacious appetite for jewels. So expensive, you approached your bank in the City to borrow more funds.'

While Graveston gaped at him, Alastair shook his head. 'I have to say, I don't think it would look good. An heir in need of cash hiring a disgruntled former employee to do away with his father, then threatening the poor widow's reputation to try to cheat her of her portion so he can drape diamonds around his mistress's neck. The penny press would be salivating at the courtroom door.'

Leaving Graveston no time to reply, Alastair continued, 'For the sake of argument, let's say the assizes believed your version of events. There's still the matter of a trial—in the House of Lords, which my uncle has run for years. I regret to say, he's no admirer of your late father, either.'

The Duke was looking less certain by the minute. 'Are you so sure the Earl would wish to become involved? After all, he didn't lift a finger for his son Max. I expect he'd be even less inclined to be saddled with cleaning up your scandal.'

'What's one more scandal to a Rogue?' Alastair asked with a shrug. 'Besides, "cleaning up" is what my uncle does best. He thrives on it, or so he assured me when I warned him about possible proceedings.'

'You've talked with him about this?'

'Of course. I'd never have pressed forward in so critical a matter without his approval.'

After giving that a moment to sink in, Alastair changed tactics. 'A distasteful business,' he said with a dismissive wave of the hand. 'It's not seemly that the noble name of Graveston, the family of the Manningtons, who've served their country since the Conquest, should be associated with such a sordid tale. Nor is there any need that it should be. If necessary, however, I'm quite willing to match my witnesses against yours. It's up to you.'

At that, he sat back and gazed out the window, calm, confident and at ease.

For a long time, the only sound in the room was the tick of the mantel clock. Finally, the Duke said, 'What does the bitch want?'

'If you take that tone,' Alastair snapped, 'I shall be forced to proceed regardless. I'm quite willing to let Society weigh my reputation against yours, in the court of public opinion or in the Lords. A hero of Badajoz, frequent leader of the "forlorn hope", valiant defender of Waterloo against a provincial aristocrat who has done—what have you done? Ah, married a wealthy girl and attempted to coerce a helpless widow. Now, would you like to rephrase your question?'

His expression simmering resentment, Graveston stared at Alastair with sullen eyes. 'What does the Dowager want?' he said at last, enunciating each word separately, as if they were being pulled out of him.

'*She* wants nothing. What I want, though, is merely what is due to her. She will waive dower, while you facilitate transfer of the reasonable amount already stipulated in your father's will— yes, I've seen a copy of it, already filed for probate—plus what was bequeathed to Lord James. Who is, as you've pointed out, the son of a duke and should be reared as such. I want you to cease your harassment and abandon any attempts to prosecute her, a process that would in any event never get further than the local court you could control. Win a judgement against her in the Lords? That horse won't jump, Graveston. You have the title and a lucrative estate. Why not show yourself worthy of both?'

The Duke sprang up and took a turn about the room. 'Just—let her go, with no retribution? You cannot know what it was like to have your mother, who lived for your father's approval and wanted only to please him, ignored, scorned, once he was besotted by *her*. I might have understood it if she seemed to care for him, for anything. But all she ever showed was an icy disdain. Still, my father was consumed by her! He had no time for me; I was packed off to school, and when I was older and protested his excessive absorption in her, he even raised his hand to me!'

Despite his disgust for the Duke's campaign for revenge, Alastair could hear in the man's voice the lingering pain of an abandoned boy who'd seen his beloved mother humiliated and discarded. He knew only too well how abandonment and humiliation could fester within, a canker in the gut.

'It must have been difficult,' Alastair said quietly, a reluctant sympathy tempering his disdain. 'But that neglect was the fault of your father, not the Dowager, who had no more choice over your father's actions than you did.'

'Choice?' he scoffed. 'What was there to choose? He made her, the daughter of a nobody, into a duchess!'

'Impossible as you—and he—seem to find it, she had no desire to be a duchess, as her behaviour made quite evident. But I understand the need to exact retribution for the unfairness of it all. I suggest a remedy with a more suitable opponent.' Alastair lifted his hands and flexed them into fists. 'Me.'

The Duke's scowl turned to astonishment. 'Meet you? For fisticuffs?'

'We can resolve this here and now, man to man, out of the vulgar public gaze—more fitting behaviour for the heir to a great and noble title. Or we can have fisticuffs by lawyer, in full view of gawking spectators in the gallery of the Lords and in front of print-shop windows. That way, I promise you, you will surely lose, dragging your title and name into the mud when you do.'

Graveston frowned, looking furious—but uncertain. 'You can't seriously think a few well-placed blows could right all the wrongs done to me and my mother.'

'Nothing can undo that—not fisticuffs, nor a public vendetta against the Dowager that would shame you more than it would her. All one can hope for is to assuage the sting of past injustice, and let it go,' he advised, the truth of those words in his own situation resonating within him.

He held up his fists again. 'That is, if you're man enough. Or would you rather vent your spleen on a woman?'

'I'm no coward, despite what you insinuate,' Graveston snarled.

'Then meet me. Expend that anger and resentment, and call it done.'

While Graveston appeared to weigh the matter, Alastair added, 'It's difficult to give up a grievance, especially one well founded. But it's better for the soul.'

'A ridiculous solution,' Graveston muttered.

'Perhaps. Before I leave you to stew in bitterness, might I ask the courtesy of knowing your intentions? If you won't tell me, I shall feel compelled to proceed with the evidence I've gathered.'

Anger and frustration played across the face of a man too engulfed by tumultuous emotion to mask them. 'Very well,' he said at last. 'Fisticuffs it is. Not here, though.'

'Certainly not. I wouldn't wish to damage any of your father's carefully collected knick-knacks,' Alastair said, running his finger over a vase on the table beside him.

'Heathen!' Graveston said with a reluctant smile. 'That Greek hydria from the third century BC is probably worth more than your entire stable.'

'Ah, a stable! That would be just the place.'

And so it was that the Duke of Graveston and Mr Alastair Ransleigh of Barton Abbey retreated to the stable, banished the gawking grooms and coachmen, claimed an unoccupied stall and proceeded to try to pummel out each other's frustration.

Having obtained what he sought, Alastair intended to go easy on the peer, but found to his surprise that the young Duke held his own pretty well. He even managed to land two or three well-disguised feints that were going to leave Alastair with a bruised jaw for the foreseeable future.

Sometime later, after they were both panting and bloodied, Alastair held up a hand. 'Shall we call a draw?'

Holding his sides, the Duke nodded. When he

could catch his breath, he said, 'You were right. It doesn't change the past, but it did…help.'

'I'm glad,' Alastair said in perfect truth. A man who would persecute a woman was despicable. But a man who could finally realise he was in the wrong, alter his course—and could throw quite a respectable right hook in the bargain—deserved a second chance. 'Then we are agreed.'

Graveston sighed. 'I've spent the last five years dreaming of revenge for my mother…and myself. It's hard to let that go. There's the temptation to keep fighting, even at the cost of tarnishing my reputation.'

'Shooting your best hunting dog to take down a pigeon? Not wise.'

'No—though oh-so-satisfying. But…yes, we're agreed. I'll inform my solicitor not to delay any longer the execution of Father's will. Your Dowager will get her properties. I'd prefer that she and the brat not use the Dower House, though. I'd prefer they remain out of my sight permanently.'

'I see no difficulty there. She has no more desire to set foot at Graveston Court than you do to see her here, and since the boy will inherit other properties, there's no need for him to reside here either. In return, I'll pledge that as long as you keep our bargain, I'll not present my evidence to the Lords.'

Pleased to have achieved the results he wanted, Alastair felt he could be magnanimous and forgive the insults Graveston had flung at him. Smiling, he offered his hand.

Reluctantly, the Duke shook it.

'One last bit of advice. When you take your seat in the Lords, I'd still be wary of my uncle.'

'Thank you; I'll remember that.' Graveston shook his head. 'I'll never understand the fascination she elicits in men. She certainly won a strong champion in you.'

'So she did. If you're tempted to forget our agreement, remember that.'

Chapter Twenty-Two

Euphoria in his heart, Alastair set off for Barton Abbey, riding as fast as he could change horses. He knew Diana was anxious, despite her trust in him. He couldn't wait to set her worries at rest.

Finally, they could move on to resolve the situation between them, resume the progress of their relationship that had been arrested when the threat against her demanded her removal to safety under his mother's roof.

How would she choose to resolve it? Anticipation and anxiety warred within as he contemplated her possible reaction.

She'd more or less said she wished to resume their physical relationship. Would she allow more than that? Could he be satisfied with less than a full commitment from her?

Ah, how he wished to cosset and care for her! Shower her with so much attention and love that the grim years with Graveston receded into distant memory, blurred by time until they seemed like events in the life of a stranger.

Would she let him?

The only thing he knew for certain was he didn't want her to walk away.

Three days of hard riding later, he had arrived at Barton Abbey in the late afternoon. Leaving his lathered horse at the stables, he had jogged to the house, impatient to bathe, change, and seek her out as quickly as possible.

A bare half-hour later, his still-dripping hair slicked down and his damp shirt sticking to his back, he found her at her easel in her north-salon studio.

He'd approached quietly, easing the door open, anxious to drink in the sight of her for a moment before she was aware of his presence.

How lovely she was, he marvelled, his heart contracting with joy and longing at the sight of her. Even better, her expression looked intent but serene as she studied her canvas, with no dark shadows of worry beneath her eyes and the once-wary set of her shoulders relaxed.

After a moment, some sixth sense must have alerted her she was under scrutiny, for she stilled, then looked over at him. 'Alastair,' she cried, the happiness in her voice the sweetest music to his needy ears.

Unable to resist, he paced towards her, picked her up and swung her around in his arms when she ran to meet him, then sat her down and kissed her thoroughly.

'Ah, how much I've missed that!' he murmured, cradling her to the rapid beating of his heart.

She looked up at him anxiously. 'It must have gone well. You wouldn't look so happy, if it had not.'

How much he wanted to sweep her into his arms, carry her up to his chamber, and make love to her for a week! 'I could be happier. But alas, that will have to wait a bit longer. Come, sit, and I'll tell you all about it.'

Contenting himself, for the moment, with one more quick kiss, he escorted her to the sofa and gave her a full accounting of his interview with the Duke of Graveston.

'He will truly let it go?' she asked, her tone disbelieving. 'Are you sure?'

'I think so. But if he should change his mind, he's been warned.'

She gave a little sigh. 'So there's still the possibility he might try to destroy your reputation.'

'Though we can't totally eliminate the risk, I think it unlikely. If it should happen, we'll deal with it. Your ultimate vindication is sure, even if he were so unwise as to proceed.'

'As is scandal and disrespect to your name, if he should proceed.'

How he wished he could set her mind completely at rest! 'Sweeting, we can't live in fear of shadows.'

'Live in fear of shadows,' she repeated with a sad smile. 'Ah, Alastair, I've done that for so long, I don't know how to live in sunlight.'

'You'll learn. I'll help you.'

'After all those years in the shadows, I know I'm…damaged. I don't know how to forget them, how to heal. If I can heal.' She traced his cheek, her touch tender. 'You deserve so much more. Someone whole, whose love has no shadows.'

It wasn't the full-fledged avowal he longed for, but… Once, sensing how close she was to telling him everything he wanted to hear, he might have pushed her for more. But she'd been pushed and manipulated enough. More than that, if they were to have a future together, it would have to be her choice, free and clear.

He gave her a wry smile. 'Diana, there is no one for me but you. For too many years, I tried to deny it, but after finding you again, I no longer fight that truth. I love you and I want you in my life, in whatever way you are comfortable. I'd prefer you as my wife, but I'll take whatever you can give me. Mistress. Friend. Adviser. Just let me stay close and help you heal. If you needed friends and allies against a duke, you'll need them even more battling the demons of the past. But that's what I desire. What do you want?'

She rubbed his hand, her expression anxious. 'I'm still not sure. A place of my own, to start over.'

'You can stay at Barton Abbey until the provisions of your husband's will are carried out. Which, by the way, buttress your position. Despite the animosity between you, Graveston left a substantial sum to you and an even more handsome one to your son. Not quite the act of a man at war with his wife.'

'It was war, though, most of the time. The Duke had won his trophy, but he could not make me compliant. Having given up all I wanted and everything I loved, defiance was all I had left. It…confounded him. He'd never met resistance that couldn't be broken. After all, he'd been raised since birth to believe the world should rearrange itself to suit him; he had only to express a desire and it was gratified. I think he found it incomprehensible that a woman, especially one who'd not been born into the highest aristocracy, would not abandon her childish op-position and go from reluctance to delight that he'd deigned to make her a duchess.'

'He should have believed it,' Alastair said. 'You told him forcefully enough.'

'It took him a long time to finally realise it. Years of tracking down and then removing everything that meant anything to me, until he had nothing left with which to try to control me.'

Alastair hadn't wanted to ask—the prospect made him sick to contemplate—but somehow the words forced themselves out. 'Not even beating you?'

'Ah. Beating. That was perhaps most frustrat-ing of all to him. Eventually he realised—unlike, I suspect, his poor first wife—that I had no fear of physical punishment. What was physical pain, com-pared to the agony of all I had lost, what I would never have?'

Rising, she paced away from him, making a cir-cuit of the room. Though he wanted to go after her, pull her into his arms, offer comfort, he knew he had to leave her be.

Finally, she looked back at him. 'I've had time these last few weeks, finally free of his menace, to think about all that happened. I found myself wondering if I did indeed overestimate his power. Perhaps he would only have threatened, but never actually used Papa's debts to put him in prison or find perjured witnesses to ruin you. All I knew was that I loved you so much, I would rather die than destroy you. He understood that and was shrewd enough to use it.'

'That doesn't make him less despicable in my eyes. I do wish, though, that you'd doubted his influence enough to come to me then.'

'So do I. But wishing won't change the past. By the end, I think in his own way, he was…fond of me. Not that he would have let me leave him, but I think he respected my courage in resisting him, even as it infuriated and perplexed him. Of course, a Duke of Graveston could not admit he'd been wrong; he never returned the books or paints or musical instruments he'd had taken away. But when he came back from London, things would appear. An exquisite antique Greek vase in my sitting room. New gowns and costly furs in my wardrobe. His way, I suppose, of reaching out, asking for peace between us. If I had deferred to him then, even a little, he might have considered his victory finally won, given me back all he'd taken and treated me as less of a prisoner. But after years of suppressing all emotion save defiance, I didn't know any other way to be. I *couldn't* yield to him—if I had dismantled any of the barriers that had kept me upright through years of siege, I risked the whole edifice tumbling down.'

She sighed. 'It may be bad of me, but I'm glad he's dead, and I'm free at last.'

'Perhaps one day, you'll be able to forgive him. But I can't deny that I, too, am glad he's dead and that you are free to do whatever you want.'

'What I want,' she repeated, shaking her head. 'Once I knew exactly what I wanted—you. Us. Our future together. When I had to give that up, I merely survived, holding on to the few pieces of myself by resisting. Now that I don't have to fight any more, I'm not sure what to do, where to go. I spent nearly nine years of my life virtually alone, pushing back against the forces of the world, first Graveston, then his son. Like a game of tug of war one plays as a child, pulling and pulling and pulling, until suddenly, when your opponent gives way, you fall backward into nothingness.'

'Is that how you feel—that you've fallen into a void?'

She shivered and rubbed her arms, as if chilled. 'Yes,' she admitted in a whisper. 'I loved you. I always loved you. I never stopped. But I pushed the emotion deep within, until it was frozen far below the surface of my thoughts. When I was a child, tromping a winter field with Papa, intent on finding a particular plant, I'd go on until my toes and fingers were numb. Once home by the fire, I'd slowly unthaw, feet and hands burning and tingling in pain. I don't know how long it will take me to unthaw my heart from all the years with Graveston, or how much pain there will be. It's…frightening, to not know who you are any more.'

He couldn't help it then; he had to take her in his arms. To his relief, she clung to him willingly. The shivering increased, until he realised, for the first time, she was weeping.

Her sobs grew in intensity until her whole body shuddered in his arms. His heart aching for her anguish, he tightened his grip.

'I'll be here for you always, however long it takes. Whatever happens. You'll never be alone, never again afraid,' he whispered into her hair. 'I love you, Diana. I always have; I never stopped. I will always love you.'

For a long time, he simply held her, until at last the sobbing lessened, then ceased and she leaned against him, limp in his arms.

He closed his eyes, savouring the feel of her cradled to his chest. Even as his body clamoured for more, he rebuked it.

Yes, he wanted more; he wanted everything. But he was wiser now, no longer an impetuous boy, insisting on having it all *now*. Breaking a nervous, green filly, one couldn't force her; she must come to him on her own terms.

He could wait as long as it took.

After several grim years lost in an emotional wilderness, he'd once again found the centre of his universe. And he would never, ever give her up again.

Pulling away from Alastair, Diana sat up, feeling dizzy and disorientated. She'd wept—in Alastair's arms. Actually shed tears, something she hadn't done since the terrible night she'd realised she must marry the Duke and Alastair was lost to her for ever.

Embarrassment replaced surprise as she looked at the soggy cravat, now hanging limply at his throat. 'I'm afraid I've ruined your neckcloth. I'm so sorry.'

He made a gesture of dismissal. 'Don't be. I've got others. Besides, the first part of healing is letting go.' He smiled, the tenderness of his expression making her chest ache. 'I should know.'

'I'm not sure I can let go. There's so much.' She pressed her hands to her chest, feeling as if a lead weight were imprisoned there. 'So much pain and ugliness, I don't dare open up, lest it all rush out, and I...I drown in it.'

'I'll be here. I won't let you drown.'

'Attentive Alastair. So you intend to protect me?'

'In every way I can. Whatever grief and pain bedevils you, we can meet it, conquer it, together.'

After the bout of tears she felt—strange, fidgety. The idea that Blankford could no longer threaten her still seemed impossible to believe. Uncertain, her whole world shifting around her, all she knew for sure was she could not bear to be pressured.

Even by Alastair.

When he reached for her again, she held up a hand to fend him off.

'I know you care for me and want to help. But…I need time to myself—to find out how to breathe freely again. I do love you, Alastair, but I don't know if I *can* become a woman who could share her life with you. I don't even know if I can succeed in mothering my own son!'

Compelled by a distress she didn't seem able to control, she jumped up again and began pacing.

What was wrong with her? Alastair had just affirmed what she would have given her life to hear eight years ago—that he'd forgiven her betrayal and loved her still. That he wanted to help her heal. That he wanted her as his lover—his wife.

Why could she not accept that offer with joy, and move on to a future with him?

It made no sense. But with her whole body trembling in anxiety, her thoughts in turmoil, all she knew was that she couldn't.

She looked back to see him watching her, his expression unreadable, his hands rigidly at his sides, as if he had to fight with himself to keep them there.

Foolish tears stung her eyes again. 'I'm sorry, Alastair. I don't mean to hurt you, and I'm grateful—'

'Sweet Diana, don't apologise,' he interrupted. 'You've lived through eight years of torment, had your child and your very life threatened, and have only just learned you can in safety move forward. How could you not need time to let the upheaval settle before you can decide what you want to do with your life?'

Another tear escaped. 'Thank you...for understanding.'

'Shall I tell you what I suggest? Just a suggestion, of course. You shall do whatever *you* feel is right.'

That sounded less threatening. The pressure in her chest easing a bit, she said, 'Very well. What do you suggest?'

'The late Duke's will stipulates you are to receive as a widow's portion the incomes and rents from four of Graveston's most prosperous properties, the land itself to be owned in trust for your son until he reaches his majority. The estates are located on good land and should earn you a comfortable income. There happens to be a small property in this county, not too far from Barton Abbey, that the absentee owner is interested in selling. The property, Winston Hollow, is close enough for Mother to call on you. She's grown quite fond of that son of yours, and would hate to give him up. I suggest that you settle at Winston Hollow, plant a garden, paint, enjoy running a household again, as you did for your father. Take time to find yourself.'

A place of her own, staffed with servants of her own choosing. A place to rediscover who she was, to purge the mistrust, the grief, the regret of the past and build the courage to believe in a future.

She'd battled against a strong-willed master for as long as she could remember, existed under the scrutiny of his watchful, disapproving staff. Never in her life had she lived both alone and free. The prospect was both liberating...and alarming.

'Will you...call, too?'

'If you want me to. I spend most of my time at Barton Abbey; Mama is a good manager and Hutchens knows his job and the land, but an estate this size requires a lot of work, and I don't like to burden her. Call on me whenever you want advice or company.'

Alastair—close, but not pressing her to do anything or be anyone. The tension within her dissipated a bit further. 'I think I would like that.'

'Then I'll notify my solicitor to start drawing up the necessary documents for you immediately.'

If she had her own house, they could begin again as lovers. Heat fired within her at the realisation.

But she could hardly take him as a lover while protesting she needed to keep him at arm's length. Could she? After such a forceful rejection, he wasn't likely to proposition her any time soon.

Her body protested the idea of further chastity, but her skittish mind rebuked it. Everything had changed since their sojourn in Green Park Buildings, when she'd thought he disliked her and would soon tire of the liaison. While she hungered for him, she knew right now she couldn't bear the weight of any expectations he might cherish for a future.

So it seemed, for the time being, she would burn.

'Thank you. I'm sorry I…can't offer more.'

He smiled. 'You are a brave, resourceful, strong woman. You will heal, Diana. And as adviser, friend—or lover—I will always be available. But now, I must go find Mother. She doesn't yet know I've returned.'

He came towards her and she tensed, but he simply lifted her fingers for a kiss. She searched his face—was he angry, impatient, disappointed? She couldn't tell.

'I'll see you at dinner.'

She stared after him as he walked out, then turned to sink down on to the sofa.

She'd greeted him as a long-lost lover and sent him off like a nervous virgin. Almost literally pushed him away, and then been illogically disappointed that he hadn't tried to kiss her before he left.

How could she expect him to comprehend her behaviour, when she didn't understand it herself?

But she'd been uncertain all along, she reminded herself, retreating in confusion every time she'd tried to contemplate a future, putting off making any decisions until the threat of Graveston was settled.

Well, now it was, and she'd just met the first challenge by, at the least disappointing, if not actually insulting, the man who'd won her back her life.

She put her head in her hands. Alastair seemed confident she would heal in time. She could only hope he was right—and that by her intransigence, she wouldn't risk losing for ever a man she might soon decide she didn't want to live without.

Chapter Twenty-Three

The following morning, Alastair hesitated outside the door to the north parlour Diana used as her painting studio. He'd speculated many different endings to the meeting at which he conveyed the glad tidings of her deliverance from Blankford's revenge, but he'd never anticipated her withdrawing from him so completely—and right after he'd comforted her in his arms.

He'd had a hard time concealing a dismay and disappointment that cut even deeper that night when, after visions of having her fall rapturously into his arms upon hearing the news, he took himself off instead to a bed that promised to remain cold and empty for a good long time. He could only be glad he'd listened to the instincts that told him not to press her, or he might have frightened her away completely.

But the rejection stung nonetheless.

Well, enough repining. One skirmish lost did not determine the course of a war, and he was far from ready to retire from the field. He might not be able to cosset and care for her as he'd like—or make love to her for a week—but he'd pledged to aid her recovery in whatever way he could, and he intended to do so.

Besides, there was no need to despair—she *had* confessed that she still loved him, had always loved him. She might not believe it yet, but he had full confidence that the courageous, determined, resilient woman who'd resisted the intimidation of a duke would eventually fight her way out of the prison of her past, back to a free and vibrant life.

Back to him.

He just had to stay patient and lure her slowly, gently, gradually out of her self-imposed isolation.

He'd take the first step this morning. After a deep breath, he rapped on the door.

He walked in when she bid him enter, but rather than cross the room to claim a kiss, as he might have only a day ago, he remained near the door.

The alarmed expression that swiftly crossed her face before she schooled her features made him glad of his caution, even as it struck a blow to his heart. How could they have become so awkward with each other in only a day?

Ah, Diana, do you not yet realise I would never do anything to hurt you?

Pushing back the sadness, he summoned a smile. 'Mama thought you'd be at your easel. I noticed yesterday that you'd almost finished your painting of the asters. I thought you might like to start one for these.'

From behind his back, he produced a bouquet of late-blooming damask roses.

To his relief, the gesture seemed to put her at ease. 'How lovely!' she exclaimed, coming over to him.

'The cool autumn nights give the petals an interesting mix of shades—pink, salmon, cream, pale pink, with a touch of saffron. When I saw them this morning, I immediately thought you'd enjoy trying to capture the different hues.' He handed over the bouquet. 'And as James would say, they are wonderfully smelly.'

'They are indeed,' she said, bending down to inhale a deep breath of the sweet, spicy aroma.

'James dotes on you, you know. I watched him while you were gathering asters and ferns by the brook that day. He mimics what you do and hangs on every word you utter. By offering affection and responding to his needs and interests, you've made a great start at reviving your relationship. It will only grow deeper over time.'

'You truly think so?'

'I do. But you needn't trust the word of an old bachelor—ask my mother.'

She smiled shyly. 'She said much the same.'

'Well, there you have it. Enjoy the flowers.'

Curbing the ever-present longing to touch her, he made himself turn towards the door.

'Alastair!' she called as he reached the threshold. When he looked back over his shoulder, she said, 'I do appreciate you thinking of me, even if I'm… still not very good at expressing gratitude.'

'You have to start trusting that good things will happen to you. How would you react to a gift if you had no reservations, felt no fear, no sense of threat?'

She paused, considering. 'I suppose I would be… delighted.'

'Then let yourself be. For eight years, you merely endured. This is what you endured *for*—so you might feel delight, and happiness, and enthusiasm again. I'll hope to see the painting when you've finished it.' With a bow, he exited the room.

Thank heaven the estate required a great deal of work and long hours in the saddle, he thought as he headed for the stables. Else, thrown together with Diana day after day in the house, stymied love and frustrated desire would drive him mad.

He'd be glad when Reynolds finished obtaining

her new property, so she might establish her own household. Once secure and independent, in a home of her own making, she could begin to heal—and he'd be that much closer to winning her back.

Six weeks later, Diana sat at her desk in the morning room at Winston Hollow, making notes on the menus left by Mrs Jenkins, her new housekeeper. After living in the manor for a month, served by staff she'd chosen herself, a sense of anticipation had begun to replace the foreboding with which she'd awakened for as long as she could remember.

Trust that good things will happen to you, Alastair had advised. It had been difficult at first, but as she became immersed in the rhythm of her own household, taking up the duties she'd enjoyed performing in her father's house, the dread that had haunted her for so long had gradually begun to dissipate.

Putting down her pen, she gazed out the window that overlooked the gravel drive, empty of visitors, and sighed. She'd begged Alastair for time to herself, and he'd certainly given it to her—rather more than she would have liked.

Indeed, almost as soon as she'd set him at a distance—and he complied with her wishes—she'd begun to regret pushing him away. After all his care and consideration, how could she have feared he would pressure her, force on her anything for which she was not ready?

Until she'd left Barton Abbey, she'd continued to see him—in company at dinner, in passing as he rode out on estate business. Several times, he'd joined them as she walked with James, to her son's delight, showing him how to skip pebbles in the brook, tossing him a ball, and one rainy day, taking him to explore the old gatehouse that had so fascinated him the afternoon they arrived.

Often, he dropped off little gifts—a book of poetry from his library he thought she'd enjoy, a colourful plant he'd found while riding through the meadows, some fresh berry tarts from the kitchen to share with James. He was unfailingly kind, gentle, patient—and he never touched her.

Oh, how she missed his touch! The mere thought of the passionate nights they'd shared in Bath made her body throb with need and her soul ache with longing.

But as much as she yearned for him, she knew that coming here alone had been the right choice. Living under threat for so long, she'd existed in a constant state of alarm, her nerves taut, her body rigid. In the sheltering cocoon of Winston Hollow, where every activity was directed by her, where no one but herself made any demands on her, where she did not have to prepare herself each night for the next day's battles, the tenseness in her body had seeped away along with the sense of dread, leaving her feeling lighter and more relaxed than she'd been in years.

She was, in short, ready to embrace a new life. But no such life would be complete without Alastair.

While he had agreed to give her time and space, he'd also said he would call. She'd expected, once she was established in her new home, he would find some pretext to stop by. Every time there was a clatter of gravel on the drive, or the sound of voices in the entryway, her spirits leapt, expecting him.

But though Mrs Ransleigh had come twice for tea, Alastair had not appeared. Not that she could fault him—she'd been the one to bring their relationship to a halt. Necessary as that had been initially, she was finding that each day, she missed him more.

His counsel. His ready smile. The delight of discussing poetry or painting or the events reported in the London newspapers with a man of wisdom and discernment. And always, his touch.

Not wishing to press her, was he waiting for an invitation to visit?

Perhaps it was finally time to send one.

Almost upon the thought, Clarkson, her new butler, appeared in the doorway. 'Madame, you have a visitor. I put him in the morning room.'

Excitement blew through her like a fresh breeze. Since she had no other male acquaintances in the county, it must be Alastair.

'Mr Ransleigh?' she asked hopefully.

'Yes, ma'am. He's just back from London, he said.'

Perhaps that was why he'd not called earlier. Gladness filling her, she smoothed her skirts, tucked in a curl that had escaped her careless coiffure, and hurried into the morning room.

He stood as she entered, looking so handsome and irresistible her breath caught in her throat. 'Alastair, what a pleasant surprise!' she said when she could speak again. 'Can you stay for tea?'

'If you are sure I'm not interrupting. I found something for you in London; I debated just sending it over, but since I was riding by anyway, I thought I'd chance delivering it myself. I hope you don't mind.'

'No, I'm delighted! Please, do sit!' Motioning him back to the sofa, she gave instructions to Clarkson, then came to take a seat beside him.

He studied her, a smile slowly lighting his face. 'I think you *are* delighted. I'm so pleased. Running Winston Hollow was what you needed, then.'

She nodded. 'I can't thank you enough for suggesting it! I'm finding I love being mistress of my own household, with all the small routines of daily life—consulting with the cook and the housekeeper, painting in the morning, lessons with James in the afternoon, taking him and the puppy your mama insisted he bring with him for walks around the property. He's such a delightful companion, eager to explore, excited by every new discovery. I love him better each day—as you assured me I would. I can never thank you enough for making it possible for me to keep him.'

'Your pleasure—and his—is reward enough. You do look lovely—and you sound happy. Have you found at last the peace you sought?'

'I think so. Just recently, I've dared to unlock the memories I suppressed of those happy times before my marriage—wonderful memories of that spring we fell in love. I've even been able to let go some of the misery of the years after, without the flood of anguish I feared. Instead, there's been this slow…trickling away of the fear and bitterness and anger that held me as much a prisoner as the walls of Graveston Court once did. I go for days now without thinking about it.'

She laughed. 'Now, this will surprise you! I believe in time, I may even be able to forgive Graveston.'

'Then your healing will be complete.' He leaned towards her and she sucked in a breath, supremely conscious of his nearness, every nerve anticipating his touch.

Running a fingertip gently down her cheek, leaving sparks of sensation in its wake, he declaimed. *"'Her merest smile to me is a delight. Her brow uplifted, finally free of pain. Her joy like the up-rush of a lark to flight. My joy to win her back to life again.'"*

Without question, he'd written that for her—about her. Humbled, she said, 'So you've taken up your pen again?'

'Yes, I have. It seems my muse is back. Though she is still often maddeningly elusive. But here, let me show you what I've brought.' Producing a wrapped package, he handed it to her.

She peeled off the paper to reveal a small leather volume. *'Pride and Prejudice,'* she read the title on the spine.

'My sister Lissa recommended it. The author has a unique voice and a sense of humour I think you'll enjoy.'

Flipping open the book to the first page, she read aloud, *"'It is a truth universally acknowledged, that a single man in possession of a good fortune must be in want of a wife.'''* Chuckling, she said, 'Yes, I think I shall like it. Thank you so much.'

'So you can enjoy a gift now—with no fear, no sense of threat?'

'Less every day. As you promised.'

'It's gratifying to be proven right,' he acknowledged with a grin. 'You're beginning to trust that the future *will* be full of possibilities? That you *can* learn to love again?'

Did he mean her son—or him?

She knew which love she needed to affirm.

'There may be nothing as sweet as one's first falling in love,' she said softly, her heart accelerating as he fixed his gaze on her, 'except, perhaps, recapturing a love once lost.'

She watched as the intensity of his regard turned to something else. Something impossible to resist.

She angled her head up, inviting his lips. He gave her just a gentle brush with his mouth, but at the first contact, her body seemed to catch fire.

He must have felt it, too, for his kiss deepened. Any possibility of breaking it off shredding to ash and disintegrating, she opened her mouth, and with an inarticulate sound, he sought her tongue with his own.

Only her brain's insistent warning that at any

moment, the butler might return with the tea tray, gave her the strength to break away.

Breathing hard, obviously as reluctant as she was to end the kiss, Alastair let her go.

'I've missed you,' she explained, blushing a little.

'"Missed" doesn't begin to convey the enormity of it,' he muttered, moving away from her.

She caught his sleeve, pulling him back again, suddenly desperate for more. 'Another kiss?'

'You're sure?' he asked, studying her. 'You'll let yourself enjoy, with no fear, no sense of threat?'

'With you, yes.'

Tenderness softened the passion in his gaze. Pulling her into his arms, he kissed her forehead. 'No fear, no threat,' he whispered as he kissed her ear, the slope of her throat, her chin while her senses swam and tiny explosions of delight and pleasure ignited whenever his mouth touched her.

'No fear, no threat,' he whispered again before claiming her mouth.

This kiss was long, gentle, and so achingly sweet she could almost weep with the joy of it. Her long-denied body trembled and burned, eager for completion.

With surprising ease, she let go her last reserve, like a ship slipping its moorings to set off fearlessly on uncharted seas, while her unfettered heart rejoiced with love for him.

She must have been demented to have denied them this—denied *him*, for so long. 'Please, stay,' she whispered when at last he broke the kiss.

'Now?' He raised his eyebrows. 'In full daylight? With the butler about to bring tea and your son in the nursery?'

'Bother the butler and Minnie has charge of James. Oh, how I've missed *you*—and this!' She traced his mouth with a trembling finger, until he groaned. 'You will stay, won't you?'

'You know I can deny you nothing.'

'I'm so glad!' Feeling impossibly wicked, she took his hand and led him from the morning room. Tiptoeing down the hallway to the stairs, scanning around them like a pair of naughty children, they went swiftly hand in hand up to her bedchamber.

It was mad, delicious—and she couldn't wait to taste him again. And at last, to offer him all of her.

A long, leisurely time later, Alastair woke from a deep sleep to find himself in a shadowed bedchamber—with a delectably naked Diana beside him. For a moment, he thought muzzily that he must be dreaming.

Then consciousness returned, and with it, the

memory of calling on her and being finally—praise Heaven!—invited back into her arms.

Diana stirred against him. He kissed the top of her head, relishing the feel of her body against his, the silk of her hair under his lips. *Diana*, free and unafraid beside him, where she belonged.

A few minutes later, she roused and gave him a sleepy smile. 'Alastair?'

He placed a kiss on the tip of her nose. 'Yes, my beloved.'

'Am I your beloved?'

'You know you are.'

'Then…is your offer still open?'

An electric flash of anticipation instantly dispelled any residual sleepiness. 'Which offer?' he asked cautiously, trying to restrain a rising hope and excitement.

She blushed a little. 'Your offer to make an honest woman of me.'

'You mean…marriage?'

She nodded, looking suddenly shy.

He could have teased her, but he was far too eager for delay. Detaching her from his arms, he slid out of bed, pulled her to sitting position, and went down on one knee.

'My dearest, darling Diana, will you marry me, and make me the happiest man in England?'

'Amorous Alastair.' She chuckled. 'Accepting Alastair. My Alastair-for-Always. Yes, yes, a thousand times yes.'

He didn't want to ask, to give her a chance to entertain any doubts, but he'd waited too long not to know for certain. 'Are you sure?'

'The innocent, joyful girl I'd once been is gone for ever, but as I've resumed the habits of my old life, the most consistent, most important joy I remembered and have found again…is you. I've no need for wariness any longer. *He* took away and pressured and intimidated; *you* give and support and encourage, asking for nothing in return but for me to rebuild my life and be happy.'

'I did ask to be part of it,' he pointed out.

'Now I have a new life I owe to you—and I can't envisage living it without you.'

Elated, he gave her a passionate kiss, then jumped up and hurried about, gathering up his scattered clothing.

'I tell you I can't live without you, and you respond by leaving?' Diana asked, looking disgruntled.

'Absolutely! I must ride to London today and arrange for a special licence. Talk with Mama; shall we be married in the parlour at Barton Abbey or here?' He stopped suddenly. 'Unless you want a grand wedding in London? The Dowager Duchess, re-emerging triumphant in Society?'

She shook her head. 'I never wanted to be part of Society. The only thing I wanted, almost from the moment I met you, was to be your wife.'

'So you shall be, then. For ever and always, my beloved,' he declared, and gathered Diana to him for another kiss.

* * * * *

MILLS & BOON®

Why shop at millsandboon.co.uk?

Each year, thousands of romance readers find their perfect read at millsandboon.co.uk. That's because we're passionate about bringing you the very best romantic fiction. Here are some of the advantages of shopping at www.millsandboon.co.uk:

* **Get new books first**—you'll be able to buy your favourite books one month before they hit the shops

* **Get exclusive discounts**—you'll also be able to buy our specially created monthly collections, with up to 50% off the RRP

* **Find your favourite authors**—latest news, interviews and new releases for all your favourite authors and series on our website, plus ideas for what to try next

* **Join in**—once you've bought your favourite books, don't forget to register with us to rate, review and join in the discussions

Visit **www.millsandboon.co.uk**
for all this and more today!